The
Clinic

Michelle Lee

The Clinic

©2021 Michelle Lee

print ISBN: 978-1-09837-062-6
ebook ISBN: 978-1-09837-063-3

For Coquina—a rock made of shell that is strong as cement.

PROLOGUE

There are two types of sickness.

One type of sickness you can control with a medicine, a tincture, a procedure. It sits on the surface available for reach.

The other type of sickness you can't control; it controls you. No amount of medicine can quiet its charge. It runs and roils deep within, too buried to touch. It might poke its head out long enough for you to grasp it, only for it to seep through your fingers.

I was always one for complex diagnoses.

As I stared at the Virgin Mary, her tranquilizing smile boring through my thoughts, I felt a sharp pain in my chest. I clutched at it.

Hours ago in the basement of my clinic, a man was bound by rope and humiliated like a dog by a high-heeled siren with red hair in a tight, black corset—a Domme; no, a Pro-Domme. I had come to understand the difference. And the more astonishing thing is that I had come to appreciate the difference.

But now, I pled with Mary, *Please let it all be okay. Please help me get out of this mess and change my ways so I don't lose everything.*

I can't fail. It's not an option.

CHAPTER ONE

My pager buzzed, and I looked down to see the emergency code for cardiac arrest: STEMI.

"Yes!" I yelped.

It was my Cath month, and I had just come off weekend call. That meant this morning, I was logging my sixtieth hour in five days. Those were the hours I *logged*. Off the record, I was reaching the eighty-fifth hour. It seemed impossible that someone could work seventeen to eighteen hours a day, sleep five or six, eat one, and maybe shower with whatever remained. But we all did it. Residency was a bitch.

None of that mattered now because Dr. Grath paged me to assist with a cardiac catheterization, my favorite procedure, and all the attendings knew it. When successful, the procedure left me with a deliriously calm sense of accomplishment.

I picked up my pace and hurried toward the elevator. I rounded a corner with my head down, studying the EKG of the waiting patient on my phone with one hand, coffee in the other, when—

"That's hot! Shit!" I gasped.

"Oh my God! I am so sorry!" A man on the adjacent side of the corner ran to help me while pushing the rolling cart I had just slammed into.

"Are you okay?" he asked, flustered. "Let me get some towels!"

"No, no, I'm fine. I have to hurry. It's just coffee." I gauged the fiery coffee stain steeping across my blouse and into my white lab coat. I looked at my watch. It had been two minutes since I was paged. *Time is muscle*, my brain kept relaying.

I ignored the mess and ran to the elevator, pushing the "up" button frantically while wiping hopelessly at the sweltry coffee stain. The elevator beeped and the doors reeled open. I got in and hit the button for the fifth floor. The man from the cart came squeezing in as the doors closed, jarring them to reopen.

"I really am okay," I said to him impatiently, pressing the number 5 button repeatedly.

"I just feel so badly," he said, one hand on his chest. "I should have been on the other side of the hallway with that thing."

"Speaking of, where is that thing? Your cart? Did you just leave it there?" I asked, waiting anxiously as the elevator began to move.

"Oh yeah, it's only paint canvases. If anyone steals them, they need them more than I do," he said charmingly. "Besides, they're blocking the wet floor until someone can come clean it up."

I nodded and watched as the elevator climbed to floor 2...3...

"Here, I brought this at least." He handed me a paint-stained rag. "I'm gonna want that back," he smiled jokingly, and I noticed his deep dimples. He had a nice smile. Frankly, he had a nice everything.

"Thanks." I didn't have time to chitchat, and this elevator seemed to be taking a monumentally long time to climb five flights.

"Can I buy you another coffee? Or pay for your ruined clothes?" he asked.

The elevator beeped open. "No, I'm fine. Thank you. I have to go." I smiled curtly and hurried down the hallway toward the cath lab.

I scanned my badge to gain entry through the double doors and walked immediately to the scrub sinks. Dr. Grath already was at the sink scrubbing in. He glanced at my stained shirt. The scrub nurse assessed my situation and went to fetch a new scrub top.

"Good morning," he said through the running water.

"Is it?" I smirked, out of breath.

He glared at me seriously. "Yes, it is. Are you alert, Dr. Wells?"

"Yes, of course," I replied earnestly. His tone reminded me that he was not one to chitchat, either.

"Good. Did you see the EKG?"

"Yes, I looked at it on my way up."

"Okay," Dr. Grath said with his hands up. "Let's go save a life."

I nodded seriously and took in a swallow of sterile air to stifle my enthusiasm.

Three hours later, Jed Terry was being wheeled to a recovery room, and I was heading out of the cath lab back toward the emergency department. My head ached with exhaustion, but my body hummed with excitement. There was something about seeing that purple-black dye flow freely through a blocked artery that left me breathing more freely; as if my breath was trapped and released with the inflation of that balloon-filled stent.

I rubbed my temple with one hand and glanced at my watch for time check.

"Oh good, you're here. I brought you some coffee," a man's voice said.

I looked up, surprised to find the man from the elevator holding a cup of coffee and a donut. "Yes, *I'm* still here," I narrowed my eyes. "Why are *you*?"

"I brought you coffee," he said matter-of-factly.

"You brought me coffee? Why?" I asked as I accepted it with a smile.

"It was the least I could do," he grinned. *Damn, those dimples.*

"Thank you," I said, inspecting the donut. Boston Cream, my favorite. "I really need this right now, so I'd say you're forgiven."

"I'm glad," he said. "I'm Beau, by the way." He held his hand out to me.

"Faith," I said, shuffling my donut to the hand that held the coffee to shake his. His hand was rough and callused.

"I know. It's on your jacket," he smiled toward the embroidered monogram, Faith Wells, M.D.

I shrugged politely. "Guess it is. Well, thanks again. I have to get going."

"Maybe you'll let me take you to dinner?" he asked nervously. "You know, just in case you get home and realize that the stain won't come out of your shirt. I would feel better if you at least let me treat you to more than just coffee."

I laughed apprehensively. Though Beau was alarmingly attractive, and I felt a strong pull toward seeing more of that seductive smile, I knew going to dinner was not an option. I worked too much to date. At least, that's what I told myself.

"Thanks, but the coffee is plenty. I'm flattered, really, but I'm already in a relationship," I lied.

"Of course you are," he said quizzically. "In any case, thanks for letting me bump into you today, Faith. It made my day."

I smiled curiously. "Anytime, Beau. Take care."

I walked toward the elevator and caught it, sipping my coffee while the doors closed. Nonfat latte with a dash of cinnamon: *How did he know*? I smiled to myself, confused by my racing heartbeat and unexpected surge of energy.

It wasn't often that it was my heart skipping a beat in the cardiac wing.

I arrived at the hospital the next day for rounds in the CCU. It was a Saturday, which meant I would personally have to scan anyone needing an urgent echo. Why did everyone seem to need emergent echos on the weekends?

Irena, the cardiac-floor nurse, handed me a stack of files. "Do you know whose life you saved yesterday?"

I shrugged. "Jed Terry's?"

"Yes, Faith, and do you know who Jed Terry is?" she asked, as if she were asking a child, '*and what do you say*?' after receiving a piece of candy.

I shook my head. "A patient? Who had a heart attack?"

She rolled her eyes. "Next time you go outside, which we all know is never, take a glance at the corner of the building. The J. Terry building. The J. Terry Cardiac Wing, the J. Terry amphitheater, the J. Terry everything, Faith. You starting to catch on now?"

"Oh shit, J. Terry is Jed Terry?"

She smiled. "Yeah, so. There's that. Good luck with rounds today. Do you need any more coffee?" she asked with a smirk, her gold hoop earrings swinging as she spoke.

I looked at her warily. She never asked if I needed coffee.

The attending, Dr. Ross, showed up with a team of lackeys. I always made it in before the rest of the residents to review charts and chat with nurses, which was why I usually was the first paged for patients possibly needing procedures, and why I was every attending's favorite. This was my last year in residency, and I was looking forward to fellowship. Though I had applied to many hospitals as a fail-safe, I only had eyes for the Hospital of the University of Pennsylvania, "Penn," which was where I started, and where I was determined to finish.

"All right, let's get started on rounds," Dr. Ross addressed the team. "Jed Terry is up first. Dr. Wells, I want you to present."

"Of course."

The team walked toward Jed Terry's room. Jed sat up when we entered.

"Good morning, Jed," Dr. Ross said cheerfully as we approached.

Jed looked past him and straight at me. "Well, if it isn't my angel right here in flesh and bone! I thought you might have been part of an out-of-body experience," he laughed, then winced in pain.

I smiled, conscious of the other residents rolling their eyes at my good fortune of saving one of Philadelphia's most prominent philanthropists. "It's good to see your spirits up, Mr. Terry."

"Why wouldn't they be?" he said heartily, his eyes dazzling even post-heart attack. "I survived the widowmaker! I should go play the lottery, don't you think, Dr.—"

"Dr. Wells," I smiled. "Faith Wells."

Dr. Ross cleared his throat as a queue for me to stop chatting and start presenting.

"Uh, Mr. Terry—" I began.

"Call me Jed, angel. No doctor who saves my life gets to call me Mr. Terry."

I tried not to express annoyance at the liberty he took in giving me a pet name, which bothered me all the more because Angel is my mother's name, and currently my mother was missing.

"Okay, Jed, I'm going to present your case now for my team," I smiled.

I presented his case and as we left his room, Dr. Ross leaned over to me. "I'd say your fellowship application just got a stamp of approval. Good work yesterday, and excellent job presenting."

I smiled modestly, but inside I was lit up like a Christmas tree.

I finished the rest of the rounds with the team and when I came back to type notes, Irena handed me a coffee.

"For you," she said with a smile.

I glared at her. I knew Irena well; she and I had become quick friends, and as far as I knew, we were each other's only friends at the hospital. We didn't hang out—that wasn't Irena's style, which was why I liked her—but we shared snarky texts about doctors or dark, sarcastic material that only she and I found funny.

"Where did this come from?"

She shrugged while typing notes. "Dunno."

"Like hell you don't," I retorted. I looked again at the coffee and on the sleeve, written in black marker, were the words: DINNER? - Beau.

I chuckled lightly. "I'll be damned."

CHAPTER TWO

The coffee deliveries continued for two weeks, each time with a similar note, and sometimes accompanied by a Boston Cream donut, until one day I decided to end the coffee foreplay.

"Irena," I said as she set the coffee down in front of me.

"Yes?"

"Don't accept this coffee any longer please," I said nonchalantly as I wrote in a chart.

Irena pretended not to hear me as she organized papers and supplies, but Irena heard everything.

"Irena," I said more forcefully.

"Yes?" she exasperated.

"I said don't accept coffee from that guy any more, please. It has gone on for too long."

She looked at me for a moment with heavy-mascara eyes. "Tell him yourself. I'm not your secretary." When Irena pursed her lips to suppress a smile, I realized she was in on this gimmick.

I narrowed my eyes at her. "Fine." I wiggled the coffee sleeve off the cup and grabbed a red marker. I scribbled on it quickly, then flung it toward Irena.

She looked at it, then at me. "For someone going into cardiology, you sure don't have a heart."

I rolled my eyes. "I save all my heart strength for my patients. I don't have time to date."

Irena went slack in the shoulders and gave me a pouty look. "Come on, Faith. You haven't dated since I've known you, and Beau is a nice guy. You can't stay single forever."

"Can't I?"

"No, you can't. Listen, you're beautiful and brilliant, and despite yourself, you're sorta nice, too. Beau is gorgeous; *those dimples*," she exhaled. "Every woman in this hospital has tried to date him, even the married ones, but he never goes out with them. Truthfully, I was convinced he was either gay or secretly married until he approached me about you."

"He asked about me? When?"

"The day he spilled coffee on you. He came to this floor looking for you, but you weren't here. I told him you'd be in the cath lab for a while. He asked what kind of coffee you drank."

It all made sense now, how he knew my coffee and donut order: Irena was acting as his insider.

"What else did you tell him?" He had seemed unconvinced when I told him I was in a relationship.

Irena cleared her throat and put a hand on her hip. "I might have told him you were single and to ask you out."

"Irena!"

She clicked her tongue. "Whatever, Faith. You can thank me later. *After* you call him."

Admittedly, I was intrigued by Beau's persistence. Just short of stalking, it was sweet how he brought me coffee every day. I pictured his deep dimples and blue eyes.

"I don't even have his number. He just keeps writing, 'Dinner?' on the sleeve."

Irena scoffed and picked up the coffee sleeve. She broke it in half and turned it around for me to see. Written inside the sleeve was Beau's number.

I pursed my lips. "Oh. There it is."

"Call him," she said sternly as she walked away.

That night, as I lay on my couch eating Thai take-out in my small Center City apartment, I contemplated calling Beau.

As much as I wanted to call him—and I did—fear held my fingers back from dialing his number. I had never been in a relationship. I had had a few casual flings, usually with men not interested in relationships. But I had managed to avoid any kind of dating that required traditional courting or intimacy. Mostly, I blamed school and work for my lack of romantic life; my hours were insufferable. But the real reason was that I didn't know how to be in a relationship.

I grew up on West Crystal Street in a neighborhood north of Philadelphia called Castle Hill. The nomenclature (crystal and castle) might indicate my childhood was glittery and grand, but it was neither of those things. While I always was aware of that, I saw evidence of it when a city council candidate cited some grim statistics on a piece of paper slipped under our apartment door. Castle Hill graded on an A-F scale looked like this: Crime-F, Employment-F, Schools-F. The only parameters that didn't have failing scores were the cost of living and the weather.

I remember thinking the scorecard was accurate except for the school "F." I had loved school and would have graded it "A." I just didn't know any better then.

My mother, Angel, worked as a waitress during the day and as a bartender at night. I don't remember my mother ever grocery shopping. She brought food home from both jobs for breakfast and dinner, and I had subsidized lunch at school. I wasn't hungry growing up, but I was never fully satisfied, either. I was envious of the smells of food wafting from apartments as I walked past them. As I'd lift open the Styrofoam lid of another Andy's Diner box, I would fantasize about sitting around a table, the center lined with steaming food and fancy glasses like I saw on TV. None of my neighbors had fancy tables and glasses, but some of them had a mom or a grandmom who cooked, sometimes at least. And that seemed enough to fantasize about.

The train of thought inclined me to call my mom again. I called her number; straight to voicemail. I shook my head and pushed away my Pad Thai. This was the longest my mother had been away. I was used to her being gone for a couple of days, but never weeks. And I couldn't call Bobby to find out where she was, although he would know. That bastard was the reason she was gone. And that bastard would have welcomed my call with a tone of sick satisfaction. I could feel anger billowing, so I closed my eyes and exhaled it out. I couldn't let them ruin my night.

I picked up the coffee sleeve and stared at Beau's number. Calling Beau meant that I was reciprocating his interest, and I didn't know if I wanted to do that. But why not? Here was a man—a very good-looking man, and according to Irena, a nice, decent one, too—who put his heart on a sleeve, literally. Most women would swoon, yet I was toiling with the piece of cardboard as if there was anything to contemplate. I knew why I hesitated: I veered toward men who were unavailable. And I did that because it was what I knew to do. It was safe and it contained my vulnerability. I grudgingly acknowledged my mother's propensity to do the same, and sighed as my thoughts once again circled back to her.

Nothing Changes if Nothing Changes, read a sign in a coffee shop I frequented. I had stared at that sign more times than I could count while mulling through homework. If I wanted to change my life, I had to change the way I knew to do things, the way *she* would do things.

I dialed Beau's number.

"Hello?" he answered casually.

"Beau, hi. This is Faith. Faith Wells," I said, not knowing exactly how to start.

A short pause, then, "Faith Wells." I could hear his grin through the phone. "I could not be happier to hear your voice."

I bit my lip to suppress my smile. "I called to tell you that you won. Your persistence paid off. I was wondering if you'd like to meet for dinner or a drink sometime?"

"Yes!" he said enthusiastically. "How about now?"

I looked down at myself. I finished a ten-hour shift an hour ago and hadn't showered. My hair was in a messy bun and my feet were swollen and achy. Thai food boxes and wrappers were strewn over the coffee table.

"Yes, perfect," I said, surprising myself at the impulsiveness. But there was something about Beau's forwardness that baited me.

"Great!" he said. "Are you near the hospital? I live on Locust, off of 18th Street, but I could come up that way."

"Let's meet in the middle," I said. I didn't tell him that the middle was exactly where I lived. "How about we meet at The Rock Bar in thirty minutes?" The Rock Bar was a swanky little spot whose specialty was anything "on the rocks."

"I will be there in thirty minutes, Faith."

I winced and put a hand on my forehead. "See you soon, Beau."

CHAPTER THREE

I was a magician when it came to getting ready quickly, and thirty minutes later, I walked up 21st Street toward The Rock Bar.

Beau was standing next to the entrance in jeans (dressy jeans, not the artist's jeans I saw in the hospital) and a plaid shirt under a black sports coat. His hair looked bedhead-perfect and his eyes reflected brightly off the city lights. He held a small bouquet of flowers.

"Wow. You look stunning," he said breathily as I approached. I didn't know what was stunning about black pants and a red sweater—maybe it was the heels? Either way, I'd take it.

"You brought me flowers?"

"Uh, yeah." Beau handed me a bundle of red baby roses no bigger than an appetizer plate. I wasn't going to ask where he got flowers on a Thursday night.

"I'm so glad you called," he grinned, his dimples disappearing into the abyss of his cheeks.

"Me too," I smiled, as I took in the rose's scent.

We found two seats at the end of the bar. I ordered a whiskey sour. Beau looked at me, impressed. "I'll do the same," he told the bartender. To me, he said, "I've never known a woman who drinks whiskey."

I put my finger up to indicate he hold that thought, then I hollered to the bartender who was walking away.

"Oh, and some wings and fries please? Two orders of fries. With that dipping sauce." The bartender nodded.

"Hope that's okay," I said apologetically to Beau.

He laughed. "It's exactly what I would have wanted to order but would have been afraid to on a first date."

I blushed.

"So, Faith, tell me something about you. How did you get your name?" Beau took a small sip of his whiskey, wincing.

"My mom named me. She said that my birth *gave her faith*," I mocked.

"Faith in what?" he asked sincerely.

I shrugged. "Just faith in everything, I guess." In my mind: *Faith that I would change her life for the better, that my birth would bring my dad back*. It didn't, of course, but that's what she hoped for on that sunny June day I was born.

"That's nice," Beau said.

Our food came. Beau looked at the heaping piles of garlicky French fries.

"You won't regret this," I said as I grabbed a glistening skinny fry. I was about to pop it in my mouth, but instead, I held it up for Beau to eat. He flashed a smile and took a bite. I was alarmed at how satisfying the exchange felt and without thinking, I ate the other half.

"Those are amazing," he agreed. "I especially like that they come with my own personal feeder," he said suggestively about me. My heart skipped a beat.

I held up another fry. He took it with an exaggerated, "Mmm!"

I laughed harder than probably warranted, but I couldn't help but find Beau remarkably endearing. He seemed soft, but not delicate; honest, but not pure. And those goddamned dimples.

"You know, you're easy to be with," he said, putting a hand on my knee.

"Am I?" I asked, surprised. My knee was burning from his touch. I usually heard that I was difficult to be with; I was closed off or too serious about work.

"Yeah, you're very, I don't know, 'you.' I could tell from the minute we met that you don't pretend to be a certain way. It's refreshing, truthfully." He grinned while studying my face.

I flustered a little as I chased down a handful of fries with the last of my drink. I found Beau easy to be with, as well. It was the first time in a long time, maybe ever, that I was on a date and not strategizing how to keep someone at a safe distance, or avoiding certain conversations, or finding a way to end the date quickly.

"What led you toward a career in medicine? Were your parents doctors?" Beau asked, diverting his attention back to the fries.

I shifted uncomfortably. These were the types of conversations I tried to avoid. Did Beau want to hear that I went into medicine because in eighth grade, I felt safe for the first time in my life when I should have felt scared as I watched paramedics, doctors, and nurses zap life back into my mother's stopped heart—twice?

Folded up on that cot in her hospital room, listening to the rhythmic beep of the EKG machine that told me Mom was okay, I fell into the deepest slumber I had ever remembered. I knew that Bobby wouldn't come to the hospital; it was too public. For three days, Mom and I shared conversations and laughs that were lucid and normal, though haunted with withdrawals. Those were some of the best days of my adolescent life, and it was then that I had resolved to become a doctor who could fix her heart if it ever stopped again. Did he want to hear that? Most likely not.

"Uh, my mom was a motivating factor," I answered safely. "Enough about me. Where are you from? And why are you at the hospital so often?"

"I'm from Jersey. Near the Shore. My dad was in construction. He and my mom retired to Florida a few years ago. I have a brother in New York and a sister in Virginia." Beau shrugged. "I'm pretty basic."

Basic sounded blissful. Beau probably grew up with a fancy table full of food. "And why are you at the hospital so often?" I asked again.

"I'm an artist. I mostly do commission work, but I have a few pieces in galleries. I go to the hospital once a week to paint with patients. Mostly the kids in the cancer ward, but I go to any kid who is in the hospital for a long time. Painting is a good distraction."

I smiled admirably. I did one round in the pediatric cancer ward and I nearly jumped off the roof after every shift. It takes special people to keep a smile on for suffering children.

"Once a week?" I asked dubiously. "So, have the past two weeks been a special occasion? Because you've been at the hospital every day." A coffee and a smirking Irena waited for me each day.

"No," he grinned. "I came to bring you a coffee and to catch you in the hallway. You're hard to catch, though," he added with raised eyebrows.

I squinted quizzically. "Why? Why did you keep bringing me coffee? I wasn't that charming when we met and I certainly wasn't charming by not calling you for two weeks."

He smiled at me thoughtfully. "I'm drawn to you."

I narrowed my eyes at him. What kind of answer was that? An artsy one. But it made my heart flutter.

"I'm drawn to you, but I don't know exactly why," he continued without reservation, and I found myself captivated by Beau's confidence, just short of arrogant. "Of course, you're gorgeous," he stated as though undebatable. "I'm sure a lot of people are drawn to you. But it's more than that. I find you very interesting, very complex. I don't know how to explain it beyond that."

My heart was speeding past a flutter now. I imagined as an artist, he might feel similarly when seeing a painting for the first time. I had gone through Philadelphia's art museums with people who stopped in front of a painting and paused. I looked at it and thought, "Pretty." But they saw much more in that painting. The way the brush strokes made the peaks of the water seem icy, or how the light illuminated a signifying figure. My brain was too practical, too scientific, to appreciate art the way artists did. But Beau saw things beyond the surface. He was looking at me beyond the surface, and though I should feel vulnerable by that, I instead felt warm, which confused me.

"I'm sorry," Beau chuckled. "Did I make you uncomfortable?"

"No. I—" *Yes*, I admitted to myself. But it was refreshing. I had spent so long being alone, hiding, that I didn't realize how much I had wanted to be seen.

I took a sip of my drink. I wasn't good at talking about feelings, and as I strategized how to respond to Beau, my phone buzzed. Impulsively, I looked at it. As a doctor, I was used to being a slave to my phone and pager, so I didn't think twice about poor manners. It was Irena.

"I'm so sorry, but I have to take this. It's the hospital," I said.

"Of course," he agreed with a grin.

I wasn't on call, but Irena rarely called me without having a reason. "Hello?" I answered, pressing a finger into my free ear to hear Irena over the bar noise.

"Faith, your mom. She's at the hospital. I think you should come, and hurry."

"Irena, what? My mom? Is she okay?" I stood up abruptly, the bar chair scraping the floor loudly.

"She's in the ED," Irena said. "I was down there assisting, and I saw her come in. I'm not on the case, so that's all I know right now. But—well, that's all I know right now."

Even if Irena were on the case, she wouldn't have been able to give me details, but she was friend enough to tell me my mother was in the emergency department.

"I'm on my way," I began making my way toward the bar exit. "Irena, tell them it's alcohol and cocaine. They need to watch her vitals closely. She could crash at any moment."

"I'll tell them," she said. Irena already knew this; she was one of the only people who knew about my mother, which was why she called me immediately.

"Who's on call for Cardio?" I asked.

"Dr. Kane," she answered.

"Good. Kane is good. I'll text him when we hang up. But Irena, she could crash, I'm telling you. Watch her. I'll be there in ten."

"Got it."

A cab lolled to a stop in front of me. I reached for the door handle desperately and flung it open.

"Faith!" I turned around to see Beau behind me, carrying my purse.

"I'm sorry!" I hollered, getting into the cab. "I'll text you."

His arms dropped to his side, and he nodded as I directed the cab to the hospital. I looked back briefly, then he was lost as the cab joined the traffic.

I'm sorry, Beau, I texted. *There was an emergency at the hospital. I had to leave.*

He responded:

No worries, I understand. Is everything all right? I could bring your purse to you.

Shit, I'd have to text Irena for cab money.

No, I'll get it another time, I wrote, then deleted. I retried with, *Sure, thanks,* but I deleted that, too.

I couldn't respond. I leaned my head back against the seat. I should've known tonight, too, would get ruined. I knew Bobby wouldn't be at the hospital. But if he was, I would stab him with a scalpel, so help me God.

CHAPTER FOUR

This was where everything seemed to move in slow motion, dream-like and wavy in my memory.

I arrived at the ED entrance and flung open the cab door, leaving it ajar. Irena was waiting for me. She leaned into the cab window to hand the driver some cash, then closed the cab's back door after me as she turned to follow me in.

"She's in room 10. Her rhythm is all over the place, Faith," she said as she caught up to me.

Irena badged me in and I half-ran toward room 10. Dr. Graham, the ED attending, was at the bedside with two other nurses. When I arrived, they looked up at me with somber stares.

I ran directly to my mom, who was moaning listlessly.

"Mom," I said, shaking her shoulders. "Mom, it's Faith. Come on, look at me, Mom."

She rolled her head toward me. Her wobbly eyes stilled for a moment, locking on my face, and a fraction of a smile crinkled the corners of her eyes. "Hi sweetheart," she slurred.

Then machines beeped wildly.

Dr. Graham lunged forward. "She's coding! Grab the cart! Start compressions!"

"Mom, no!" I hollered. At that moment, I couldn't think like a doctor. I felt my mom's hand go limp in mine, like it had twelve years earlier, and I froze.

Irena grabbed my arms and gently pulled me away, saving the ED nurse from having to do it. I knew the protocol: I wasn't on the case and as family, I would have to stand back as the team tried to resuscitate her.

The next thirty minutes felt like hours as doctors, nurses, machines, and sounds whirred in all directions. Irena stood next to me, assuring the doctors and nurses that I wouldn't interfere. "I have her," she told them.

My thirteen-year-old-self flickered on and stared through the lens of my eyes, remembering the confusion of watching my mother's heart stop the first time. Then, a nurse had taken me out of the room and sat with me in an exam area. She had given me a drink, a "nicee," which tasted like crushed ice and ginger ale and cranberry juice.

This time, I wasn't taken to an exam room to wait. This time, as a fellow doctor, they let me watch as my mother rested lifeless on the table, her body jerking with each defibrillation, until finally I heard Dr. Graham say, "I'm calling it. Time of death 23:10."

Dr. Graham, sleek with sweat, looked at me sorrowfully. "I'm so sorry."

I stared at my mother, her black hair splayed on the pillow, her cornflower blue eyes in a silent stare. All I could think about was that people always told me, "You got your mother's eyes!" I closed my eyes, her eyes, and pictured her face when life flowed through her. I could feel her presence, although only her shell lay on the table. I took a deep breath in, and that's the last I remembered before waking up in a hospital bed.

An IV was attached to my arm when I awoke.

I was in one of the triage rooms; Irena was typing at a rolling computer stand.

"Irena," I said hoarsely.

She looked up and came over to my side. "Oh hey, you passed out. I popped an IV in you. You're in shock and probably dehydrated and definitely exhausted." She spoke authoritatively, but with soft undertones.

"Where's my mom?"

Irena looked at me contemplatively. Perhaps she wondered if I didn't remember that my mother had died moments ago.

"I mean, where's her body? Is it still in room 10?"

She grimaced. "She was taken to the morgue."

I nodded.

"I took this off her hand. I thought you might want it now." She handed me my mother's opal ring. The stone was as black as her hair. I winced looking at it, remembering holding her hand and playing with the stone.

"I have something else," Irena said. She handed me my purse and the small bouquet of baby red roses.

"Where did you get this?" I asked weakly.

"Beau brought it. He's been sitting in the waiting room. He heard you say something about your mom as you rushed out. He was concerned."

I put my hand over my eyes, but the IV got in the way. "Can you take this fucking thing out now? I want to go home." I was agitated, and I knew this was just my way of dealing with pain. Whenever tears threatened, bitter resolve stepped in to corral them and fight the emotional battle instead.

"Sure." Her short, brown ponytail bobbed as she removed the IV efficiently. She glanced at my face and I could tell she wanted to say something about tonight: *Are you OK?* But Irena knew that I wouldn't be receptive to that type of question. I wasn't one to talk about my feelings or hug it out. Neither was she, so she finished with a cotton swab and tape, then turned back to the computer.

I sat up and gathered my things. I looked at the roses, thought about throwing them in the garbage, but decided against it. "I'll see you tomorrow," I said as I pushed off the bed.

"Tomorrow's your day off."

"Then I'll see you Saturday," I said defensively.

"Tina can cover my shift. Let me come home with you for a bit. We don't have to talk. I'll just sit on the couch while you rest."

I scoffed. "I'll be fine, Irena. Thanks. Just—just let me be."

She stared at me unconvinced, but she knew better than to pursue. "Drink some electrolytes and try to sleep."

I walked out of the ED, the double doors whooshing open, then closing again. The bright lights and waiting room buzz felt muted, yet pronounced. I had almost reached the doors to the outside when I heard, "Faith."

I pivoted slowly to see Beau trotting up. "I nearly missed you. You walked right past me. I told you, you're hard to catch!"

I looked at him gravely. I wanted to be angry at him for waiting for me. I wanted to tell him to go away, that I'd call him tomorrow, but I also had an urge for him to wrap his arms around me.

"Faith, are you okay?" He put both hands on my shoulders and looked closely at my face. "What's wrong? What happened?"

I stared at him blankly. I couldn't speak. I wanted to close my eyes and pretend everything away.

He pulled me to his chest and stroked my hair. "Let's go outside and get you some fresh air." He walked me outside slowly, holding me up until we reached a bench. "Do you want to sit for a minute?"

I blinked a *yes*, and he understood it. We sat down and he cradled me into the crook of his arm. He took his lips to the top of my head and breathed in my hair, then rested his cheek on my head. "Sssh, it will all be all right. Whatever it is, I've got you."

I closed my eyes and a solitary tear slid down my face. It felt foreign. I swiped at it quickly and sat up. "I need to go home."

"Okay," he said slowly. "I can get you a cab. But do you mind if I follow you home? Just to make sure you make it okay?"

I shook my head. "I'll be fine."

"Please. For my sake. Call me chivalrous, but it's late and I don't feel good about letting you go home by yourself."

"Please, I do it all the time," I said, as I stood to hail a cab.

"Wait, Faith," he gently swiveled me around. "You're clearly upset. Are you sure you don't want to just sit a little longer? Or grab a bite to eat? Maybe talk about what's bothering you?"

"Beau, you have to stop."

"Stop what?"

"Just stop, I don't know, being so goddamn nice."

He chuckled.

"I'm serious," I continued. "You don't want me, trust me. You're a nice guy and I'm—"

"You're what? Not nice? Come on, Faith."

"I'm broken," I said sharply. "My life is not pretty and nice like yours. I'm complicated and my life is messy. You want to know what happened in there?" I challenged with a slight shriek. "My mother died."

His mouth dropped open. "Oh my God, Faith. I'm so sorry. "

I interrupted him. "She overdosed," I shrugged. "Yeah, and it's not the first time she has overdosed, and it's not the first time her heart stopped because of it. It's just the last time. And the worst part is that she was all I had. I have no one else. I don't have a brother in New York or a sister in Virginia. I don't have those things that solid people have. I am alone and probably always will be, and probably always should be. I'm broken, Beau, and I'll break you if you get too close to me."

I went to stand up, but Beau pulled me back down and wrapped his arms tightly around me. "Now you listen to me, Faith," he said soothingly in my ear. "I'm going to take you home and I'm going to stay with you until I know you're okay. If you won't let me, I'll go back into that hospital and make Irena do it. And I don't buy that shit about you being broken. But I do believe that you're used to being alone, which is why you're trying to push me away. Tonight though, you're not going to be alone. Tonight, I'm staying with you."

My defense mechanism *was* telling me to push him away, but the part of me that was hurt and mourning, the part of me that was still in shock, the part of me that was tired of being so alone, went limp in his arms. My shoulders slacked and I whimpered, "I don't want you to."

"Yes, you do," he said, stroking my hair.

"I can do this on my own," I whined.

"I know you can," he said softly.

His smell was warm, like cedar and sweet sweat, and I didn't want to move. My body hurt and a well of tears sat behind my eyes ready to burst, but an unexplainable dam kept them trapped.

"Twentieth & Sansom," I finally said.

"That's where you live?"

I nodded into his chest.

"Okay, I'll get you home."

Beau held me tightly as he hailed a cab. We didn't speak on the ride or as he supported me into my apartment, took off my shoes, and tucked me into bed. I felt so tired that I wondered if I would even wake up once I fell asleep. In all my years in med school, after countless hours interning, never had I felt so tired. It was an all-encompassing exhaustion; one that made even the nerveless parts of my body hurt.

I closed my eyes and surrendered to the chasm of grief.

CHAPTER FIVE

The sun rose and with it came mourning.

The first thought that raced through my head as I stared at the dewy light seeping through the blinds was that I couldn't call my mom. It seemed a profound void to not have the ability to just pick up the phone and call her, even though most of the time I didn't expect her to answer. The possibility was not there anymore, and that realization felt fragile.

I looked at the clock. It was nine a.m. I peeled myself out of the bed, grabbed some comfy pants and a Penn sweatshirt, and walked toward the bathroom. I brushed my teeth and hair and washed the smeared makeup from my face. I stared at my reflection in the mirror, but in it, all I could see was my mother: Mom's long, straight black hair, Mom's purply-blue eyes, Mom's pale skin and rosy lips.

I heard a chair slide from the kitchen table and stopped to listen. I didn't forget that Beau had taken me home, but I hadn't paid much attention to what he did after I went to bed. Apparently, he was still here. A swift sense of fretful relief pulsed through me.

I poked my head out of the bathroom. "Hello?"

I heard footsteps, then Beau appeared around the corner holding a cup of coffee. He was wearing glasses and jeans and a T-shirt. His disorderly sandy blonde hair tousled in all directions stylishly, but unintentionally so.

"Hi," he said, resting against the side of the hallway, maintaining comfortable distance.

I postured similarly in the bathroom doorway. "You're still here."

He smiled delicately and nodded. "Yeah, I'm still here." Those simple words felt so strong. "Would you like some coffee?"

I almost wanted to laugh at the congruence: Beau, waiting for me, holding a cup of coffee when I finally emerged like the first day we met at the hospital. But laughing was not in my repertoire today.

I nodded morosely. "Sure."

He turned toward the kitchen and I went back into the bathroom to pull my hair into a bun. When I walked into the kitchen, Beau was buttering an English muffin. There was a plate of cut fruit, two steaming cups of coffee, and the bouquet of baby red roses he brought to me the night before in a drinking glass of water on the table. A folded newspaper laid in front of a pulled-out chair. I looked around the apartment; everything seemed in order. The blankets, usually messy and strewn all over the couch, were neatly folded and placed in a large basket by a reclining chair. My medical books were stacked on the coffee table and two candles were well spaced on either side. All the scattered dishes in the apartment were now drying on the rack next to the sink, and the counters were wiped and cleared of clutter. The apartment wasn't cleaned up, just touched up, but the effect was reassuring.

"Have you been here all night?"

Beau set the English muffin in front of me and sat down. "Most of the night," he answered. "I left this morning to shower and change my clothes. Grabbed some breakfast and fresh coffee for you. Eat if you can," he said, nodding toward the table. "You have a long day ahead of you. It will help."

My stomach sunk thinking about what was ahead of me; so many decisions to make. I made decisions every day about how to save lives, but I didn't make decisions about the un-saved lives. I didn't want to face it.

I took a sip of coffee, then looked up at Beau. "Thanks for bringing me home last night. You don't have to stay; I'm fine. I have a lot to do today, like you said."

He cleared his throat. "My uncle owns a funeral home near Mayfair. I could make a call, if you'd like."

I stared at him indifferently. My brain was telling me I needed to be alone right now, sort through the facts, make a plan, and execute on it. Meanwhile, a little tug, as slight as a hummingbird pulls nectar, told me to trust Beau and accept his help.

"Sure. Thanks."

He smiled, relieved. "Good," he put his hand out toward me. I stared at it warily.

"Faith, today, and maybe for the next little while, I just want to be your friend, if that's what you need. You said you are used to being alone, and I admire that, but if there's ever a time to let someone help you, it's when you've lost someone close to you. So, if it's all right with you, I'll stick around for the next few days and just—" he shrugged. "Just be here."

His hand remained on the table, palm facing upward, fingers extended. I looked up at his eyes, earnestly blue, and reached out to lay my fingertips on his. He curled his fingers slightly and that small gesture filled my chest with a burn so prevalent, I thought it might seep open.

I nodded. "It's okay with me."

Even though my chest didn't seep open, Beau had found a way to seep in.

The next few days played out with robotic efficiency.

Beau's Uncle Seb was a saint. He actually looked like Saint Francis. I only knew this because Saint Francis was Mom's favorite saint. There had been a magnet of St. Francis d 'Assisi on the fridge, and Mom had a statue of him holding a pigeon on her dresser. She had used the statue to hold her jewelry, but sometimes I caught her kneeling in front of it with her folded hands in front of her closed eyes. I had wished she said her prayers out loud so I knew if they were the same as mine. In my early years, those prayers included my dad coming back; in later years, they included my mom coming back.

Though we hadn't attended church regularly during my growing-up years, Mom had always made it a point to go to the Midnight Mass service on Christmas Eve. I had looked forward to that Mass all year. It was the one time I saw my mom's face soft and still as she closed her eyes to the echoing sounds of the choir. I had stared at her tranquil face, orange with the lambent lighting, and prayed Mom would take me to Mass more. It was the only place I saw her at peace.

For many years, I carried a rosary and followed my own set of rites that seemed in line with a committed churchgoer. I prayed at night. I made the sign of the cross when I passed a cemetery or heard someone use the Lord's name in vain. I read Bible passages that made little sense to me but convinced myself they were impactful.

I thought my mom would be proud of my efforts, but she would roll her eyes amusingly and caution, "Be careful with all that praying. Religion can starve your soul as easily as it can feed it." I didn't know what she meant, but I was willing to take the chance with my soul: For a while, praying was the only thing that gave me hope.

"May I suggest a Celebration of Life Ceremony for your mother?" Beau's Uncle Seb asked me softly. My mind stuttered back to the funeral services as I sat in a chair across from Uncle Seb's desk.

"What exactly is that?"

"Sometimes the family chooses to celebrate their loved one's life rather than focus on their departure. This might include special people speaking and sharing memories of your mother. Or, some people choose to show a video or photos of their loved one who has passed."

None of that sounded appealing to me. In fact, I was debating on having a service at all.

I shook my head. "I don't think so."

He nodded with a pursed smile. "Perhaps something simpler, then. An affirmation might be nice. It's simply a period of time, as short or as long as you wish, in which friends and family can come pay respect to your mother and her family."

I shuddered. I didn't know how many people would show up for an affirmation; Mom had estranged most people in the last few years. Still—and perhaps it was because of my quasi-catholic upbringing—I felt the need for a service, even if just a small one.

"An affirmation sounds like a nice option. Where would I hold this type of service?"

"You can use the chapel here, if you'd like," Uncle Seb smiled warmly. "Sometimes, especially in the case of cremation, the family creates a table with the urn and some photos of the departed loved one."

I shuddered again. There weren't a lot of photos of Mom, and the ones I had taken with my phone over the past couple of years were none I would want people to remember her by. I'd have to dig through the chest in her apartment for some photos.

I nodded. "Okay. I'll bring some photos. Is that all I have to do?"

"Yes, Faith. We'll take care of everything else. Here is my number," he said as he handed me his card. "Call me if anything comes up. Otherwise, we'll reach out with details of the arrangement."

"Thank you very much," I stood and shook his hand.

Beau was waiting outside the door reading a book when I walked out. He stood and took off his glasses. "Was Uncle Seb helpful?"

I smiled meekly. "Yes, very helpful. Thank you, Beau."

He put his arm around me and we walked out, my head leaning in his nook.

CHAPTER SIX

The key turned slowly into the lock of my mother's apartment. Music pumped nearby and in the distance, a woman's voice hollered a complaint about someone's trash in the hallway. I pushed the hollow door open with a creak before walking in. I hadn't been to my mom's apartment in weeks and wondered if she had, either.

I walked in slowly, closing and locking the door behind me. I flipped the light switch. It was dead. I crossed the living room carefully, toeing in front of me before stepping, until I could draw back the curtains. Dusty light cast through the apartment; piles of wrappers, dishes, empty boxes, trash, and litter took form. I shook my head, recalling when I would finish my homework on the couch or play Monopoly with Mom on the coffee table when a snowstorm closed the bar. A cold wave of nostalgia shivered up my spine, and I wondered if she was here looking at that couch with me. I wished I knew which form of my mom went onto the next life, if there is a next life: Was she the mom I saw at Christmas Mass? Or the mom toward the end?

I had a brief urge to clean the apartment, but it fleeted quickly. That asshole, Bobby, could deal with this mess. It was his apartment after all; or at least, he paid for it.

I breathed in sharply and made my way to my mother's room, stepping lightly until I drew back her curtains, as well. The chest I came for sat beneath the window. I cleared the clothes off a chair, pulled it up to the chest, and opened the lid. A waft of piney cedar stung my nose as I pulled out a stack of photos and papers. Mom kept anything of importance in this chest: birth certificates, baby blankets, poems, photos. She had always said that if there was a fire, we were only to save this chest. I thumbed through the papers, pausing to read a poem entitled, "In the Midst." My lip trembled as I read a passage dated shortly after my birth:

> *And as I reach through the rubble of life,*
>
> *I find a sliver of Faith.*
>
> *Blue-eyed and puckered,*
>
> *And I hope that your despondent clutches*
>
> *Will release me.*
>
> *Just for a while.*
>
> *Just long enough.*

I felt tears sting the back of my eyes, which I blinked back quickly. I wished that I had known my mother better, that she would have let me into her world. When I was growing up, Mom had a manic sense of staying busy. She woke and worked, worked then slept, and in between (and often times during) she would drink to accomplish both. She didn't attend school meetings, not that there were many of them, and she didn't enjoy a meal with me while talking about our day. But that wasn't because she didn't care; it was because she didn't see the relevance of it. She always provided for me and there was a rhythm about our relationship that suited both of us. I didn't know if my childhood was normal because I didn't have a benchmark. But I did know that until Bobby started coming around, there was at least a sense of order and predictability. And after Bobby, there was no sense at all.

I moved on to some photos and landed on one of Mom with long, glossy black hair parted down the middle and a gleaming smile. She was stunningly tall and lean in her tight jeans. I flipped to another one of her holding me as a child. I must have been two or three years old, and we looked like we were laughing, laughing as though we were being wildly tickled. I wondered why I never remembered my mom being as happy as she looked in that photo. Her eyes were bright, and her face was full and flushed with color, not lean and gaunt as I was used to seeing her. In that photo she looked, I thought to myself with a faint smile, like a mom.

I found two plastic bags with take-out boxes in them and emptied them. I filled both bags with photos and papers I wanted to keep, and left the rest. I went to my mom's closet and grabbed the red scarf she always wore to Christmas Mass. I stuffed it into one of the bags.

Suddenly, I heard a click and a creak. I paused, bags in hand, and listened intently. The apartment door opened. My heart thudded against my ribs. There was only one other person who had a key to get in: Bobby Clay. An old, familiar feeling of dread hummed through me. This time, my mom wasn't here to field Bobby away from me. I heard thick footsteps cross the living room toward the bedroom door, stumble once, then recover. I looked around in a panic and picked up the statue of Saint Francis, shaking the jewelry from his neck.

"Is that you, Faith?" he called out in a strong lullaby. "I wondered if I'd run into you here."

My breath shallowed as my heart raced through my ears. I swallowed heavily and debated whether I should run out and try to race past him in the living room, or if I'd have to wait until he entered the bedroom to swipe past him. It was too late; Bobby's robust frame came into shape in the window-lit doorway.

"It is you," he smiled cunningly. "How are you doing? You must be pretty shaken up." I half expected him to lick his lips while scanning my body, and an oscillating angst I had felt a hundred times swept through me.

"I was just leaving," I said shakily.

He looked at the Saint Francis clutched tightly in my fists. "You weren't going to hit me with that, were you?" He chuckled slightly. "There's no need for violence, Faith. Especially at such a sad time. We just lost an Angel, you and me."

My stomach lurched at the way he said my mother's name with a paltry manner of ownership.

"Don't say her name," I said icily. *You piece of shit.* "I'm leaving now," I said as I attempted to walk past him and out the room.

He tried to stop me, but I jumped back before he could touch me.

"Woah, relax," he said, entertained.

"What do you want, Bobby? There's nothing left here for you," I said as rage crept up from belly, but fear filled my chest and began sliding down my arms.

"Of course there's something left. Look at this mess. Someone's got to clean it up, huh? Make sure everything is taken care of?"

The rage continued to web through my veins and my fingers were starting to feel the tingle. "You didn't come to take care of anything for her, Bobby. You came to save yourself, to cover up anything that could lead to you."

He teetered his head back and forth. "Maybe. But I have to admit that I am sad as I look around this place. Your mom was a beautiful woman; it's a shame what became of her."

The rage in my body grew warmer. "What became of her? You became of her! You ruined her life when you started doing drugs with her! Or did you forget that part?"

He snorted uncomfortably. "Your mom was a grown woman who made her own choices."

"Bullshit!" I hollered. "My mother was fine until you came along and charmed her and made her feel like you'd take care of everything. But you never wanted her for anything other than something pretty on your arm and someone to party with, and when you were done with her, you would disappear, leaving her for weeks pining for you."

Bobby rolled his eyes and smiled. "I loved your mother. We had an arrangement that worked for us. She knew what she was getting into. And I did take care of her. I paid for this apartment. I paid for a lot of things."

I scoffed. "Oh, you paid for a lot of things, all right. Specifically, cocaine. You got my mother addicted to drugs so that she'd have to stay addicted to you."

"I think you have the wrong perception of me, Faith," he said, hardening his tone. "Sure, your mom and I partied together, but I didn't get her addicted to drugs. I can't take the blame for that. I tried to help her. I loved her."

"Stop! Just stop!" I shouted as tears stung the back of my eyes. But I would never let them fall and give that prick the satisfaction. I edged closer to the door for an easier escape. "You were the gateway drug for her. You always gave her just enough. Just enough money to get by, just enough of an apartment, just enough of your lies. And when you were done partying with her, filling her nose full of coke and her heart full of empty promises, you'd disappear back to your perfect family and your perfect law firm, and you'd keep her tucked away as your dirty little secret. And as long as you gave her enough, always just enough, she stayed exactly that: your secret, pretty muse."

He flinched imperceptibly and his face sobered. He didn't look entertained anymore, and I wondered if I had gone too far. I gripped Saint Francis tighter.

"I did what I could to help," he said stoically.

"Is that what you tell yourself at night as you're lying next to your boring fucking wife thinking about my beautiful mother who is lying cold in a morgue because of you?"

Bobby's eyes got wide and he started puffing loudly. "I didn't kill your mother! She ruined her own goddamned life!"

He stood tall and faced me firmly. I clenched the statue, though I felt the rage that fueled my bravery dissipate quickly, as though someone sucked it right out of me.

"Your mother was miserable before she met me. When I met her, she was a sad fucking waitress at the diner with no life in her at all. I gave her life. I put color back into her cheeks. She was happy when she was with me. And yes, we partied. A lot of people do, Faith. But it's not my fault that she turned into a low-life junkie. That's on her."

I willed the rage to come back and fill my body with the bravery I had minutes before, but I was met with fear, instead. My legs felt like jelly and my arms felt too weak to hold up the statue. I had been calculating that if he charged me, I would have to hit him across the face; the body would not stop him. But it would have to be just across the cheek, not high enough to hit his temple, but not low enough to where I'd miss the opportunity to knock him out.

As if he could sense my fear, he stepped closer. I held up Saint Francis like a baseball bat, but the realization that I didn't have the mettle to hit him made the statue feel heavier.

He snickered. "Go ahead and put that down now. Come on, you've been through a lot. You've lost your mother, and you probably feel confused and alone. I can help you. Let me help you." His tone had turned soothing and plausible. "You're even more beautiful than your mother."

I recoiled as that hungry look he wore when I was younger returned to his face. I could almost see him salivating.

He took a step toward me, and as swiftly as a boxer ducks from a punch, I grabbed both bags and darted past Bobby, running from the room. I took high, quick steps to jump over anything I might trip on. I heard Bobby swivel and walk after me. "Where are you going? I'm not going to hurt you. Come back! Faith, come back!"

And that was the last time I would hear Bobby Clay's voice.

CHAPTER SEVEN

I walked faster than most people run for five blocks and dipped into the tunnel to catch the train back to Center City. Every step I took felt heavy, like I was stepping in mud, and I kept glancing behind me to make sure Bobby didn't follow me. But I knew he wouldn't follow me down to the train corridor. The train might wrinkle his $5,000 suit.

I stood in the crowded train car, holding onto the canvas strap that hung from the ceiling and feeling as impotent as it did. I felt the need to cry, but tears were stuck inside a cubby of guilt. I should have hit him, I knew I should have, but my arms were so heavy. I couldn't make sense of it.

I quivered as I recalled his smug grin. I realized tonight was the only time I'd been alone with Bobby. Though I had seen that hungry look on him before, my mom was always quick to usher Bobby off. Tonight, I was alone, and those wet eyes made me cringe as they had when I was younger.

I remembered the first time my mom brought Bobby home. I was sitting on the couch doing homework and he trailed into the apartment after her. "Faith, hi, honey. This is Bobby. Bobby, Faith," she pointed quickly, as she brushed past to get to her bedroom. "I'll only be a minute!"

Bobby took a seat on a chair adjacent to me. He pulled the legs of his creased suit pants as he sat, and I noticed how shiny his paisley socks seemed.

"Whatcha working on there?" he asked, leaning forward on his knees. His eyes felt sticky.

"Math," I answered without looking up.

"Ah," he said, craning closer to look at my algebra page. "I never did like math. X's and y's that make a z," he chuckled. "It doesn't matter much in the real world."

I wholeheartedly disagreed, but I didn't care to engage in conversation. My mom always told me not to trust a man who tried to be my friend. "Men should be friends with people their own age."

"You look like your mother," he smiled intently. "Anyone ever tell you that?"

I remained silent; a creep sped up my spine.

My mom swept out of her bedroom with fresh clothes and a plume of perfume. "You ready?" she asked as she eyed Bobby. The toggle of her eyes from him to me told me that she read the awkward interaction.

"I'm ready," Bobby said. "I was just helping your daughter with some math."

Which he was not.

"Okay," my mother laughed nervously. "Faith, there are still some chicken fingers in the fridge. You're good, right?"

I nodded a smile at her.

"'Kay, then," she said, as she put on her jacket and guided Bobby to the door.

They left and I hoped Bobby would be a name I didn't hear after a couple of dates. But he stuck, and after a few more exchanges that left me with my skin crawling, I started excusing myself right away when he showed up. I'd walk to the Free Library of Philadelphia and stay there until I knew they'd be gone. Eventually, my mom must have come to the same conclusion as I did about Bobby—it was unnatural the way he looked at me—so she would casually preempt his visit with, "Faith, did you want to go to the library for a little bit?"

I thought of all the nights I lay in bed as a teenager fantasizing about ways to make Bobby disappear, ranging from amateur plots to hit him between the eyes with a slingshot to more sadistic conspiracies of pushing him down the steep apartment stairwell.

Today had been my chance to make him disappear, or at least to have left a mark on his smug face. But I didn't. For the first time, I felt something I had never felt for my mother concerning Bobby: Empathy. I could never understand why she stayed with him, why she put up with his inappropriateness, and (I suspected) his temper. But today, I understood how large he seemed when you were alone with him. And I was angry that I allowed him to make me feel small.

My stop came, and I mechanically stepped out and followed the herd of people ascending the stairway to 22nd Street. The crisp air blew the presence of Bobby off of me as I walked home, and I forced myself to redirect my thoughts. Bobby was now officially in my past. I would never have to hear about or see him again, and that breathed satisfaction into me.

As I reached for my apartment door, a cloud of strong smells filled my nose. I recalled that I had allowed Beau to meet me back here tonight. I reflected with some humor at how this man who was practically a stranger yesterday had earned a key to my apartment, even a temporary key.

"Hey, hon," he hollered as I opened the door and cautiously gazed in. He was at the stove stirring something in a pot. I walked in slowly, dropped the bags on the couch, and removed my jacket. *Now he's calling me 'hon?'* I wanted to dislike it, but I didn't.

"What are you cooking?"

He walked over to give me a long hug, swaying me back and forth; his strong body easily engulfed my frame. I accepted with my arms at my side at first, then moved them up to return his pine-scented embrace.

"It's nothing fancy. It's just some chicken soup," he said casually. He removed my scarf and coat and slung it over the arm of the couch. "But it's medicine for the soul," he grinned and took me back in his arms.

"It smells good," I mumbled, buried in his embrace. As I looked past his shoulders to the table that he set with bowls, cutlery, napkins, and glasses, my shoulders shook softly, and I squeezed my eyes willing the dam to break and the tears to fall. And though they didn't, I felt a flood of emotions wash over me.

"I'm sorry, Faith," he rubbed my back tenderly. "This must be so hard for you."

I nodded. But the emotions weren't for the loss of my mother nor for my horrendous night.

This was the first time I had walked into a home-cooked meal.

"I like this one the best," Beau said, holding out the photo of my mother and me. It was the same photo I reflected on in her apartment.

"I like it, too, but I was trying to find a photo of just her to frame for the funeral." I shuffled through the handful of photos I gleaned from the cedar chest. Most of the photos showed my mother with her hand splayed in front of her face or covering her mouth or half an eye. I found it odd that I was just now realizing how camera-shy she was.

"Maybe having a service for my mom is not the greatest idea," I said pensively.

"I think it will be nice. You may not realize it, but having closure is important." He said this as if he knew what he was talking about.

"Have you ever been to a funeral?"

"I come from a big family, so yes, grandparents, uncles, aunts…"

I nodded. I had never been to a funeral service.

"Listen, don't worry about a thing," Beau said reassuringly. "Uncle Seb will take care of the details. It will be a nice service for your mom. Is this the photo you like then?" He held up the photo of me and my mom, the only photo that showed her uninhibited smile.

"I guess. I just wish there was one of her by herself, but with that smile."

"Then I'll make it work. I know someone who can take images and make them into whatever you want, so if you want your mom by herself, by herself she will be."

"Really?" I asked, hopeful.

"Absolutely, but I better get going so I can make sure it's done by Saturday," he said as he collected our dishes to take to the sink.

My heart sunk at the thought of Beau leaving. I got up and followed him to the sink, carrying our water glasses.

"Maybe you can look into it tomorrow? It's already getting late. Surely, your friend won't be able to do anything tonight?" I asked as more of a statement.

He ran the water and started rinsing the dishes. "He's kind of a night owl," he said over his shoulder. "He'll still be up."

I bit my lip nervously. An unfamiliar feeling coursed through me: I didn't want to be alone.

"But maybe," I said loud enough for him to hear over the water and clinking dishes, "it would be best if you just—"

He turned off the water.

"Stay," I finished in the awkward quiet.

He contemplated, trying to decipher the intention of my words.

"You want me to stay?" He turned to give me full attention, slinging a dish towel over his shoulder and resting his hands behind him on the sink. *God, he made domesticity look so hot.*

"Yeah, I do." I meant it. And I wouldn't have meant it if it were Irena or anyone else. I wanted only Beau to stay.

"How about I stay until you fall asleep?" he offered. "You need some rest. But I'll come back tomorrow if you'd like."

My pulse fastened thinking of him leaving until tomorrow.

"I want you to stay until we both fall asleep," I invited.

He laughed nervously and looked down at the floor. Beau had been flirty and charismatic up until the point where I fled from our date at the bar. After the hospital, he had softened into more of a friend or a familiar lover. But now, as his physique poked through his shirt, but not presumptuously, a strange pull nudged at me to inch forward and dive into his dimples.

"Please?" I asked softly.

He lifted his head slowly and put his hands out for me to come close. I sauntered closer.

"I'd love to, really, I would." he said slowly, as if calculating how to politely decline. "But—"

"I want you to stay, Beau," I said resolutely.

He tipped his forehead so that it was touching mine. I was dizzy with his heady scent, and I let my hands wander around his muscular chest as if in search of something lost.

"Faith, you can't imagine how badly I want to be with you," he sighed lustily.

"Good," I smiled relieved.

"I want to stay, Faith, but I can't stay in *that* way."

I slackened.

"I'll hold you until you fall asleep," he said as he pulled his head back and moved a strand of hair behind my ear. "You're so beautiful when you sleep."

I blushed and scoffed sulkily. "Don't you think that's a little unfair?"

"That you're so beautiful?"

"*No*," I retorted. "That you've seen me sleep, but I haven't seen you. C'mon…stay."

"I just—" he shifted. "This might sound ridiculous, and God knows I'm going to regret saying this," he laughed. "But I don't want us ruined because you and I rushed into things at the wrong time."

I knew what he really meant. He didn't want to be with me while I was fragile. He didn't want a desperate invitation. I could appreciate it seemed that way, but what Beau didn't realize was that my most fragile part, the part that kept me up at night with worry for as long as I could remember, was now lying in a morgue waiting for Saturday's service. And the silver lining was that it allowed a part of me to be free.

"I'm fine; I really am," I said, answering the question I knew he'd been wanting to ask since yesterday.

"It's okay if you're not," he said genuinely.

That small response, that permission, made the well of tears behind my eyes threaten to break the dam again, but I'd be damned if it didn't hold strong.

"But I am," I contested. "I know this is going to sound insensitive, but as much of me that is sad, the same amount of me is relieved. My mother hasn't been well for a while. This didn't come out of nowhere."

"That doesn't necessarily make it easier, I'd imagine."

"But it made it predictable. And in my profession, you come to anticipate certain outcomes," I said pragmatically. Beau's stare made me realize how cold I must seem and I feared he might think I was sociopathic if I didn't give a little more explanation. "Look, I'm not heartless, and this hurts. It does. But I've been waiting for that call, so now I have to focus on getting through the next few days. I'll have time to process the rest later. And I will, I promise."

He smiled empathetically. "I believe you."

I grinned a *thank you*. "So, you'll stay?"

"I'll stay," he confirmed, cupping his strong, lightly calloused hand behind my head. "But nothing past first base," he said with his golden grin.

"Deal. Can we start now, though?" I asked before leaning in to kiss his neck.

"I should probably finish these dishes," he replied, lifting his chin to let me graze beneath it.

"The dishes can wait until tomorrow," I pouted out slowly between kisses.

He moaned, then finally relented by bringing my face to his. "Yes, they can." Then he pulled me in for a kiss that made my knees buckle.

For the next ten minutes or so, our lips communicated without words. Moans and sighs and the occasional giggle, as if Beau and I were watching a movie of our lips falling in love. And for ten whole minutes, I didn't think about my mother or work or succeeding or failing or anything else that kept me up at night. I thought only of this kiss and the smell of chicken soup in my kitchen, and the man behind both of those things.

And though we didn't go past "first base," that night Beau taught me things about my heart that I would never learn in med school.

The day of the funeral came with a thunderous boom. A rainstorm had swept through the city, shaking the buildings with each cracking rumble.

I stood in the small chapel arranging, then rearranging, the flowers and photos that surrounded my mother's pearly urn on the table. I stared at the urn that contained the last of my mother and felt a sardonic sensation pulse through me. After all the life we live, the feelings we feel, the bonds we make, in the end, we can be bottled up in iridescent cream porcelain. It seemed such a simple conclusion to the great complexities of life, and I wondered if it was only I who found it to be placid.

I heard the echo of the door open and in walked Beau carrying a rectangular object wrapped in loose plastic. He reached me out of breath and shaking the rain from his sleeves.

"Wow, is it coming down outside or what?" he exasperated as he trudged over and gave me a wet kiss on the cheek.

"What's that you're holding?" I eyed the object he gripped.

"Oh, this is the photo of your mother I promised." He went to a closet and pulled out a small easel and set it up next to the table with the urn. He unwrapped the photo, its back facing me, then set it gently upright.

I gasped when he stepped back. An oil-painted canvas of my mother, whose features were naturally of cold colors—black hair, pale skin, red lips, purple eyes—had somehow transformed to tones as warm as a sunset.

"Did you do this?" I asked Beau as I stepped closer to touch my mother's angelic face.

"Yes. Do you like it?"

My throat caught. "It's perfect." I realized in that moment, studying my mother's glittery eyes, that the reason I loved her smile in this photo so much was because it was something I saw only once a year at Mass on Christmas Eve: Sober.

"Your smile is like hers," he said.

"Really?" I had been told many times that I looked like my mother, but never because of our smiles. It occurred to me that through this portrait, Beau was one of the only people who had seen my mother smiling uninhibitedly. And perhaps he also was one of the few who had seen me smile the same way.

"She's beautiful. I wish I could have known her," he offered.

"I wish you could've too." But in some twisted way, it felt appropriate that this was how Beau was meeting my mother—the best of people always comes out at their funeral.

"Thank you, Beau. Thank you for this painting."

He smiled as if to say, "It was no bother."

I stepped closer to him. "And thank you for being here."

"Faith," he said, wrapping his arms gently around my waist. "There is no where on earth I'd rather be."

I hugged him intensely because it was the only way I knew how to express the overwhelming emotions that were spilling out my pores.

The door echoed open again and Uncle Seb shimmied in with a wheeled cart holding a flower arrangement so large that it would require two people to carry it. It was full of mostly white lilies.

"Another one," Uncle Seb said out of breath. "This one must be from someone special!"

I narrowed my eyes at the flower arrangement speeding toward me. Only one person I knew would send something so extravagant, so hyperbolic.

"Wow, that's a flower arrangement!" Beau exclaimed.

I didn't smile. I just reached out and grabbed the card from the staked pin and read it silently: "For an Angel." -B.C.

Bobby Clay.

"I'm sorry. I think there's a mistake. These flowers don't belong here." I told Uncle Seb.

He looked confused. "I'm quite certain they do. They were delivered with your mother's name—"

I cut him off. "I know and I'd rather not explain, but these flowers don't belong here. That's all I can say. Can you please take them elsewhere? Donate them to the next funeral. I don't care what you do with them."

Uncle Seb looked at Beau, who shrugged. Then he politely carted them back up the aisle.

"You okay?" Beau asked, concerned.

I crumpled the card into my pocket as if it were a gum wrapper. "Yeah, I'm fine. Thanks."

And just like that, Bobby Clay ruined another beautiful moment of mine.

CHAPTER EIGHT

I t was Match Day.

I barely slept as it was, but last night, I stared at the city lights through the slats of the blinds, unable to calm my mind enough to sleep.

"You're going to get in," Beau said sleepily beside me after I tossed to a new staring position. I appreciated Beau's confidence, but there wasn't a resident who was getting sleep tonight, especially one applying for a cardiology fellowship, one of the most competitive fellowship programs to get into because of its limited number of slots. Of course, it wasn't enough for me to get matched to any program—I wanted to match at Penn.

His arm flung over blindly to console me. "Get some sleep, babe."

I clutched at his hand like one grasps at a lifeline, careful not to wake him, but I needed this hand that had comforted me through the past year of ups and downs and all-arounds. This had been my hardest year of residency. The hand that rested on my chest was the hand that held me after a hard day at work. It was the hand that patted my back after I accomplished something no other resident had accomplished. It was the hand that stroked my face tenderly to wake me for the next round of chaos. And if I matched into the fellowship program I desired, this hand would be the one I'd reach for over the next three years of an equally challenging caliber.

I knew my own two hands were enough to get me through life; they had gotten me this far. But, I realized, it wasn't about *needing* Beau's hands to get through life. It was about *wanting* his hands to hold through the journey.

I finally flung the blankets off and got out of bed around five-thirty. I wasn't due at the hospital today, but I got there by six o'clock anyway, burying myself in work until matches would be posted at noon. I took huge bites of breaths to calm the surge of anxiety that would wave in my chest as the clock ticked slowly toward noon. My back felt tight. My watch felt heavy on my wrist as I glanced at it every minute or so.

At 11:40 a.m., twenty minutes before I could log in to see my fellowship fate, I got a text from Beau.

Meet me at the Serenity Garden.

Meet him at the Serenity Garden? No, I couldn't possibly. That was in the other building, by Oncology.

You're at the hospital? Are you volunteering today? I replied.

Yes, I'm here. No, I'm not volunteering. Come over. This will be a nice place to see your match.

I thought about his suggestion. He was right. The Serenity Garden is peaceful and the fresh air would do me some good, no matter what the result was.

Ok. On my way.

I walked briskly to the other building, unaware of the people I was passing. I checked my watch compulsively.

Finally, the elevators opened to the fifth floor, and I made my way toward the Serenity Garden. I opened the doors to find Beau waiting for me in dress pants and a charcoal-colored blazer.

"Do you have a meeting today?" I asked, surprised by his sharp appearance. His everyday attire was casual, and damn, he looked good polished. Good enough to have distracted me. *Shit*, I glanced at my watch.

"You have four minutes," he smiled. He was holding something behind his back.

"What are you hiding back there?" I asked with a smirk.

"It's a surprise. For after your results. But this is for now." He handed me a coffee. On the sleeve was written, "Good Luck."

I tipped my head. "Thank you, Beau." I walked toward him to give him a kiss. He leaned over and kissed me sweetly, but wedged the coffee between us enough that I still couldn't glance at what was behind his back.

"You ready then?" he asked excitedly.

"Yeah. I think so," I said. *One minute left.* I logged into the website that would display my match. "God, I'm so nervous."

"You're going to get in," Beau said confidently, although he looked nervous, too.

Noon.

Results.

Penn.

"I'm in! I got into Penn!" I screamed as I stared at the results on my phone that confirmed I had made it into the fellowship program at the Hospital of the University of Pennsylvania. I would start and finish in the same place, just as I had wanted.

I looked up to celebrate with Beau, but quickly averted my eyes down. Beau was kneeling on one knee. He held out a small bouquet of baby red roses with a gleaming ring nestled in the middle.

"You were hard to catch, Faith," he said with his incredible smile.

I teepeed my hands in front of my mouth. "Oh my God. Beau...."

"But now that I have you, I plan to keep you forever. Be my wife, Faith. Marry me."

So much had led up to this moment. My mind reeled back to the past year of finding love with Beau and the past decade of working toward a career in medicine. My heart flooded with pride that both efforts were being met with solid commitment.

"Yes!" I beamed.

He stood and kissed me passionately, our smiles pressed together. He slipped the ring on my finger. Some people nearby started clapping, and we turned to acknowledge them with our elated laughter. Beau lifted his arm in a triumphant fist pump, egging their applause on. I buried my face in his chest at the attention but couldn't stifle my joy.

Today was Match Day. Double Match Day.

We settled on a small beach ceremony in Florida where his parents lived. I toggled with the idea of getting married in a catholic church, but in the end, I didn't want to face the lopsided pew flock. Surely, the bride-side would be sparse.

The ceremony was lovely and reflected everything I loved about our relationship: simple, unassuming, and warm. Beau's dad walked me down the aisle and Irena served as my Maid of Honor and only guest. Beau's mother and sister had arranged nearly everything, which I had gratefully welcomed. I could save lives, but so help the soul who relies on me to make place cards or source taffeta for guest chairs.

We took a three-day honeymoon in an upscale Florida resort before returning home to Philly for me to start my fellowship. We were settling into our new norm of busy schedules and heavy metal on our ring fingers when Beau sprung an idea on me.

"Let's have a baby," he said while picking up a piece of tuna sashimi from a plate we shared.

I choked. "A baby? Now? You must be kidding."

"I'm serious. I mean, we both want kids and there will never be a good time to start."

In truth, Beau really wanted kids, and I really wanted to make him happy. One of the aspects of Beau's life that I admired was the traditional one: siblings, family get-togethers, photo albums full of smiling children on the beach. But having a baby scared the hell out of me.

"I thought we agreed that we'd try after my fellowship, once I found permanent placement?"

He teetered in thought. "Yeah, I know, but that will be years. Do you really think it will be easier to have a baby when you're starting your career at a practice?"

He was right. I couldn't foresee an ideal time to start a family for the next five years, at least. I did a quick head calculation and surmised that if I planned a pregnancy correctly, I could stay on course for my fellowship. Then a panicky image of when I did rounds in the maternity ward came to mind: women on bedrest, complications that led to longer-than-anticipated healing times. I couldn't afford to have this go any other way than status quo.

"What if it doesn't work out and I fall behind on my program?" I asked, concerned.

Beau's eyes widened; he realized I might actually agree to this. "Then we'll deal with it. You started med school a year before your colleagues did anyway, so really, you'd still be right on course if there was a delay."

"I guess so," I contemplated. "But my schedule, Beau—I don't know how I'll manage a baby."

"My schedule is flexible, so I'll take care of the baby while you're finishing your program. Maybe we can get a nanny. With a British accent."

"I don't know," I flustered.

"Come on," he tugged at my shirt near my belly. "You're going to be the best mom. And the hottest," he added.

My stomach roiled. The best mom? Another thing I didn't know how to do. I looked at Beau's face and pictured a chubby baby with his dimples, and I couldn't resist.

"She has to have a British accent," I said.

He shifted with excitement. "So, is that a *Yes*?"

I breathed in and narrowed my eyes. "Yes. Let's give it a try."

There was a reason people "tried" to have babies.

"We'll try again," Beau rubbed my shoulders as I grimaced at another plastic applicator indicating I was not pregnant. Beau knew better than to give me a condoling, "I'm sorry, honey," or, "It's not your fault." He knew that I didn't take well to pity.

"I'm a doctor; I can feel that something is wrong. I'm going to call Dr. Desmond," I said.

"Whatever you think is best," Beau replied placidly.

I rubbed my lower lip and calculated my options. My brain was clinical by nature; it always had been. As a child, I dosed my medication after getting strep throat in the fourth grade and learned how to alternate between ibuprofen and acetaminophen at exactly the right hour. I learned how to dilute mom's vodka just enough where she wouldn't notice. And when the neighbors would leave their babies with me, I learned how to thicken their baby formula with a tad of rice meal to keep them fuller for longer (which always earned me a scold from their mothers for "using too much").

I had tracked my ovulation, read all the reproductive material I could find, and felt confident that getting pregnant would be as easy as every schoolteacher, church nun, and woman in my apartment building growing up warned me it would be.

But month after month, that damn applicator came back negative, slumping my shoulders and bruising my innate pride. All the years I spent reading about genetics and the role they play in health, sitting on my doctor's pedestal of "your body is your body," and here I sat wanting to change this aspect of mine.

There was something almost portent about the negative line on the stick that also resonated a hung feeling in me: Maybe I shouldn't mess with nature. *There's a reason my body isn't allowing this pregnancy right now,* I tried to tell myself. Yet the part of me that clasped at the marvels of modern medicine with eager fists also told me that we had a way around infertility for a reason.

And so we went to see Dr. Desmond.

"The bad news is that you have polycystic ovarian syndrome," Gerald (Dr. Desmond) started. "In other words, you're not ovulating normally."

I sighed. PCOS was my self-diagnosis so I couldn't say I was surprised.

"The good news is that it's quite common and there are medications that can help. Clomiphene is my first choice to start."

Before coming to see Dr. Desmond, I had brushed up on my notes from when I did rounds in Obstetrics and had researched the most common and safest routes of dealing with infertility. I knew that Clomiphene was a practical suggestion. I also knew that it came with a certain risk that I didn't want to consider.

"The risk with taking fertility drugs of any kind, of course, is the increased chance of becoming pregnant with multiples, typically twins," Dr. Desmond confirmed.

Beau perked up. "Twins?"

And while it seemed a drop of hope fell into the pool of dread for Beau, a drop of dread fell into the pool of hope for me. I was already anxious about what kind of mom I would be. Let's face it: I didn't have a deep well of knowledge to draw from, and I worked eighty hours a week. Beau had convinced me that he would take care of everything at home so that I could focus on my career, and we could hire a nanny to allow him to still paint. I trusted him and knew that he could pull from a resource I didn't have, one rich with family life and traditions.

But twins? It didn't sound like double the fun; it sounded like double the risk of failure.

My heart plunged thinking about failing at anything.

CHAPTER NINE

Juliet came first, already as determined as her mother, and secretly, I was proud of her for beating her brother out of the womb. Matthew came shortly after, quiet as a mouse.

"Is he okay?" I panted, panicked. He didn't cry. Then, a small wail.

"A healthy baby boy!" Dr. Sue announced proudly. She was the only traditional doctor who said, "You can do it!" when I told her I didn't want to schedule a C-section. Relief washed over me. I had given birth to two healthy babies with Beau by my side.

My body convulsed from the trauma, exhausted from a sixteen-hour labor, but I couldn't feel pain.

I held them both on my chest, tiny and pink, and something inside of me changed. Every resolve I had formed in my life became exaggerated in that sure moment. Now, my path, my goals, my decisions, weren't only for me.

Beau kissed my head, his eyes filled with joy. "You're amazing. You're just amazing," he said emotionally as he helped cradle the babies with one arm and stroked my wet hair with the other.

I blinked at them. Though they had occupied my body for nearly thirty-eight weeks, we had just met, these people I created. The realization was confounding, and it was the first time I felt a disconnection from science. Something supernatural had happened that couldn't be explained by any medical book.

The nurse came to take the babies for weighing and measurements. "No, not yet," I pleaded. She winked and walked away. I knew she'd be back momentarily, but I wanted this moment a little longer.

They settled together as they did in the womb, and I marveled at their delicate features. Matthew was nearly bald, but Juliet had sticky curls of light hair. Matthew had a stork's bite that went down his nose, but Juliet's face was flawless. Juliet's red lips parted and she whimpered, and I felt a heat of energy rush through my chest.

My whole life had been filled with unknowns. I didn't know who my father was. I had never met an aunt or grandmother. Most days, I didn't even know when my mother would come home again.

But there were a few things I knew for certain. One, I was my mother's daughter—good or bad, or anywhere in between. Two, I was meant to be a doctor. Three, that Beau was meant to be my husband. And now, with certainty, these lives that rested on my chest were meant to be mine.

I'd give them everything. Everything I didn't have. Everything I always wanted.

They'd have it all.

"I really liked the one on West State Street," Beau said as we clicked through photos of houses for sale in Doylestown, a suburb north of Philadelphia. "It's close to the hospital and good schools."

Matthew and Juliet sat on the floor piecing together parts of a fire truck floor puzzle. The twins had just turned three, making the timing of our move to a quaint suburb perfect. Though Beau was content to raise the kids in the city and had a better perspective since he took the lead in caring for the children while I finished my fellowship, I persisted a move to the suburbs. I wanted my children to have a carefree suburban life where they waited for the ice cream truck in the summer and built snowmen in the winter.

"Are you sure you're going to be okay in the 'burbs?" Beau teased. "You've been in the city your entire life."

"I'll be fine," I assured him. "But I've been thinking a lot about something, and I'd like to put it past you."

He waited expectantly for me to continue.

"I want to open a clinic. A wellness clinic for women. And men too," I added. "But mostly for women. I want to offer a place where they can feel safe to talk about what they really need and a place that can give them all-around medical care: physical, emotional, and mental."

"Okay," Beau said slowly. I could tell he wasn't expecting this conversation. "The concept is great, but why wouldn't they just go to their regular doctor or an existing wellness center? Isn't the mind/body/spirit-thing kind of *in* right now?"

"Yes, it's *in*," I smiled. "Which is why I know it will work. But patients need insurance or heavy wallets to go to the doctor's office or wellness centers. People wouldn't need insurance to be treated at my clinic."

"A free clinic?" he asked.

"Yes, but not in the traditional sense," I irked slightly. "My vision is to offer more than general care. I want to be known for top quality medical care with a strong cardiac focus. Beau, do you know how many people I've seen over the years who come in with congestive heart failure for reasons that are fairly avoidable?"

Beau shrugged. "I'm guessing a lot?"

"Yes, a lot. I've watched doctors get irritated because a patient hadn't gone to their primary doctor before the condition advanced. But I knew why they didn't. Most of them couldn't afford to go to a doctor. Some of them didn't even have a primary doctor. My mom didn't. *I* didn't growing up," I said, putting a hand to my chest. "My mom would take me to a local church for free immunizations and shuffle me around to different clinics if I got sick, which was almost never," I added. "The thing is, few of the places were *actually free*, and those that were didn't offer *whole* care or even consistent care. You'd go if you had something acute, then you would just be a name in the filing cabinet after that."

"Yeah, I can see that," Beau said morosely. Though he didn't experience those types of struggles first-hand, he had seen and heard enough during his work at the hospital to sympathize with the authenticity of the situation.

"Some people need more than just a doctor," I continued. "They need weight loss experts, abuse care, addiction specialists. They need a place that will pull these elements together without the burden of a bill to follow. I can't offer that at the hospital or at my practice, but I could offer it at an independent clinic."

He nodded. "It could have made a difference for you guys."

I shifted uncomfortably as Beau acknowledged how the latter service could have helped my mother, thereby helping me. It had been over five years since my mother died, and I may have brought her up in conversation a mere dozen times. I didn't like talking about her; it fueled feelings of anger and sadness (then anger at my sadness) that

I didn't know how to process. Irena suggested I "talk to someone" shortly after my mother died, but I didn't find the relevance in it. What's the use? She was gone, I reasoned. Though I couldn't help her from creeping into my head almost daily.

"Anyway, I'm going to need some funding, obviously," I deflected. "There is a foundation in Doylestown called the Massenet Foundation. They provide funding for women who are trying to get back on their feet, so to speak. I've booked an appointment to meet with the founder, Anna—I can't remember her last name—but I'm hoping the foundation can help with some of the costs to get the clinic running."

"So, this is more than just an idea. You've really looked into this," he said with a tinge of alarm.

"I have. And don't be mad, but I asked our realtor also to look at commercial spaces in Doylestown. It just so happens there is a building for sale that might be perfect. It was an old ophthalmologist practice."

"You want to buy a building? Shouldn't we just focus on buying a house for now? I mean, we have all those student loan debts, and we're getting this house on a doctor's mortgage. How in the world would we afford it? Shouldn't we wait until we at least have some real paychecks coming in?" Beau was starting to look concerned.

"Of course, buying a house for our family is the priority, but this would be separate from that. I could lease or rent a space for the clinic, and maybe I will, but if we can buy one, why not? Let me just see what Anna says when I meet with her. Maybe her foundation can help. If not, I'll wait to open the clinic. But it's really important to me to try, Beau. I want to give back."

"I feel like there's more to it than that," Beau said inquisitively.

"What?" I laughed defensively.

"It's not enough to land a job at one of the most competitive cardiac practices—with one of the highest salary contracts, I should add—you need to open a clinic, too? You always have to one-up people, don't you, Faith? You have to do it all," he smiled. Beau was one of the only people who understood my drive. It came from a deep place, a place of need and hunger. I wanted my name—our name, our kids' names—on a building one day, too.

"So, can I?" I asked sulkily.

He sighed. "Where are you going to find the time to work at the clinic? And what about the kids? We've been looking forward to you getting a normal job, if you can even call it that, so that you'd have a more predictable schedule and manageable hours."

I looked at the twins and grimaced. The clinic would inevitably take more of my time away from the kids. My long, erratic hours were never a problem when it was just me and Beau; he would use that time to paint and meet up with friends in the city. But since having the twins, Beau had taken on the bulk of the parenting role while I worked and it had worn on him. No one can prepare you for the demands of being a parent; no book, no pep talk, no horror story. Everyone thinks they're prepared, that they can defy the odds, that they have what it takes to not have the enormity of parenthood take over at times. But we had fallen prey to the demands more than once. I knew Beau was looking forward to some normalcy in our schedule so that we could spend more time on the same planet, rather than passing the baton in orbit.

"Okay, maybe the clinic can wait. You're right. Let's focus on the house and starting my job," I smiled weakly.

He closed his eyes and shook his head. "No. I can't do that to you. I'll support you. You know I will. Do whatever you think is best."

I bit my lip to suppress my spreading smile. "I can make it work, Beau. I promise."

"I know. I trust you."

"Thank you, thank you, thank you, Beau!" I got up and sat on his lap and wrapped my arms around his neck. "You won't regret this," I kissed behind his ear.

Somehow the twins, who up to this point, had been contentedly playing, perked up at my attention toward Beau and kicked into gear claiming their territory.

"Daddy, Daddy, I'm hungry!" Matthew came barreling over.

"I want cheese cheese's," Juliet sprung forward.

"I'll get them!" I said, scooping Juliet up and grabbing Matthew's hand. "Do you want chocolate milk instead?" I asked, still high from Beau's approval.

"Come on, Irena," I pleaded. "Why not? You're almost finished with your program. A clinic for women is the perfect place to start as an NP." Irena had been completing a program to become a certified registered nurse practitioner in tandem to my fellowship program. She had worked as a floor nurse for more than a decade, but now she was craving life on a slower scale with steady patients.

"You'll work under my supervision," I implored. "But really, you'll run the show since I'll be at the practice most days."

She kept busy as if she wasn't hearing what I was saying.

"I don't trust anyone else, Irena," I followed her as she shuffled items around. "Besides, Doylestown is great. You'll love it there."

Irena rolled her eyes. "I don't want to leave the city, Faith. I've been here my whole life."

"I get it; I have, too. But have you ever been to Doylestown? The clinic is going to be right downtown. It's a city," I proffered. "A really small one with low buildings."

"That's called a town."

"A city by any other name would smell as sweet! In fact, I promise you, it smells much better."

She laughed. Irena loved Shakespeare. For years, she toted a coffee mug around that said, "*A fool thinks himself to be wise, but a wise man knows himself to be a fool.*" I had never known Irena to think many people wise, and whenever a condescending doctor or know-it-all patient talked down to her, she'd politely take a sip of her coffee as if to retort with its silent message.

"I don't know," she hesitated. But I had hooked her interest.

"What's there to think about? I know you have a list a dozen deep of practices to send your resume."

She shrugged.

"I'm offering you a job right now. You don't even have to give me your resume," I teased. "And it's in a great town, doing feel-good work, and you get to work with *me*," I batted my eyes sarcastically.

"It's something to think about," she relented. "I do like the mission of the clinic; working with people, women, who need solid health care. I think about when my parents came to this country: My dad was a laborer and my mom stayed home to care for us. We couldn't afford to go to the doctor regularly. Hell, I think an old, half-blind woman who lived one street over in our small Greek community delivered my brother."

"That explains a lot about Tobias," I winced.

"Speaking of Tobias, what would I do with him? You know I'm all he has."

"Bring him, too. I'll hire him to clean or work the desk at the clinic."

She grimaced. "I don't think he knows how to operate a computer."

"Then he'll clean rooms and do general maintenance. He's good with a wrench, right?"

"He could build your clinic if you asked him."

"Perfect. I might need him to do just that if my meeting with The Massenet Foundation doesn't go well tomorrow. He'll pass a background check, right?"

She tilted her head.

"Doesn't matter. I'll find a way to make it work. Start looking for a place to live in Doylestown, Irena. I'm serious. We're doing this."

She looked at me contemplatively. "All right. Let's do it."

CHAPTER TEN

The door to The Massenet Foundation opened with a clanky ring. "Hi, can I help you?" a young woman with heavy eyeliner asked as I stepped in.

"Yes, I have an appointment. My name is Faith Wells."

"Of course. Anna will be with you in a moment. If you wouldn't mind taking a seat," she gestured.

I sat in one of the four chairs in the reception area and picked up a local magazine. I landed on a page advertising a nearby dairy farm with the area's best ice cream. *I'm not in the city anymore*, I thought.

"Dr. Wells?" I looked up to see a startlingly attractive woman holding her hand out to me.

"Yes, hi," I stood, shaking her hand while staring at her superbly green eyes.

"I'm Anna. Thanks for coming in," she smiled warmly. "Right this way."

I followed her through a small floor with four desks into one of two offices in the back. Her office was decorated in calming neutrals and her desk was adorned with dozens of photos of a man (presumably her husband), happy children, and a burly dog.

"Thank you for seeing me," I said as we settled.

"My pleasure. Coffee?"

"No, thank you."

"I was inspired by your email and your application," Anna stated with pleasantly crossed hands. "Tell me a little more about the clinic you're interested in opening."

I cleared my throat. "Well, I'm moving to the area soon to take an attending position at the Cardiac Care of Doylestown, near the hospital. But I also wanted to open a clinic, particularly for women, with a focus on cardiac health," I smiled at the obvious motive. "The clinic also would offer other specialties in addition to general health care."

"Your application listed specialties like weight loss, which seems in line with a cardiac facility, but it also listed mental care and addiction help?" she asked while scanning highlighted portions of my application. "How do those things fit in?"

"Cardiac care is what I know and I chose cardiology because—" I paused. Without thought, I almost confided in Anna that my mother's addiction and cocaine-induced heart attack was what inspired me to become a cardiologist. But my filter caught the words before they came out. Still, I was jarred that Anna had that effect on me. "—I chose this specialty because heart disease kills more people than any other ailment. In addition to obesity, stress and drug abuse—particularly cocaine—lead to heart conditions, sometimes fatal."

I thought I saw her smile flinch, but it was probably because she worked with women with substance abuse daily, so she knew the statistics well.

"Indeed," she said. "And this would be a nonprofit clinic, so you'll treat people who don't have insurance?"

"Yes. That's the purpose of the clinic, really. Everyone deserves good health care. That's why we need the funding. Not just to get the clinic started, but to afford the essential staff. I'll be able to dedicate only one day per week to the clinic, so I'll need a nurse practitioner to manage the day-to-day. I'll also need a medical assistant and two people to manage the office and paperwork. Most doctors, myself included, will donate their time intermittently."

Anna nodded. "I can appreciate the motive. We have many women who come to us for help, and one of the main things they need, aside from employment, is good health care. Government health programs help, of course, but they don't cover all that they truly need."

"Exactly. And often, women with little or no healthcare coverage will avoid seeking sufficient medical care because they don't feel comfortable or don't think they can afford it," I added.

"Absolutely. There was a woman who used to come in, Patricia, who had a constant cough. She always looked tired. I encouraged her to see a doctor. She was reluctant, but she finally went to urgent care. They said she sounded like she had pneumonia and told her to go to the hospital for X-rays. There, the X-rays revealed possible pneumonia, so they gave her antibiotics and told her to follow up with her doctor. She never did because she didn't have one. Several months later, she collapsed and was rushed into the hospital with a heart condition. It turned out, it wasn't her lungs at all. It was her heart."

"Heart failure," I wagered. "That happens more often than you think. The lungs and the heart are frequently confused; they're symbiotic organs."

"Right, well, I have to think that if she'd had more regular care—a doctor who knew her—she might have been able to identify her heart problems earlier."

"It's very possible. And that's exactly the point, right? That story is many women's stories because women in particular are less inclined to put their needs above others. So, they hold off on paying a fifteen-dollar copay in place of food for their kids. Especially women who barely have fifteen dollars to their name."

Anna nodded. "Then, for some women—often times, women I work with—their back starts to hurt or they're wrought with anxiety, so they take a pill or a hit from someone else, and it's lost from there."

I narrowed my eyes slightly. She really got this. Anna understood women's struggles. And it seemed she genuinely cared about them. I didn't expect this from someone who seemed poised and pretty—sitting in a poised and pretty office in a poised and pretty town—and I found myself easily trusting that Anna was the right person to have come to for help with the clinic.

"So, you need $500,000 for this clinic?" she asked. I liked her directness.

"Yes. As I laid out in my business plan, I will try to raise some of that through donations. I have a few patients and colleagues who likely will contribute, but I'm new to the area, so my reach only goes so far. And the clinic will run independently with no affiliation to the hospital or health networks."

"That's a lot of money," Anna sighed while contemplating. "Let me make some calls and run it past my husband, who manages the campaigns. Perhaps we can raise that money for you, along with using a little of the foundation's funds. Give me a couple of weeks."

"I appreciate that," I said relieved. "In exchange, I hope you'll refer women who come to the Massenet Foundation to the clinic. Oh, and if things work out, I'd like to put your foundation's name on a cornerstone of the building."

"That would be lovely," she smiled. "What are you going to call it?"

I had written down dozens of names, but only one kept finding its way to the top of the list, despite my attempts to find a better one.

"The Angel Clinic," I finally said out loud.

"How fitting," Anna appraised.

Indeed.

CHAPTER ELEVEN

It was a sunny September day when we moved to Doylestown. Our move was welcomed by the town's annual art festival that filled the streets with canopied crafts and a veil of cotton candy and popcorn.

Beau and I walked with the twins down State Street, their awes and coos blending with those of hundreds of other children.

"I love this!" Beau exclaimed. "It reminds me of walking the boardwalk as a kid. All the noise and people. Isn't it great?"

"It's perfect," I agreed. As I strolled along with Matthew's little hand in mine, I realized the pieces to my puzzle were starting to fit.

Beau and I had closed on our house two months ago—a beautiful 19th century Victorian—as well as a two-story brownstone in Doylestown, registered now as The Angel Clinic. As I signed the closing documents, my chest swelled with pride. It would be the first time in my life not living in an apartment. We had a house, a home, where Matthew and Juliet had their own bedrooms, Beau had an art studio, and we had space to grow. It was everything I dreamed of as I labored through years of school, residency, and fellowship.

"Mommy, look!" Juliet screeched. She pointed excitedly to an inflatable bouncy house.

"Can we go in?" Matthew hollered.

Beau and I helped them take off their shoes and lifted them through the 3-foot opening to the bouncy house.

"I'm glad you encouraged us to move here," Beau said with his arm around my shoulder as we watched the twins bop from side to side. I leaned into him.

"We start interviews for the clinic next week," I boasted.

"That's great. It's really coming along. You're an impressive woman, Faith Wells, M.D." He liked to add the accreditation. Admittedly, it made me proud every time he did.

"Plus, the renovations are almost complete."

He smiled his approval while eyeing the bouncy house.

"And I think, despite herself, Irena loves Doylestown, too," I laughed.

"I'm sorry. But I have to...," he said as an apology, not hearing the last two things I had said. He beamed his mischievous dimples at me, and I knew what he was thinking.

"No, Beau," I laughed. "Don't do it."

"I have to," he contested as he took off his shoes.

I shook my head, but I couldn't stifle my laughter as he climbed into the bouncy house and tumbled the kids like laundry in a dryer. He gestured for me to join, but I was happier watching and listening to their giggles. Sometimes, I longed for the ability to channel the childlike nature that Beau could. But I had nowhere from which to draw it.

What I did have to draw from was a well of discipline and resourcefulness, which was proving helpful in my career. Just blocks from where I stood watching the kids toss around, the clinic was taking shape. With a $500,000 grant approval from the Massenet Foundation, The Angel Clinic had a crew plastering walls, installing lighting, and putting up signage. The clinic was walking-distance from the house and the house was walking-distance from the hospital, which meant I could get to all three of my workplaces within minutes.

Irena found a small apartment in town and I agreed to let Tobias live in the clinic's upstairs apartment under the agreement that he would serve as its property manager and help with clinic renovations. He was proving to be an effective foreman and a surprising find. Tobias had renovated the apartment (that he shared with several house plants and a tabby orange cat with six toes per paw) with the tasteful pallet of creams and grays, accented with old wood. It was not what one would expect from a six-eight-ish, thickset Greek man, but as I was getting to know Tobias, the apartment seemed fitting to what was inside his gruff exterior.

Irena found new flush in her cheeks by organizing the clinic's everyday details. We spent the better half of the last month creating manuals and procedures, outlining escalation paths, and anticipating a workable schedule that would allow me to focus much of my daytime energy at the practice while spending my day off (typically a Tuesday) at the clinic for specialty appointments. I had recruited several other area specialists to volunteer one day a month at the clinic: obstetricians, dermatologists, even a nutritionist.

I closed my eyes and inhaled a sense of accomplishment.

I was ready to make this town pulse.

"Hi," a meek voice barely cut through the hammering sounds from behind the receptionist area.

Irena and I turned to find a small, ballerina of a woman clutching her hands with a timid smile.

"I was wondering if you were hiring?" she asked. Her features were delicate but alluring, and though she had a mature look, I guessed she was in her early- to mid-20s.

"We are," I replied. "We're currently looking for a reception-ist and a medical assistant. Would either be something you're inter-ested in?"

"Um, yes," she replied. She had a slight crouch when she spoke as if it took great effort. "I'm almost finished with my medical assistant program. Anna sent me here, from the Massenet Foundation? They helped me with the program."

"What's your name?" I eased. If she went through a program funded by the Massenet Foundation, it was likely that she was a recov-ering "something."

"Kat," she replied. "Katerina." *Katerina Ballerina*, I mnemoni-cally repeated in my head.

"Katerina, you're almost finished with your MA program? Do you have any other experience in the medical field?"

She shook her unpoised head, her dusty brown hair shifting down her back.

"This might be the perfect place to start, then."

Her face slackened. "Really?"

"Sure. Why don't you fill out an application. Irena will sched-ule an interview." Katerina's shoulders straightened and she smiled, revealing a chastity to her drawn appearance.

"I'm Irena," she chimed in, handing her the application. "Katerina, just fill this out and bring it back when you're finished."

"Most people just call me Kat." *Fat Kat*, I tried to make the mnemonic work, but it couldn't: Kat might have weighed 90 pounds soaking wet.

"Well, is Kat the name you'd prefer?" Irena asked practically, smacking her gum louder than she probably realized.

Kat's eyebrow dipped as though she were confused that she had a choice in the matter. "Yeah. Yeah, I guess I do prefer Kat."

"Okay, then, Kat," Irena said.

Kat wandered off and I turned to Irena. "I like her."

"I knew you'd say that," Irena replied while loading staples into a stapler. She was half-sitting on the receptionist desk. "You always go soft for people who seem, you know, troubled."

"What do you mean?" I asked defensively. But I knew what she meant. Irena and I had been working with hospitals, shelters, and other facilities to drop off cards for the soon-to-open Angel Clinic, and we often left with a touched heart.

One woman stopped us in a shelter hallway as we were leaving (she overheard us talking to the office manager) to tell us she had chronic pain in her side for four years. Despite her repeated visits to the hospital, she still had no answers about why. I knew why. It was because she likely had something that would require careful testing, follow-up, and investigative work. A trip to the ED isn't the place for that kind of diagnostics: The ED triages for acute emergencies and if you don't have a life-threatening one, the department discharges you to a doctor's care. But what happens if you don't have a doctor? What happens if you are bounced from one office to the next, so no one takes the time to review your chart or collaborate with other doctors about your condition? Things get missed, sometimes a lot of things. That's what happens.

"Well, same with you," I countered to Irena. "That's why you're in this field and at this clinic."

"No, I'm in it for the money," she winked.

I rolled my eyes.

"It's good to see you soft sometimes," she said, finishing the staple refill and testing it on a stack of papers. "But I won't let you hire unqualified people just because you like them. Let me vet Kat."

"Okay. But I'm not *soft*," I sulked. I didn't get a job as one of the highest paid cardiologists at my practice, in a male-dominated field, by being soft.

"Well, your abs certainly aren't soft and I still can't figure that out. Here, label these folders," she said.

I laughed and took the folders from her hands, then looked at my abs and shrugged. If there was anyone I could be soft with, it was Irena.

CHAPTER TWELVE

"Mr. Terry, it's great to see you again," I said as I walked into the exam room.

It was my day at the practice and I had a full schedule, but Jed Terry's name caught my eye as I scrolled through in anticipation for today's appointments. I hadn't seen Jed Terry since I assisted with placing his stents during my last year of residency. Jed was loyal to Dr. Grath in Philadelphia, but Dr. Grath had just retired. I wondered if Jed had sought me out.

"My angel! How are you?" he beamed.

"I'm good," I answered warmly. I forgot that he gave me that uncanny nickname. "I was surprised to see your name on my schedule. What brings you to Doylestown?"

"I've been thinking about coming up this way for a while. It's time for me to slow down a bit, and Doylestown has the best cardiology outside the city."

I couldn't argue with that. It's why I didn't contemplate long about my decision to join this practice.

"Besides," he continued, "I must admit that I knew you came up this way, and since Dr. Grath has decided to play golf instead of being on-call to save my life, I'm giving that honor fully to you," Jed grinned. "You saved my life once, so I know I'm in good hands."

"I'm flattered, Mr. Terry. It's good to see you again."

"Dr. Wells, I told you to call me Jed," he corrected with a wink. Jed was a charming man, and I couldn't help but find him endearing. He was attractive for his age and I sensed that he knew that. Though his flirtatious disposition wasn't offensive, it was certainly confident. I wondered if there was a Mrs. Terry, but judging by the ringless left hand, I guessed not.

"Well, Jed. I took some time to review your charts. Mind if I listen to your heart while you tell me how you've been feeling?"

"I feel like a thirty-year-old locked in a fifty-eight-year-old body now that my heart works again!" He gloated, his dark eyes shining inside his tanned crow's feet.

"That's great. Big breath in."

"Not everything about it is great," he inhaled and exhaled sharply. "You see, certain parts of my body act like they're thirty, while others," he suggested toward his groin area with his hands, "act like they're fifty-eight."

I understood his implication. "Your meds could be affecting your erectile function. I can help with that," I offered with an assuring smile.

He sighed, relieved. "That'd be great."

"Did this just start happening? I didn't see anything about it in your chart."

"Nah, you probably wouldn't have. Dr. Grath kept it out of the records. He used to give me samples. I'm real private about that kind of thing."

"I understand that, but I assure you, your records are quite secure. It's important that it's documented in case something happens. Your doctors will need to know any medication you're taking."

"What doctors? I have you! And you'll know," he bantered.

"Yes, you have me now, but I'm not always going to be around. Sometimes, I'm in the office here, sometimes I'm at the hospital, and sometimes I'm at the clinic."

"What clinic?"

"I'm opening a nonprofit clinic in town."

"Just a general health clinic? Or a specialty clinic?"

"It's general, but it's geared toward women who may not have access to traditional health care. Obviously, it will have a focus on cardiac health."

"That sounds like a commendable idea, Dr. Wells."

"It's more than an idea. We're cutting the ribbon in two weeks," I said proudly.

"Two weeks? Wow," his thick, slightly graying eyebrows rose. "How did you get it funded, if you don't mind my asking? As you know, I've served on several hospital boards and have gifted a thing or two to the medical world. It's an expensive venture."

"It is certainly expensive," I agreed. Though the $500,000 grant from The Massenet Foundation had made it possible to open the doors to the clinic, we were a long way from offering cutting-edge services. The equipment needed and bodies required to run the equipment would cost about the same as the initial investment. My time already was stretched so thin that the plan to run funding campaigns wasn't even making the short list. For now, I'd have to make do with what we had and figure out the rest later. Or, maybe I could address it now.

Jed's pool house probably cost more than I'd need for the next phase of my clinic.

"Why don't you come by for the ribbon-cutting, Mr.—sorry—Jed," I corrected quickly. "It would be my honor to have you as my personal guest."

"The honor would be mine, Dr. Wells. When is it?"

"Two weeks from this Saturday. It's the Angel Clinic on West Court Street." I wrote down the address of the clinic and handed it to him. "Just in case."

"The Angel Clinic?" he guffawed. "I'll be damned! I must not be the first person to call you their angel!"

I smiled humbly. "Actually, Angel was my mother's name. She passed a while back."

"I'm sorry," he said uncomfortably. Realizing the irreverence of the nickname he had given me, "I'm sorry if I offended you by calling you my angel. I didn't know—"

"Oh, no, please. Of course you didn't. It's okay, really. Thank you."

"I will certainly stop by to wish you luck," he smiled, holding up the piece of paper with the address.

"I look forward to seeing you then, Jed. In the meantime, I'm going to sneak you some samples, but I want you to schedule a stress test. You're due."

"Yes, Dr. Wells," he smiled compliantly.

"How was work, honey?" Beau asked as I walked through the door at 11:11 p.m. "Make a wish. Hurry."

"I wish there were 240 hours in a day instead of twenty-four," I sighed. The kids were in bed already, and Beau was sitting on the couch with a beer and a book. I plopped down next to him.

"Long day?" he asked, offering me his beer.

I accepted gratefully and took a long drink. "Aren't they all?"

He offered a dimpled nod.

"Thanks for this," I said, lifting the beer.

We quietly mulled as we deliberated which words to play next. I wanted to say *Goodnight, love you. I'm going to go take a shower.* I'd down the beer, stand longer than I needed to in the steaming shower, crawl into bed, and go to sleep. Maybe I'd get lucky and have an after-shower rejuvenation to pick up a book or finish the show I started watching weeks ago.

But I knew that kind of indulgence wouldn't take well. It had been weeks since Beau and I had been intimate, and if I could guess what he'd care to say, it'd be something along the lines of *Do you want to take a shower together?* If I could answer without consequence, the answer would be: I didn't. I was just too goddamned tired.

"How was *your* day?" I asked safely.

He shrugged. "It was good. Busy. I thought I'd be able to work a little, but the contractor came about the bathroom, so my day got swallowed up. Then the twins had music lessons, it was dinnertime, and somehow it was 11 p.m. and you're home."

"So, you haven't unpacked your canvases yet?" The small solarium off the study was dubbed as Beau's art studio, yet the boxes remained taped. I spent the summer acclimating to my responsibilities at the practice and getting the clinic ready to open, which meant Beau, as usual, took the brunt of getting the kids settled into Doylestown.

But I still didn't understand why he didn't unpack the boxes. It almost seemed like he kept them hulled up to remind me that while I enjoyed my career, he could not. Or, maybe my guilt just saw it that way.

"Maybe this weekend we can set up your studio?" I offered.

"Sure, sounds good." He nudged my ribs with his finger, a sex-temperature-taking poke. I sometimes dreaded that nudge and it had nothing to do with Beau: He was still as sexy as the day we met. But I resented that I had worked sixteen hours today and now I had to drum up enough energy to have sex. A hundred steps backward for womankind crossed my mind: *Would it be wrong if I just took a little nap while we had sex?* Yes. Wrong on too many levels.

Beau had been so patient as I worked long days, nearly every day, and he had done an impressive job getting the kids ready for school and establishing routine in a new town. Though he didn't complain, I felt the unspoken pressure of patience wearing thin. It wasn't fair for me to leave him alone for everything, especially in the bedroom. And Beau did smell good, like soap and musk, as if he showered right after his workout but still had residual sweat on the surface of his skin.

I scooted closer to Beau on the next nudge.

CHAPTER THIRTEEN

I knew she was different the minute she walked in: The air became thinner and more difficult to breathe as if there wasn't enough to share with such a presence. She walked with a rhythm, one foot directly in front of the other, but she had a slightly off-beat step every four steps or so, but with no real pattern to it. I wanted to instantly dislike her, but I was enamored.

"Can I help you?" Irena asked. I watched from the printing machine while I waited for health forms to print out.

"Yes, hello, thank you. My name is Mara, and I understand you might be looking for a receptionist?" Her voice was steely and firm but had an elegance to it; it was almost sovereignly.

"That's correct, we are. Would you like an application?" Irena asked disenchanted.

"I brought my resume, if you please. But I'm happy to fill out the application, as well," she replied, her full, buoyant, black hair swung against her armpit as she spoke. It was not jet black as my mother's hair; it had a hint of radiance to it, as if it saw the sun enough to soak up its warmth.

Irena took her resume and handed her the application. "You can just fill out the first page and sign the last. Skip the stuff in the middle."

The woman's full lips stayed pursed, but her dark eyes half-closed as she nodded in gratitude.

I tried to seem distracted, but I wanted to watch this woman. It was not every day that someone intrigued me enough to make me want to watch them.

Irena scanned the given resume and stopped abruptly. She turned around. "Hey," she said quietly in my direction. She nodded for me to look at the resume and pointed to an entry of employment indicating that Mara had worked at Simon-Cross-Hamilton, a powerful Philadelphia law firm.

I shrugged and mouthed, "So?"

Irena moved her finger to reveal Mara's role at the law firm: Esquire, Junior Partner. We looked quizzically at each other. Why would a lawyer be applying for a receptionist job? At a nonprofit health clinic? Then, Irena moved her finger again to point out the dates of employment: Esquire was her last listed job, and it was more than three years ago.

Mara flowed back to the desk minutes later, handing her application to Irena. Irena scanned it quickly, as if she cared, then said, "I noticed on your resume that you once worked for Simon-Cross-Hamilton?"

"That's correct."

"The Philly law firm?"

"Yes."

"You're an attorney?"

"Was an attorney." Her face, the color of creamed coffee, took a slightly protective turn.

Irena, who had a hard time hiding exactly how she felt on a good day, narrowed her eyes. "Forgive me, but aren't you a little over-qualified for this position?"

"I would think being overqualified was a good thing. I would be surprised if another candidate could manage paperwork as effi-ciently as I can. I'm an accomplished conversationalist, and should a confrontational situation occur, I'd adequately contain that as well."

"Fair enough. It's just that—-"

"Mara, hi, I'm Faith," I interrupted and walked up beside Irena. Mara's thick black eyes looked over at me. "I think what Irena is getting at is that perhaps this job will not keep you interested, seeing how you are a very qualified attorney."

"Was an attorney," she corrected again.

"Was an attorney," I repeated slowly. I wasn't much better than Irena at beating around the bush. "Can I ask why you are not prac-ticing anymore?"

"Because I can't," she answered openly.

I waited for more explanation but she had concluded her sen-tence. This was when Irena, if I were not present, would have become impatient with a *Thanks, I'll call you, don't call me.* But I was intrigued. Mara was not confrontational with her short responses, just pointed. And now my curiosity was piqued.

"Can I ask why that is?" I asked boldly, but with sincerity.

Mara stared at me thoughtfully before answering. "Perhaps you should take another look at the first page of the application, Question 12."

"Perhaps you can just tell me," I challenged softly.

"You have a record," Irena stated with an aha flair, staring at Question 12's filled in checkbox: *Have you ever been convicted of a crime?*

Mara stood still while an uncomfortable quiet settled around us. I understood what Mara meant now when she said couldn't practice any longer; she must have been disbarred. Of course I wanted to know what circumstance might have led to Mara losing her license, but would it really matter? This clinic was a place for second chances, or third, or fourth; a place where one is not judged by who they were, but who they are. Mara's skillset was undeniable: A former tax attorney could easily handle the paperwork of a receptionist. And I could look past poor choices or circumstances as long as she wasn't one thing.

"I have only one question before the job is yours," I said. Irena cleared her throat as if to queue that she was not comfortable with my offer. I ignored her. "Whatever you did—were you dishonest about it?"

Mara answered without pause: "Never."

Mara was overqualified for the receptionist position but she was perfect as a practice manager.

It took two days for Irena to warm up to Mara, as is Irena's wary way with anyone, much less a woman who could have won a beauty pageant plus a Mensa IQ Award. Mara won over Irena when she brushed her fine-toothed legal comb through every document, organized them easily, and suggested a new prioritization scheduling routine. Irena quickly realized that having Mara manage the practice— creating forms, hiring staff, keeping records, managing payroll, coordinating schedules— would allow her to do what she really wanted to do: care for the patients.

But the clincher in winning Irena over was Mara's home-baked baklava, a platter of which Mara had brought to share on the day before the ribbon-cutting. Irena's eyes widened at the stacks of layered phyllo pastry, sticky with honey. "Where did you get baklava around here?"

"I made it, of course," Mara replied.

"You made this baklava? You're not Greek, are you?" Irena asked, confused.

Mara smiled. "No, I am from Azerbaijan. This is a family recipe." She said *Azerbaijan* in a way that made her sound even more elegant, if that was possible.

"Mmm. It's similar to my family's recipe, but this is lighter. Is there lemon in it?" Irena asked, licking a flaky piece of phyllo from her lips.

"No. What you taste is likely from the serbet. It's the Turkish version of honey; it has a lemony taste to it. I like Greek baklava very much, as well," she offered.

"Maybe I'll bring some in," Irena reciprocated.

A bond was formed.

"Ooh, baklava?" Tobias came from nowhere. Tobias was everywhere and nowhere often. He floated around the clinic, fixing this, adjusting that, and though his heavy presence should have been obvious, he was oddly more of a wallflower. "Can I have another one?" he asked after gulping the first rectangular pastry down with one bite.

"Of course, Tobias. Have as many as you'd like," Mara replied. Tobias let out a giddy woot and reached for two more. Mara smiled gently, amused by Tobias' pleasure, and I saw a sensitive side of Mara that I hadn't seen until now.

"How about you, Kat? Would you like one? You should claim it now," I said as we removed the thin, white paper from several new exam room chairs and adjusted the swivel to the appropriate height.

Kat shook her head. "No, no thank you," she said quietly. I wondered if Kat ate many pastries at all; her thin frame seemed lacking in nutrients. And sunlight. She was almost vampire-pale. "But I will take one home, if that's all right."

Irena walked over and held a piece up for me to bite. "Oh, God, that's good," I savored. "Save two for me. Tobias, I'm talking to you!"

He held his hands up in surrender. I winked, and he grabbed one more.

We didn't hear the sound of the door open, but we heard the click-clack of steps approaching. A red-haired woman with cat glasses appeared.

"Oh, sorry," Irena apologized with a full mouth. "Can I help you?"

Mara, who was leaning lightly against the desk turned to face the red-haired visitor.

"Hi. My name is Shiloh," she said congenially. "I saw the sign in the window that you're hiring for a receptionist?"

"We are," Mara took lead, and though I expected Irena to be offended, instead, she turned around and popped the other half of her baklava in her mouth as if to demonstrate that Mara *had this*. I was happy to see Irena and Mara finding some rhythm; I was comfortable that the clinic would run smoothly on the days I couldn't be here.

"Are you interested in applying for the position?" Mara asked pleasantly.

"Yes. Baklava?" she observed, looking past Mara at Irena and Tobias, who were still hovering over the platter.

Mara nodded.

"I spent a summer in Greece between eleventh and twelfth grade," she sniffed deeply. "Ah…the cinnamon. That's what I smell most. My boyfriend thought I was crazy because I could sniff out baklava from a mile away. I went with him to Greece, which was a bad idea, for the record, but that's for another time."

Mara smiled warmly and Irena had stopped chewing to listen to Shiloh's story. There was something magnetic about Shiloh; she was alluring like a siren, yet instantly relatable.

"Want some?" Irena asked Shiloh. Tobias shot Irena a glance like she had offered his last meal to a stranger.

"Oh my God, yes!" the fiery girl replied, then pursed her mouth playfully. "I mean, yes please. Food excites me. Sorry."

Tobias sulkily walked over and handed a piece of baklava to Shiloh.

"That's a good color on you," she said to Tobias as she gratefully picked out her piece of baklava. We all instinctively turned our attention toward Tobias' baby blue T-shirt, which I hadn't noticed all day. "Is that Egyptian cotton?"

Tobias turned from sulky to flattered as quickly as a light switches. He ran his free hand over his chest. "Peruvian Pima."

"It's nice," Shiloh complimented in a non-flirty manner.

"Why don't you fill out this application while you enjoy the baklava," Mara said, bringing attention back to where it belonged.

Shiloh nodded and clacked away on her heels (matched with a black plaid pencil skirt and emerald green blouse) to fill out the application.

Everyone looked at me as the barometer of how they should feel about Shiloh. "She seems nice," I said, even though I wanted to say that she seemed a myriad of other things: interesting, beguiling, and slightly disconcerting. "Let's hope she has some experience. Our doors open tomorrow, for God's sake, and we have no good candidates for a receptionist."

They nodded and we all went back to our pre-opening day work, chatting loudly and calling out checklist items. Moments later, Shiloh returned with the application.

Mara scanned it briefly. "Shiloh, I would normally want to schedule a follow-up interview, but we open tomorrow, which means we're a little short on time. Would you be open to an interview now?"

"Of course," Shiloh replied with marked poise, her professional decorum coming to the forefront.

"Okay," Mara scanned the application. "It looks as though you've had receptionist experience at a personal physician's office as well as a telecommunications company?"

"Yes, that's correct," Shiloh answered.

"Are you experienced with multiple-line phone systems?"

"Yes. In both of my previous jobs, I managed multiple calls at the same time. Which phone system does this clinic use?"

Mara stared at her blankly, then looked down at the phone. "CoTel," she answered, as if she knew all along.

"I'm not familiar with that system, but I'd be happy to do a trial run so you could determine how I manage incoming call traffic.

Time per call, time until resolution, lost calls, missed calls, the usual statistics…."

Mara looked briefly at me. I shook my head as if to say *It's not that fancy of a phone system.*

"That won't be necessary; I trust your confidence in the matter," Mara said to Shiloh.

"Okay. If the phone system has APIs, then I can build you a program that captures that data and displays it on a dashboard," Shiloh offered. "I did that in my last job."

Mara kept an assured look on her face, yet I doubt that any of us knew what an API was.

"So, you would consider yourself proficient in traditional software programs?" Mara asked.

"Yes," she half-laughed. "Yes, absolutely."

"Can you elaborate on which programs you're familiar with?"

"All of them," Shiloh answered confidently. "It would be easier for me to tell you which ones I'm not proficient in. And I type over 100 words per minute. Accurately."

Several more questions and answers alternated before Mara looked up and smiled. "It seems that you have the skillset required for this position, Shiloh. Tell me, other than what we've discussed, what qualities do you feel are important for a receptionist to possess?"

"Well, aside from making operations run seamlessly up front, I realize that I would be the first impression of this clinic, which means you can rely on me to take care of my personal appearance, offer a pleasant welcoming to our patients, and of course, speak well. I'm not married and I don't have kids, so I can work extra hours when necessary."

Her facial expressions were charming and cryptic at the same time, as if she were sharing a secret with you. As a bonus, Shiloh had answered all of the questions human resource rules didn't allow an employer to ask but that they really wanted to know.

We could add astuteness to her list of qualities.

"Thank you all for being here today," I started, addressing a crowd of fifty, give or take. Beau and the twins stood nearby.

For weeks, I struggled with what to say at The Angel Clinic's ribbon-cutting ceremony. Beau encouraged me to get personal—share something about my mother or my childhood—and for a minute I thought I might. But I decided against it.

I didn't want people to know that I grew up in the streets of Castle Hill to a single, alcoholic mother who was never home and later died of an overdose. I wasn't ashamed of these things: If judged stares were all I had to deal with, so be it. I didn't want people to know of my past because I didn't want pity.

In grade school, I always was "that poor, bright girl with the mom who, you know, has a problem?" Almost all the kids in my school had a mom or dad with a problem, but I might have been the only student who cared about school. I didn't view school as an obligation or a warm lunch. I saw it as my way to a better life. I watched TV shows with doctors and lawyers, learning that the way to a fancy table full of glamorous food was by being one of them. And after my mother's stay in the hospital when I was in eighth grade—that pivotal moment that solidified my decision to become a doctor—I realized that to be a doctor, especially one who fixes hearts, I would need a lot of schooling. School became my priority.

But it was a steep climb to get into med school, especially Penn Med. I didn't have alumni parents to follow in their footsteps or transcripts from an elite boarding school. But I worked with what I had. I leaned heavily into one particular teacher, Mrs. Neiran, who took a special interest in me. I could tell Mrs. Neiran only worked at our school to "make a difference." She drove a BMW and wore high-quality, pressed clothes. I especially loved her shoes, which never looked worn. When I told her that I wanted to be a doctor, she helped me navigate the world of scholarships, grants, and special applications far after the time that I was in her class. She never said it, but I knew that she went home to her upscale life and talked about "this girl with such potential" who she was going to "help make a difference in her life." And I let her because Mrs. Neiran was authentic in her motivations, if not ignorant in her intentions. But also, I let her help because she really did know how to get me where I needed to go.

Even though I earned my way into college and later med school, it always rode on me that it was partly because Mrs. Neiran pitied me. Pity changes everything. Pity drives charity, and charity gives control to the giver, leaving the recipient indebted.

I didn't want to owe anyone anything.

If someone was going to donate to my clinic, it would be because they believed in me, not because they pitied me. Therefore, my speech would reflect the future, not the past.

"Today is a special day because tomorrow we open the doors to The Angel Clinic." A small round of applause circulated. "The Angel Clinic is a place where people can come for top-quality health care, regardless of what kind of card is in their wallet—credit card, insurance card, or no card at all. As a doctor, I took an oath, as many of you did, that we will 'remain a member of society, with special obligations to all fellow human beings, those sound of mind and body as well as the infirm.' I am proud to share this obligation with some of the most talented doctors, nurses, and technicians in the world who are here today and have generously offered to donate their time and services for this clinic. I thank you from the bottom of my heart, cardio pun intended." A conciliatory laugh from the crowd.

"I'd like to also thank the Massenet Foundation for its extraordinary grant that made opening this clinic possible." Another wave of quiet applause as Anna and her husband, whose arm was adoringly around Anna's waist, humbly raised their glasses.

"And of course, this clinic would not be possible without the support from the wonderful Doylestown community." I looked around the crowd and spotted Jed Terry holding a glass of champagne near the back.

"Though the doors of The Angel Clinic open today, we still have work ahead in making the clinic a full-service facility. As many of you know, cardiovascular disease is the number one killer for both men and women. As a cardiologist, my mission is to provide preventative cardiac care to lower those statistics. My first focus will be to raise funds to purchase a cardiac stress system. These systems can be costly, upwards of $100,000, so I have my work cut out for me! But with the help and support of all of you, I am confident we'll get there." Another small applause broke out.

"And now it's time to cut this ribbon and enjoy this lovely heart-healthy spread provided by Sunflower Bakery. But first, I have a final thank you: To my husband, Beau, who somehow puts up with my wild ideas and allows me to run with them. Thank you, honey." Beau smiled and the twins giggled.

Ribbons, especially red ones, reminded me of arteries, so cutting the ribbon automatically sent a signal to my brain to reattach both strangling ends. But I felt exhilarated as I realized that sometimes we cut an artery not to reattach it, but to redirect it.

So that it can thrive elsewhere.

CHAPTER FOURTEEN

"Dr. Wells, I think you should come in, and quickly," Shiloh said in a low voice, speaking close to the phone.

I set down the book I was reading to the twins. This was the first night I was home for dinner in weeks, and I insisted that Beau lock himself in the studio while I managed the kids. And though my choice of book that showed similarities and differences in bodies among different animals was boring the twins to tears (I could never choose fun books like Beau could), they were enjoying some couch time with Mom.

"What's going on, Shiloh?" I asked.

"Um, it's kind of hard to explain, but there's a gentleman here named Jed Terry."

"Is he okay?" I asked, a flit of panic behind the words.

"He's okay, yes. It's his friend, who, uh, needs some help."

"Shiloh, can you please be more specific? Isn't Irena there?"

"She left fifteen minutes ago. Kat and I were just closing up when Mr. Terry showed up. He was knocking on the glass. I recognized him from the ribbon-cutting, so I opened the door. His friend was groaning and walking oddly, and Mr. Terry helped him in."

"What the hell, Shiloh? Call an ambulance!" I grunted myself to a standing position, the twins falling from both of my sides with a disappointed, "Aw."

"Yeah, but Mr. Terry said to absolutely not call an ambulance."

"I don't remember putting Mr. Terry in charge of my clinic," I retorted as I worked my shoes onto my feet.

"He insisted that I call you. He said that you were the only person who could help with this situation. That it wasn't an emergency but that you needed to be called. I'm sorry," Shiloh pleaded. "He was very persistent."

"Shit," I sighed. "I'll be right there. Have Kat take his vitals—and Shiloh, if anything seems off, call an ambulance."

"Got it." She hung up.

I knocked softly on Beau's studio door: No answer. He likely had his headphones on, listening to loud music, so I walked in. His back was to me, but he saw my reflection in the window and turned around.

"Hi," I winced.

"Hi," he said jovially, brush in hand. He turned off his music.

"I'm so sorry, Beau. But there's an emergency at the clinic."

Beau looked at his watch, confused. "Isn't the clinic closed?"

"Someone came in as they were closing up. They need me for a consult."

"Can't they go to the hospital?"

"It's complicated. It's a special patient. I know his history, so they need me to come in."

Beau looked at me thoughtfully; his dimples flexed, but not with a smile. He set down his paintbrush. "Okay," he yielded.

"I'm sorry. I really wanted you to have this night to yourself."

"It's okay. Duty calls," he said as he stood and kissed me blankly on the forehead as he walked past to tend to the children.

I lingered in the doorway, the heaviness of disappointing Beau pushing on my chest. Then I walked toward the garage, grabbed my purse, and drove to the clinic.

It took only minutes for me to drive, park, and walk into the clinic; it could have been faster to walk.

The lights in the front reception area were dimmed, but the lights in the hallway with the exam rooms were bright. Shiloh was not at the desk, so I assumed she was back assisting Kat. As I approached the only exam room with a closed door, I heard a man holler, "I don't know!"

I entered the room to see a man with a disheveled suit lying on his stomach with his elbows on the table. Jed Terry sat in a chair fiddling with his phone.

"Ah! Dr. Wells, thank you for coming in," Jed said loudly with relief. "This is my friend, Andrew."

"Hey," Andrew whimpered.

"Hi Andrew, I'm Dr. Wells," I directed toward him as I shut the door behind me. He appeared to be in his mid-40s and was clearly in discomfort, yet I couldn't see any visible injuries. "What brings you in, Andrew?" I asked, walking past Jed to address Andrew directly. Kat handed me a chart with his vitals. Though his pulse was higher than normal, likely from the excitement, all other vitals seemed normal.

"There's something—" he started, "there's, uh, something—" he exhaled forcefully. "Do all these people need to be in here?" he asked, panicked.

I looked at Jed with a queue for him to leave, but instead he blurted: "Andrew has something stuck up his you-know-what." He put his hands up and raised his eyebrows in a *don't judge me; it's not my thing* manner.

Shiloh, who was only in the room to ensure Kat wasn't by herself, excused herself quickly and left.

Andrew's head dropped and his forehead slapped the exam table with humility.

My mouth gaped open for an instant before I scooped it up. "Okay. There's an object in your rectum, Andrew?"

"Mmm-hmm," he mumbled without raising his head.

"Do you know what type of object is in your rectum? And how long has it been, uh, up there?" I asked. It had been a long time since I did rounds in the ED for non-cardiac-related matters. I was not quite prepared for this call tonight. I wasn't prepared for any after-hours calls from the clinic, for that matter. I glanced incriminatingly at Jed.

"Okay, Andrew, first, there's nothing to be embarrassed about. This type of thing happens all the time," I said truthfully; this was rather routine for the ED staff, I recalled. "Second, I don't think I can help you here. You really need to go to the hospital. They have the equipment necessary to address this easily."

"He won't go to the hospital," Jed said. "He came to my house, for God's sake. As if *I* could do something about it. I didn't know where else to take him." Jed leaned against the wall with his arms folded, a laugh waiting to fire.

"Why won't you go to the hospital, Andrew?" I asked.

"I can't," he replied sorrowfully. "I'm on the Board of Trustees."

Oh, I realized. It was one thing to go to the hospital with an issue one might consider "typical;" it was another thing to walk into the ED with this type of problem. Though HIPAA protected a patient's privacy, it didn't protect from people's mouths spewing details they shouldn't. An incident like this surely would instigate someone telling the story without names but with enough detail to identify someone of Andrew's stature. Even if Andrew was lucky enough to evade rumors from leaving the hospital, he certainly wouldn't avoid the ones circulating among the treating staff, or among those who had access to his records.

"Okay, Andrew. I'm going to need to do an examination. We'll step out while you undress and put on a gown."

"I don't think I can bend over to take off my pants. Won't it lodge it up there further?" he asked, terrified.

"No, it doesn't quite work like that," I assured him. "We'll be back."

As soon as we stepped outside, Jed turned to me. "I'm sorry, Dr. Wells. I didn't know where else to go." His salt-and-pepper hair was tousled and he wore a cashmere sweater with tan slacks. The casualness somehow gave him a younger look.

"It's okay. I'm just not entirely sure I can help him here. I'll try, but I'm afraid he's going to need to go to the hospital if I can't."

"He won't. He'd rather go home and, you know, wait to see if this will all *pass*. So that he could put this all *behind* him," he snorted softly, waiting to see if I found the humor in his remarks. I did.

"I'd strongly advise against that," I said, stifling my snicker.

"Thing is, he can't really go to many hospitals around here. If he doesn't serve on the board, it's likely that his father or mother does.

"How do you know him? Can I ask?"

"Well, everybody knows the Yales," he answered. *Of course:* *The Yales* were one of the most well-known healthcare families in the Philadelphia region.

"But he worked for me when he was just out of law school," Jed continued. "He's a very good attorney. Worked on malpractice cases and hospital lawsuits mostly, but he'd help me out from time to time with other things."

"I see. I'm going to go check on him. I think it would be best if you stayed out here during the exam. Shiloh can make you some coffee or tea," I offered. Shiloh raised her eyebrows and looked over with her black-rimmed glasses and red lipstick. She looked like a pin-up girl, not one strand of her glossy red hair out of place, even after a day's work.

"My pleasure, Mr. Terry. Which would you prefer?" Shiloh asked.

"Excuse me," I bowed back toward the exam room, beckoning Kat to follow. I opened the door as Andrew lay face-down again. Kat grabbed the exam light and we both gloved up.

"Lie on your left side, Andrew. Just try to relax. Can you explain to me what is in your rectum?"

He sighed, embarrassed. "It's a vibrator," he said so softly I had to ask again.

"A vibrator!" he repeated loudly. "About the size of a pickle."

I winced at the visual but remained professional. "How long has it been up there?"

"I don't know. I guess a couple of hours. Right after it slipped from her grip and *disappeared,* she drove me straight to Jed's house. Then, Jed brought me here. Listen, you're going to keep this off the record, right?"

Though I wanted to ask who "she" was, and what he meant by "off the record," those questions were not important right now. My obligation was to the medical problem, which was removing this object, so everything else would have to take a *back seat.* God, I wished Irena were here for this.

Though rectal exams are unglamorous, they are necessary and routine: A doctor gets desensitized about performing them.

"Well, the good news is that it's close enough that I think I can grab it."

"Oh, thank God," Andrew expelled.

"The bad news is that this is going to hurt a little bit, Andrew. If we were in the hospital, I'd offer you some type of anesthetic. But we don't have that here."

"It's okay. Just get it out," he pleaded.

"Kat, can you hand me the forceps please? No, not those ones. The smaller ones. Yes, those."

"Oh!" Andrew exclaimed as I carefully probed and located the object. But I couldn't pull it out easily; the forceps kept slipping. *Damn it.*

Knock, knock. Who would be knocking at the door right now? There were only two possible answers, neither of which I understood. Jed certainly didn't want to be in here for this, and what did Shiloh need so urgently? *Knock, knock.*

"Kat, can you please tend to that?" Kat nodded, then returned and whispered in my ear. I looked at her contemplatively. "Andrew, I'll be right back. Sit tight," I said, then immediately regretted my word choice.

I opened the door to find Shiloh in the hallway. "Shiloh, what do you have for me?"

"This," Shiloh said, holding up a tube of lidocaine and a long, blunt metal probe usually used for Doppler ultrasounds. It was still wrapped in autoclave sterilization plastic. "This will help. Sometimes you need to put something on the other side of the object to create room for it to come out. The lidocaine will help with the pain and help him relax a little."

"You've done this before?" I asked suspiciously.

"Yes. Several times."

The look on my face must have said enough because she continued. "This type of thing happens all the time to dommes. The rookie ones, at least."

"Dommes?"

"Yes. Dominatrices? Dominatrix," she clarified.

I stuttered to process the designation. I knew what a dominatrix was from TV, but how it was relevant now, I didn't know, unless—"Are you a dominatrix, Shiloh?"

"I don't know," she replied cautiously.

"Well, you mentioned it," I said impatiently. "Obviously, there was a reason for it."

"Can I assume this conversation is off the record and won't jeopardize my job?"

There it was again: the "off the record" question. "Yes. Why not."

"Then, yes. I am. Or, I was, before my business partner moved. Now, I'm a receptionist. Who kind of misses it, truthfully." She added the last part almost nostalgically.

Before I could react, the door opened and Kat walked out. "Um, Dr. Wells, are you coming back in?" she asked timidly. "Andrew is getting nervous."

I nodded, then turned to Shiloh. "You've seen this happen before?"

"Probably more than you have," she smirked.

"And you have—" I didn't even know how to ask, "—removed these types of objects before?"

"It's easy if you relax them a little."

I bit my lip. Everything about tonight was unconventional (and "off the record," if everyone's wishes were granted) so I took a gamble: "Could you help me with this, Shiloh? If Andrew is okay with it, of course?"

Shiloh rubbed her finger along her jaw line while the other arm sat in a folded position. "Okay. I'll help," she said whimsically. "For old time's sake. But first I have to reapply my lipstick."

I sighed, relieved, then a little confused: *Reapply her lipstick*? Then I sighed again because I couldn't believe I felt relieved that my receptionist was going to help me with a medical procedure. But hey, an expert is an expert. Is a professional chef more qualified to bake bread than someone who has been doing it for fifty years in her kitchen?

I opened the door to the exam room (after Shiloh reapplied her lipstick). "Andrew, this is Shiloh. Shiloh is going to assist."

Shiloh slowly walked over to Andrew and stood directly in front of him. Her posture was tall and forceful. Andrew immediately stopped whimpering and stared up at her like a child begging his mommy for one more ice cream.

Without saying a word, Shiloh took a pair of gloves and slowly put them on: the left first, then the right, and when she was done, she cracked her knuckles. Kat and I watched, mesmerized.

"Now, Andrew," she said in a calm, authoritative voice. "You're going to stop whimpering." Andrew closed his mouth obediently. "And you're going to keep your mouth shut unless you open it to say your safe word. Do you understand me?"

Andrew nodded, and I noticed his entire body relax.

"Andrew, I give you permission to speak. *Once*," she enunciated with vigor. "Tell me your safe word."

"Waffles," he mewled.

Shiloh walked around to sit next to me. She winked at me as she grabbed the probe. "When you have a grab with the forceps," she whispered, "I'll insert the probe carefully, staying to the side. It should create enough room for you to pull it out easily."

Dumbstruck, I nodded. I went back in with the forceps. Andrew let out a groan, but not one of pain.

Shiloh quickly responded, "I said no sounds!" She slapped the table and shouted forcefully. I fully expected Andrew's body to tense as much as Kat's and mine did. But instead, his body relaxed further, allowing me to easily grab the object. Shiloh went in almost in tandem and sure enough, the object, a pink vibrator the size of a small pickle, came out with ease. I plopped it in the metal tray Kat was holding. Kat quickly discarded it with wide eyes.

"Okay, Andrew, we dislodged the object," I said, masking my relief. I covered him back up and removed my gloves.

Shiloh removed her gloves, as well, and returned to stand above Andrew. He crooked his neck to stare up at her compliantly. Without tipping her head down, she said, "Andrew, this session is over. But a word of advice: Don't patron amateurs."

I marveled at the exchange, at the way Shiloh commanded Andrew so effortlessly. Kat stared at Shiloh with a wide mouth as if she had just witnessed something both horrifying and alluring. As curious as I was about what had transpired, as the physician, I had to assume control. "Shiloh, that will be all. Thank you."

Shiloh gave one quick nod and walked out of the room in role with her confident stride, as if entering and leaving the room were the equivalent to a director calling, "Action!" and "Cut!"

I didn't know what type of movie I had just watched. But I knew that if I were scanning the channels and landed on it, I'd probably stop to watch it again.

As long as no one knew.

CHAPTER FIFTEEN

People tend to put doctors on a pedestal: If you follow your doctor's words and actions, you will survive. In fact, you will thrive. And it's not always about medical advice. We can give marital advice, child-rearing advice, any type of advice, and people assume we have the answers. We know everything. *The doctor said so.*

But the truth is that we have the same problems as everyone else. And last night's incident left me reflecting quite a bit. My feelings were conflicted, ranging from fear that I crossed a boundary by letting Shiloh help me, to a sense I couldn't quite pinpoint. Repulsion? Admiration? Dare I admit it: *Intrigue?* I was more interested in Shiloh than ever, perhaps more than I should be. I found myself contemplating how and when I could probe more about her, particularly about her dominatrix past. Or was it her present? I couldn't decipher based on our quick interaction. I was eager to learn more, but I'd have to wait for the right opportunity.

I had just finished working the early shift at the hospital and was now headed to a four-hour evening shift at the clinic. I didn't anticipate spending as much time at the clinic as I had been, but it turned out that I was stopping by almost every day, sometimes for an hour, but sometimes for a full shift. We had an abundance of appointments hitting the books but a lack of revenue. I was behind on my fundraising initiatives.

I pulled the lightweight scarf off my neck and folded it into my briefcase as I walked up to the clinic's rear entrance. The early spring sun had warmed throughout the day, no longer making my scarf necessary. Half the staff stood outside cooing around a large delivery the size of a refrigerator box as two men in navy uniforms wheeled another large box toward them on a dolly.

"What did we order?" I asked with some alarm.

"I don't know. It came with a card," Irena handed it to me.

JT Enterprises proudly offers this PC-based cardiac stress system as a donation to The Angel Clinic. The card went on to describe how JT Enterprises was a proud local contributor, yadayada, I skipped over. Signed: *Jed Terry.*

"Holy shit," I said. "Jed Terry donated a cardiac stress system."

Irena's jaw dropped. "An entire system? That had to cost a fortune!"

"I am aware of that," I said, still in awe.

"Ma'am, would you like us to set this up somewhere, or schedule another day to do that?" one of the men in uniform asked.

"Tobias, can you direct them to exam room 4?" I asked. "The larger one in the back? Have them set it up there, please?" He nodded and motioned for the men to follow.

"Tobias," Mara called after him, studying the packing slip. "I'll come with you. I want to ensure everything is accounted for and in working order." Mara strutted after him with her long black, silky hair bobbing softly against her crimson blouse.

"Did you know he was going to do this?" Irena asked, still perplexed.

"No," I shook my head.

"Did you mention that the clinic needed this? Maybe during the opening day reception?"

"Not specifically. He must have heard me talk about it in my speech. Maybe he got inspired. He's new to the Doylestown area. Perhaps he is trying to make his mark here," I offered. But I knew what this donation was. It was a thank-you gift.

Irena and I looked up as the sound of crunching tires approached. A glossy, cream-colored vintage Mercedes convertible pulled up behind the clinic, rims agleam, and top still fastened as if it, too, might shed its clothing as the day progressed.

"I see the delivery made it!" Jed strolled up casually. He wore a collared shirt under a gray sweater with pleat-free slacks and expensive-looking leather shoes.

I smiled. "Jed, to what do we owe the honor? Both in your presence and in your present?"

"Well, as for my presence, can't an old friend stop by to see how things are going?" he bantered. An *old friend*? I wasn't quite sure when we became old friends, but I amused him.

"And as for the present," he continued, gesturing toward the large boxes, "It's a tax write-off. What can I say?" he grinned charmingly. "Can I come in for a cup of coffee? That gal up front really knows how to make a mean cup." I eyed him curiously. Shiloh made him a cup of coffee from a standard doctor's office bulk supply last night; average coffee at best. Then I remembered last night and shuddered.

I was hoping to file the incident deep in the cabinet and not revisit it for a while. Instead, here it was visiting me.

"Of course. You're always welcome." *Old friend*, I wanted to add cynically. I glanced at Irena as I turned to lead Jed into the clinic and rolled my eyes amusingly. She cleared her throat in acknowledgement and followed us.

"Mr. Terry," Shiloh said as we approached the front desk, almost as a description rather than an address. Her demeanor turned instantly coquettish, and I wondered how she turned that characteristic on and off so easily, and with such intuitive timing.

"Hi there, Shiloh," Jed beamed. "You got any of that delicious coffee for me?" Jed picked out a butterscotch candy from a jar on the front desk and popped one in his mouth, his eyes twinkling at Shiloh.

"My pleasure."

"Shiloh, first—" I said, slightly irritated that Jed was seemingly here to just "hang out," and equally confused. "Can you get me up to speed on what's on deck this evening?"

"Consults in exam rooms 1 and 2." She handed me the evening appointment schedule. "Irena has a patient in room 3. There's a follow-up visit that I was going to put in room 4, but I'll have to wait for one of the other rooms to open up now that they're setting that machine up in there."

"Busy night for a—?" Jed started, then stopped mid-sentence. I looked up, curious as to why he stopped speaking, and I realized why as I felt her presence approach me from behind.

"Good evening, Mara," I said without turning around. I was busy observing Jed, whose seemingly fixed grin was replaced with fluttering eyelids and parted lips.

"Dr. Wells, I've verified everything is received and in working order if you want to sign here," Mara said with a smooth cadence, holding the receiving slip out for me with her long, bronzed fingers. She didn't look up at Jed, who was staring at her intently.

"You can sign it. I trust you," I said.

"Very well," she said. "Excuse me, I have some office work to tend to."

She sauntered off, her gait like a slightly off-rhythm drum beat to which you found yourself nodding along.

Jed cleared his throat. "Is she new? I haven't seen that woman here before. Or have I?" he asked, mostly to himself.

"She was at the ribbon-cutting ceremony," I answered. "Although, she kept herself busy through most of it."

"What's her name?"

"Mara. Her name is Mara."

I was grateful that Jed's visit didn't include discussing last night's events, but I was not as grateful that it included something else: a solicitation for drugs.

He wanted more Viagra. Jed hung around small-talking with Shiloh, popping butterscotch candies as if they were peanuts, for about thirty minutes before he approached me between exams.

"Jed, I don't have any samples here. I don't carry them around in my coat pockets." I turned them inside out for dramatic effect.

"Maybe you can order some for me?" he grinned, the crinkle of his eyes bewitching.

"I can ask my rep for some samples but it might take a few days. Why don't you just let me write you a 'script?"

"No. Can't do that. There's only one thing more vulnerable than a person's bank account, and that's his medical records."

"Surely you can't avoid that for sake of keeping face!" I laughed. "You're on five medications as it is!"

"Yeah, but everyone after a certain age is on some type of cholesterol or blood pressure medicine. I can't control my heart. But as a man, and call me old-fashioned, I should be able to control *other* organs."

"You shouldn't see it that way. It has nothing to do with your manhood, or whatever. But nevertheless, I understand." It was just some Viagra, for God's sake. Let the man have some fun.

Although... "Jed, here's the thing—remember if you take the Viagra, you can't take nitroglycerine within twenty-four hours, so you need to call 911 for any chest pain. I'm serious about that. Also, if you already feel light-headed that day, you should not take one. Deal?"

"Deal, Doc," he winked.

"Stop by in a few days."

"Will do." He trotted off.

"Oh, Jed!" I called after him. "Please thank your Board again for the donation. It will really make a difference in the type of service we can offer here." Thanking the Board, I realized, was my underhanded way of saying, "I don't owe *you*."

He shrugged, as if I thanked him for giving me something as paltry as a quarter for a parking meter.

My chest thudded a loud beat as I wondered if accepting this donation would be the start of something that I couldn't see, like eating a steak marbled with fat. One steak, once in a while, had little to no effect on the heart. But eating one every day could clog the arteries quickly.

But who worries about that when the steak tastes so good?

CHAPTER SIXTEEN

"How long has your chest been tight?" I asked.

Joan looked at me, embarrassed. "Couple years," she answered quietly.

I removed my stethoscope and smiled at her. Though treating patients who had waited longer than recommended to seek cardiac care happened from time to time in private practice, it was almost the norm at the clinic.

"I want to schedule a stress test for you."

She sighed apprehensively. "How much does that cost?"

"We can do it here at the clinic. It will cost you nothing," I said proudly. I was still getting used to offering patients this expensive procedure at no cost, thanks to Jed's—JT Enterprise's—donation. And it felt amazing.

"When was the last time you had your bloodwork done?" I followed up.

"When I had my last child."

"And when was that?"

She hesitated once more. "She just turned twenty-three."

"Then I'd say you're due," I mused. "Kat's going to draw some blood and get some lab work done. It's also no charge." I beat her to the question.

She didn't respond. She stared nervously past me while she knotted her hands together.

"Joan? Does this sound like a plan to you?" I sensed her reluctance.

"It's just—Dr. Wells, I'm grateful, I really am. But I've had people tell me that things were free before, then I get bills, and collectors try to get money from me. I don't have money like that. I just want to know why my chest is hurting me."

"I know," I acknowledged. A scar on my left thumb pulsed as a reminder of a time I sliced it opening a can as a child. My mother wouldn't take me to the hospital, even though I could have used a few stitches, for fear of the bill that would follow. "They always get you," my mother would say. "They charge a hundred dollars for gauze, and the next thing you know, I'm making payments for the rest of my life for six little stitches."

"Joan, look at me," I said. "There will be no charge for anything I recommend for you. You have my word."

She smiled, then her lip quivered. "I trust you. Thank you, Dr. Wells."

I put a warm hand on her knee. "My pleasure, Joan."

I left the room and beckoned Kat to manage Joan's labs, but not before pausing a moment to recognize that Joan would get the health care she needed because of this clinic. And if I had to go through ten more lifetimes of worrying about my mother, enduring Bobby Clay's demise of her, and fighting my way through school to make this clinic happen, I would do it all again.

In a heartbeat.

"Dr. Wells, may I have a moment of your time?" Mara asked as the clinic processed its last patient of the night. It had been a long day, and the pain in my feet and back dipped and peaked like an echocardiogram reading.

"Of course, Mara. What can I help you with?"

"I wanted to give you a financial health check of the clinic."

I sighed. I knew this was long overdue, but it was something I just didn't want to address. Since opening the clinic six months ago, I had not gone through with my fundraising initiatives, as planned. I completely underestimated just how much of me there was to give. Between working at the practice, rounds at the hospital, shifts at the clinic, and trying to maintain any semblance of being a wife and mother, I found myself drowning in a sea of time. Sleep was something I got accustomed to missing during years of med school, but it had become an even scarcer commodity in an effort to juggle my numerous roles.

Harder than balancing time was making it seem like I had everything under control so that none of my roles would be taken away from me. If my practice thought my clinic was interfering in my performance, they might squeeze me out slowly by filtering new patients to other doctors. Ultimately, they could vote me out if I were to not carry enough weight.

More pressing of a matter was Beau and the twins. There was an unspoken language Beau and I had come to talk in that often rotated defensiveness, resentment, then a shove under the rug to feign optimism and acceptance. Reset and repeat, it felt like, more often than either of us would have liked. The worst part was that I knew of all my obligations, Beau would wait the most patiently, so he often got put on the back burner. I hated myself for doing that to him.

But back to the front burner.

"Sure, Mara, let's go sit down for this," I said, rubbing my back. She followed me to my small office and sat across from me.

"Page one is our Accounts Payable and Accounts Receivable report," she said, handing me a folder. "As you can see, we are fine at present."

I shrugged, pleased.

"Page two," she continued, "shows our six-month projected expenses and revenue."

I grimaced. This sheet showed a lot of parentheses, which I knew were negative amounts. In medicine, math was crucial, but my brain calculated dosages and test results so consistently that financial accounting became elusive at times. Beau managed our finances at home, Mara managed the books at the clinic, and our accountants handled everything at the practice. My job was to make the money to keep the lights on for all of them.

"Okay, this sheet doesn't look as great, obviously. Just give me the short of it," I said.

"We need money. Quickly," she said evenly.

Just then Shiloh appeared in the doorway. "Sorry to interrupt, but I wanted to see if you needed anything else before I left for the night?"

"I don't think so," I replied. "Thanks Shiloh. Have a good night."

She hesitated briefly before smiling and clacking away in her crocodile heels.

"I hope she didn't hear us talking," I said.

Mara seemed uninterested. "Likely not. But if she did, then there's no harm."

"I disagree. I don't want the rest of the staff to stress about the financial dire of the clinic. This is my responsibility."

"As you wish," she nodded unconvinced.

"You think we should let them know that we're going broke?" I asked incredulously.

"I think there is power in numbers. I wouldn't suggest alarming the team with details. But involving them in a plan rather than keeping them in the dark could be more effective than doing things alone."

"I don't know. There's not much they could do." I said almost as a question.

"You prefer to handle this matter alone. I will help however I can," she said calmly. "Perhaps you can ask the Massenet Foundation for another grant?"

"No, the $500,000 grant was already the largest they had approved to date. I can't ask them for more only six months after opening." I rubbed my lip remembering that I had a meeting with Anna next week to go over the grant allocations. "What about our traffic of people with private insurance? Has that increased?"

"No. We have not been marketing our capabilities for cardiac screenings. Perhaps this is something Shiloh and Kat could brainstorm?" she proposed, and already I could see her suggestion to "involve the team" take form.

"Let's see what they can come up with," I agreed reluctantly.

"What about the gentleman who donated the cardiac stress system? Jed Terry, I believe his name is?"

I nodded. He had already been circulating in my mind as a possible short-term solution. "I'm sure he would donate more, but I have to be careful about the timing. It looks a little unsavory to ask after he just gifted an expensive piece of equipment."

"I agree. But surely he has friends."

I pictured Andrew Yale, whimpering on his side.

"Yes. I don't know how to get to them though," I said.

"Perhaps we host a social function."

"With what budget?" I asked confused.

"We could entertain a dinner or cocktail hour at the clinic to thank Jed and to get to know some of our neighbors. We could invite some of the business owners in Doylestown. Much of fundraising is just connecting with people. They keep you in mind when their accountants encourage donations for the year. You know, Tobias is a very talented cook."

"We couldn't host it here!" I laughed out loud. "Where would we put everyone?"

Without smiling, she offered, "We could have an al fresco dining experience in the back parking lot. It looks like a lot of gravel now, but with the right decorations, it could be quite lovely."

I couldn't visualize our parking lot becoming an outdoor dining area, but growing up surrounded by concrete, I learned a long time ago that outdoor spaces were not natural to me. I assumed it was a cultural difference that made Mara seem quite confident in the prospect; even Tobias and Irena had created patio gardens in their small apartments. When I gawked at Tobias' garden beds, full of herbs and vegetables I couldn't identify, he shrugged, "I'm Greek."

"I don't know, Mara. I don't really have time to plan something like that."

"I will take care of it. Tobias and I will cook to keep the costs down. The team will help with the set up."

"We won't be able to pay them overtime," I eyed the spreadsheets Mara had prepared for me. "I thought you were going to suggest I lay someone off; not up hours."

"I don't think anyone would expect overtime. Dr. Wells, may I say something bold?"

I shrugged.

"As we've already established, you prefer to do things alone. But I can't help but wonder if that is because that is the only way you know."

I stared at Mara, contemplating my answer.

"I knew a woman like you: beautiful and intelligent. There also was something about her that was guarded. Just when you thought you were getting close to her, you realized she was just out of reach, holding you at a distance.

"The only person she let in was one of our partners at the firm: She fell desperately in love with him. It didn't take long for their relationship to go from steamy and sexy to dark and dangerous. Everybody knew it. But she kept to herself. She didn't talk to anyone about anything other than work. One coworker, Angela, approached her when she noticed bruising around her neck, but she barked at her and made some excuse. A month later, she showed up to work in a leg cast. Everyone grimaced. Angela bravely approached her again and said with more firmness, 'I think he's is hurting you. I can help.' But again, this woman denied it and pushed everyone away."

I listened intently, but I was uncertain where Mara was going with this story. Did Mara think I was being abused? I pictured Beau, his dimpled grin, and scoffed at the thought.

"The week her cast was removed," she continued, "she set fire to the partner's Shore house where he had thrown her down the stairs one night. He was high, she later found out."

"Oh my God," I replied, wincing. I thought of my mother strung out some nights, not herself.

"She didn't deny her crime, but in the first week of her sentence, Angela went to visit her and said, 'I wish you would've let me help you.'

"'It wouldn't have made a difference,' she had told Angela. But Angela had countered that it would have. 'The same cameras he'll use to show that you set fire to that house are the same cameras that would have incriminated him in your abuse. The same cameras that one of our clients installed. I came across the invoice. Of course, that scumbag expensed it. I tried to tell you about them, but you wouldn't listen. I'm sorry.'"

Mara stopped and waited for me to say something.

"I'm sorry to hear that," I consoled. "Mara, I don't mean to sound insensitive, but I'm not sure why you're telling me this."

"Because that woman was me," she said in a firm voice. "And if I hadn't been so guarded, if I had let other people in, if I had stopped feeling like I had to fix everything alone, I could have avoided three years in prison. I could still have my career as an attorney. I could have put the right person behind bars."

"That's why you went to prison," I reflected. And the leg cast might have had something to do with her slightly offbeat stride. "You set his house on fire?" I was intrigued.

"I did. And I'm not proud of it. But I'm not proud that I let him abuse me, either," she said, inhaling memories. "I came to this country many years ago. I put myself through college, then law school. I worked hard to be where I was: Partner at one of the largest law firms. Part of my protection plan was to hide my past, not get too close to anybody. But he broke me. I was broken."

Mara said the word that stung me—broken—and my heart felt a jab for her.

"I look back and realize that much of my action was desperation. I felt alone and helpless. My family, my sisters, were in Azerbaijan. My boys were grown and had left for college, and our relationship had become strained because they suspected the abuse but knew I wouldn't leave, which created a distance. I was alone. I felt alone, at least. But part of that was choice: I didn't let anyone in. Not the right people, at least."

"I've never heard you speak of your children," I deflected.

She blinked her eyes sorrowfully. "Two boys, one year apart. We haven't spoken since I went to prison, but I'm hoping to change that."

"Where is their father?" I asked. I guessed the Shore house inferno man was not their father based on her timeline.

"Their father is still in Azerbaijan. I left the country with my boys when they were very young. Their father also was abusive. When I left him, I told myself I would never let a man hurt me again. I guess history has a way of repeating itself."

"I'm so sorry, Mara. I know it's not easy sharing that."

For a moment, I contemplated sharing a piece of my past, the part that witnessed my beautiful mother get taken advantage of by a powerful man. But I couldn't bring myself to dredge it up. *Why bother?*

"I'm just a survivor, Dr. Wells, as you are."

I winced warily. *Why would Mara suspect I was a survivor?* Perhaps Irena had leaked something about my past because I couldn't recall talking about it with Mara. I was curious about her comment, but I let it go. This was her floor.

"I learned a lot through my experiences," she said. "I learned there is value to letting people see your vulnerabilities and to accept help when needed. I'm still practicing, but I can tell you that I feel safe here at the clinic. Which is why I'm sharing my story with you. There is a family here. A family that you chose, and you've chosen well."

I tipped my head in agreement.

"Which brings me back to where we began: Let us help. We can raise the money for the clinic. We can get creative. You don't have to figure this out by yourself. Trust us."

I smiled humbly. I had been so busy dividing myself between different roles that I didn't pause to see what was happening right under my nose: This clinic had birthed a family.

"All right, Mara. Let's do it, sister."

CHAPTER SEVENTEEN

The energy in the clinic buzzed as the staff prepared for our Evening Under the Stars.

Tobias spent much of the day in the back parking lot constructing something that resembled a large deck with open framing, pergola-like. Kat and Shiloh created guest lists and invitations. Mara and Irena planned menus. I would walk in some days to find all five of them briefly huddled about some detail or the other.

"Dr. Wells," Shiloh asked as I walked up from a consult. Her garnet hair was pulled neatly into a curled updo, like a sexy, modern-day Lucille Ball. She didn't wear her glasses today, and for the first time I noticed her hazel eyes underneath the swooped eyeliner. "I was wondering if you had Jed Terry's address. And perhaps Andrew Yale's?"

I shifted uncomfortably. Shiloh and I hadn't spoken of the "night of the Andrew," and Kat hadn't mentioned it either. Although, I wouldn't have expected Kat to bring it up; Kat communicated more with curt nods and smiles than with words.

"I can get Jed's address, but I don't think we'll need it," I answered. "He should be coming in any day."

"He has an appointment?" she asked, surprised.

"No, not exactly. He's coming to pick up something," I said distractedly. "Anyway, you can hand him the invitation then, and one for Andrew."

"Perhaps I can ask him if anyone else would be interested in coming?" She sounded hopeful.

"Sure, you can. He likes you. See what he says," I smiled.

"He likes my easy company. But what he really likes is seeing Mara," she said evocatively.

Shiloh had noticed it, too: Jed's jaw drooped when he saw Mara, and there was a noticeable change in his normally pert vibe.

"So maybe Mara should ask him?" I gauged.

"No. We need to keep her the reason he would come. I'll find a way to ask him. Leave it to me."

I nodded. I had full confidence that Shiloh could manage a conversation with Jed after seeing how she so easily influenced Andrew. I wanted to say something to Shiloh about that night, but I couldn't bring myself to ask her what I really wanted to know: How did she learn to do what she did?

"Dr. Wells, I could use a hand in room 3," Irena swept up to the front desk like a gush of wind. "What are you girls gossiping about?"

"Nothing," I said quickly, walking toward room 3. "Just invitation stuff for the dinner."

It couldn't have worked out better if we had sent Jed Terry an invitation to pick up the invitation because later that day, Jed strolled into the clinic, trailed by Andrew Yale.

"Dr. Wells!" Jed exclaimed as he reached for a butterscotch candy. "You remember Andrew."

I had just finished my last appointment and was going over some notes with Irena. "Yes. Hi, Andrew. How is everything?" I asked slowly.

Irena smiled politely at the duo, her wary, city eyes scaling them head to toe.

"Good," Andrew replied curtly, eyes averted. He was dressed in a well-tailored blue suit with a yellow tie. He looked polished but unnatural, like a kid at church whose mother made him dress up for Easter. He glanced at Shiloh, sitting up straight in her black jumpsuit and heels, then he looked away quickly.

"Mr. Terry," Shiloh said, avoiding eye contact with Andrew not because of intimidation, but almost as punishment. "I'm glad you stopped by. I have something for you." She handed him two envelopes.

"Oh, look Andrew, one for you!" Jed winked and handed Andrew the envelope. They opened them in tandem.

"A dinner. At the clinic?" Jed amused. "*Al fresco*, it says."

"We want to thank the donors and patrons of the clinic. The clinic will be transformed," Irena commented as convincingly as she could. She was not one to charm, but she recognized Jed's potential as a regular donor, so she made the effort.

"I think I can make it work," Jed said, peering behind me. "Everyone from the clinic will be there, I assume?"

"Yes, everyone will be there," Shiloh answered with an easy tone. "You are welcome to bring a guest, if it suits you," she fished.

"Nah, I'd come alone. So would Andrew, right pal?" he snickered at his distracted friend. Andrew nodded.

"We'll add you both to the list," Shiloh said, pleased.

"Before I wrap up for the night," I interjected. "Jed, would you care to follow me back to my office?" Irena stopped smacking her gum and I could feel her glance cautiously at me. I knew I'd have to field questions from her later.

"You bet," he replied, grabbing another butterscotch. He tossed one to Andrew, who fumbled to catch it. "Come on back with me, Andrew."

"Uh, Jed," I struggled. "Perhaps it would be best if you came alone. For confidentiality reasons."

He winked at me. "Ah, it'll be okay. I'll waive my HIPAA rights. C'mon, Andrew."

I led the duo back to my office and shut the door behind them. I walked behind my desk and reached into a drawer. "Jed, I invited you back here to give you these," I said as I placed a handful of Viagra samples in his hand.

"I've struck gold! Or blue, rather," he laughed, then he took a seat and motioned for Andrew to follow suit. I wasn't expecting them to get *comfy*, and I reservedly took my seat across from them.

"Dr. Wells, Andrew has something he'd like to ask you," Jed said, waiting for Andrew to pipe in.

Andrew cleared his throat. "So, the girl up front—"

"Shiloh," I filled in.

"Right. Shiloh," he stuttered. "Well, I was wondering what her status was? Does she work outside of the clinic? Do you know of any other jobs she, uh, may have?"

"I think you could probably ask her that question," I answered, confused.

"Okay. I just didn't know if you two were close. It seemed like you might be the night I came in," he replied awkwardly. For a man of Andrew's position and power, I found it curious that he seemed timid when he walked into this clinic. Though he made eye contact with me, which was more than he did for Shiloh, his words were brief and shallow. While it invoked a small glimmer of empathy from me, it likewise made me skeptical of him. I didn't like when I couldn't get a clear read on someone.

"Andrew, just get to the point. Jesus," Jed said while fiddling with a Rubik's cube, one of the only ornamental items on my desk. It helped me think.

"Thing is," Andrew said. "I was wondering if Shiloh was a domme. Actually, I know she is; I could tell by the way she acted the night she helped with, you know, my predicament," he blushed.

I gasped slightly as I contemplated how to answer. Thanks to Shiloh, I now knew what a "domme" was, but I was taken back by Andrew's nerve of bringing up this matter with me. What did I have to do with Shiloh's past dominatrix role, and why would Andrew ask me instead of her?

"Again," I scoffed. "I think you could probably talk to her about this. To be honest, it's getting late. I think we should all probably call it a night."

"Andrew needs your help," Jed piped in impatiently. "He has a proposition for you."

"I have a very particular interest," Andrew said quickly, sensing that he was losing me. "One that is dangerous, so I need someone experienced such as Shiloh. And I need a professional to be on hand should things not go according to plan."

"What's your special interest?" I asked out of curiosity.

"Autoerotic asphyxiation."

My eyes narrowed in alarm. "Asphyxiation? That could kill you."

"Well, I know," he said casually. "But I'm not into the hard-core stuff. I just like a little tightening from hands, or a belt, or a collar. Just enough."

"A collar?" I snorted. "I'm sorry, but I don't think I can help you." This was becoming a go-to phrase when it came to Jed and Andrew walking into my clinic.

"Dr. Wells," Jed said. "I know this is out of your comfort zone. It's out of mine too, trust me," he chuckled. "But I gotta tell ya, I've got friends in high places, and you'd be surprised how common this is for them."

"That may be," I feigned disinterest. "But I'm still not able to help you with this."

"That's a shame," Andrew said. "Because I would be willing to pay substantially for these services. I'm sure the clinic could use a few extra donations?"

My capacity to entertain this ludicrous and offensive conversation peaked. I turned to Jed first: "This is my fault."

They looked at me anxiously, then at each other, then back to me.

"It's my fault that you're here," I continued. "I crossed a line helping you that night. I should have called an ambulance, but I thought, 'Why not try to help?' But now I remember why I should follow protocol— because when I cross a line, it gives you the liberty to cross it, too."

"Dr. Wells," Jed said carefully, "I didn't mean to—"

"No, stop, Jed, please. I think enough has been said here tonight. Jed, I'll see you for your next exam. And Andrew, I'll see you around, maybe." I stood up and grabbed the keys from my coat pocket to indicate it was time to lock up.

"Dr. Wells, please," Jed tried again. "We can pretend this conversation didn't happen. Andrew wanted to tag along tonight, and I didn't think you'd be so offended by his question, but I can see now that it was wrong of us to approach you. I was just thinking about how the money could help you. I'm sorry."

"Thank you. Goodnight, gentlemen," I said.

"Can we still come to the dinner?" Andrew asked, unfazed.

Shit, the dinner. Right now, Jed and Andrew were our two most promising contributors on our attendance list, and the clinic desperately needed their future contributions. The proper ones.

"Of course. See you both at the dinner," I said with a straight face. Jed looked apologetic as he followed Andrew out. He stopped at the door, hesitated, then turned to leave my office.

I exhaled loudly. *The nerve of these men.*

CHAPTER EIGHTEEN

"Mommy? What does this say?" Juliet asked sleepily as she ran her little fingers over the embroidery on my scrubs pocket. I got home just in time to tuck the kids into bed.

"This says, 'Faith Wells, M.D., F.A.C.C.'" I pointed out each raised letter.

"What does it mean?" she asked in her tiny voice. She had the same blue eyes as my mother—as I—had, but her hair was lighter than ours.

"Faith Wells is my name," I said playfully. She giggled. "And M.D. stands for Doctor of Medicine."

"Mmm-hmm."

"F.A.C.C. means Fellow American College of Cardiology," I said slowly.

"You fix hearts. That's what Daddy says," she said.

"Right. I fix hearts. I also make people feel better when they're sick or hurt."

"I got a boo-boo today at school," she said, pulling her leg out of her covers to show me.

"Oh," I rubbed it earnestly. "Let me take a closer look at that." I pretended to look close, then playfully bit her leg like a hungry dog. She screeched, "No, Mommy!"

Our laughter subsided and I stared at her admirably with more love than I knew what to do with.

"Is that why you're gone all the time? Because you're fixing people?" she asked.

My heart dropped. I knew I wasn't home as often as I would've liked, as they would've liked, but I had an endless list of responsibilities. The hospital, the practice, the clinic—they were all sucking up more time than I had anticipated.

"I'm not gone *all* the time," I said exaggeratedly. "I'm here for dinner," I teased raising her leg to playfully bite again. She reflexed a kick to stop me.

"But yes, Juliet," I said seriously. "When I'm not home, I am fixing people."

"What would happen if you didn't fix them?"

"Well, some would go to another doctor to get fixed. Some would get better on their own. And others would stay broken."

"Or some might die," Juliet stated matter-of-factly. For a split second, I was shocked by her pragmatism, but then a resounding pride filled my chest. *You are my daughter*, I reflected in her ability to deduce.

"Yes. But not on my watch," I winked.

"I want to be a doctor when I grow up. Like you, Mommy," she said sincerely. My heart tipped over and spilled its contents into my eyes. I blinked heavily to hold back the emotion.

"You'll be the greatest doctor, Juliet," I said determinedly. "And I will help you."

"Thanks, Mommy," she yawned a smile.

"Goodnight, Doctor Juliet," I said as I turned off her light and played her sound machine music.

I paused outside her door.

The conversation from earlier today with Jed and Andrew had left me with an uneasy feeling, yet I couldn't pinpoint why. Was it because they had the gall to approach me to facilitate some kind of kinky service, which left me to wonder how they must perceive me? Did they see me as someone they could take advantage of? The idea made the blood boil in my veins. I thought of my mother: in control one day, out of control the next because of a man who took advantage of her. I watched as Bobby Clay slowly scratched at her independence, a little skin at a time, until she was entirely raw; fully dependent. That would never be me.

But perhaps it was those exact insecurities feeding my disdain.

What if Jed and Andrew approached me as a competent doctor and businesswoman? Not a woman they could push over, but rather, a woman of credence that they could let into their circle? By profession, doctors were confidants, a person one could go to with whatever problem—big, small, or kinky—without judgment. Obviously, I had established a sense of trust from Jed, who adopted me as his preferred doctor; trusting me with problems he was embarrassed to share with other doctors.

My blood tempered to more of a simmer as my thought process pinged side to side.

Would it be the worst thing to have the trust of high-powered people? Such regard was what I dreamed of as an out-of-place student in a world full of people who had connections. I had been fighting for the top for as long as I could remember, and it's a longer climb when you start from dead bottom. I watched as my peers easily got interviews with the help of a phone call from Daddy, while I had to stay after class, write extra papers, find a creative way to catch the eye of the right people. When I gave birth to the twins during fellowship, I took one week off, then dragged my swollen body back to work, shooing off the comments: "What are you doing here so soon, Faith? Didn't you just have a baby? Have *two* babies?" But I was the only woman in my program, and I was not going to let the men get ahead and give creed that a woman couldn't keep up in a man's world. Even if it meant I had to change my post-birth dressings while pumping breast milk in a bathroom stall so I didn't miss a beat.

And now, I was gaining notoriety in the Philadelphia medical scene, the most recent Top Doc magazine stating beneath a flattering picture of me in a lab coat: "Faith Wells, M.D., is making waves in Doylestown as she opens a nonprofit medical clinic with specialized cardiac focus." None of my male counterparts had opened a non-profit clinic while managing their jobs and their families. I had done that. I was doing that.

And goddammit, sometimes connections weren't a bad thing. Sometimes connections could get you to the top quicker, like putting a missing rung on the ladder. In cardiology, connections saved lives. You connect an artery and blood flows freely.

Isn't that what I wanted when I pursued a career in medicine? The big checks and the fancy table full of food? And connections so that when my kids want to go to college or chase a dream—when Juliet wants to be a strong, female doctor—they won't have to scrape and claw and crawl on their fists to accomplish their goals while their peers glide through on roller skates? No, they won't have to do it by themselves.

Mommy could make a call for them.

CHAPTER NINETEEN

"Shiloh, do you have a minute?" I asked casually as I typed the last of my notes.

"Yes, Dr. Wells," she replied attentively.

I looked around to make sure we were alone. It was a week before our Evening Under the Stars dinner, and I had been doing some thinking about our guest list.

"I wanted to ask you something personal. You don't have to answer."

"Okay."

"You mentioned once that you were a dominatrix—or are—I don't remember, exactly." I shrugged one shoulder. "We were a little preoccupied."

The corners of her mouth twitched with the slightest smile.

"I was wondering if you would tell me more about it."

"About domming?" she asked, her cat glasses raised with her eyebrows.

"Yes." I looked around again to make sure we were alone.

"What do you want to know?"

"I guess I want to know what it involves."

She lifted her eyebrow curiously. My instinct to immediately refute my interest in participating as a domme was held at bay. I wanted Shiloh to talk.

"I'm not educated about it. I mean, the only thing I know about *dominatrix*," I said in a lower voice, "is what I see in the movies: whips and chains and leather," I smirked. "But what I saw that night—the way you made Andrew submit entirely with very few words—it intrigued me. There was an art to it. Your persona was obviously practiced and it completely overwhelmed the room. Even I stopped to watch you," I laughed slightly.

Shiloh's mouth pursed a smile. "That's the idea of it."

"What do you mean by that?"

She stared at me hesitantly, straight back and crossed legs, then slackened. "The idea is that you have total control. It's all about control."

"Control? Not sex?"

She scoffed. "Sex? No," she said defensively. "That is a common misconception. It's more of a psychological service than a sexual one."

"So, you don't have sex?"

"Never."

I stared, processing. Shiloh could sense my confusion. "I'm sorry, but you don't have sex? What exactly are they paying for?"

She rolled her eyes. "They pay for the experience. The escape. They pay for the fantasy and the fetish. Most of all, they pay for a place to feel free."

"Free of what?"

"Free of whatever burdens they carry. Some carry the burden of making a lot of money. Others of calling the shots all day. Some carry the burden of feeling dirty, feeling like a freak, and living in a world designed only for the pretty."

My chest thumped. I knew that feeling. I knew that feeling every day of my life.

"You'd be surprised," she smiled. "Most of my clients—in fact, all of them—were very high-powered, reputable figures. Lawyers, judges, politicians, doctors." She paused expectantly after saying *doctors*.

"I think you can tell by my face that I am surprised to hear that. I don't know any doctors who participate in this type of," I searched for the word…"Activity?"

Shiloh laughed. "Activity? I like that." She grabbed a fingernail file and started filing her nails. "Who goes around talking about it? Do you know any of your colleagues' sex lives? What they do in the shower? What they write in their diary? What they pray about? Likely not." Her file tapped the air after every question.

"These men—I'm assuming it's men?" I was skeptical to assume anything anymore.

"Mostly. For me, yes. Only. Women are not my specialty."

"So, these men… they pay for you to do what exactly? If not sexual?"

"Who said it wasn't sexual?"

"You said it was more psychological than sexual."

"More, not entirely."

"And you said you don't have sex."

"We don't."

"So, what do you do for them?"

"It's different for everyone. That's part of the art. Sometimes a client thinks he wants one thing, but he really wants another."

"And how can you determine what they want?"

"I imagine it's the same way you do, Dr. Wells," she said factually.

I stammered. "I'm not a dominatrix."

"No, but patients come to you saying they have this symptom or that, and you must filter through their words and focus on their symptoms."

I teetered my head in acknowledgement.

"But that's not enough," she added. "The good doctors—the good dominatrices; the Pro Dommes—also rely heavily on intuition. Intuition is what makes them a master of their craft."

A flashback reeled: I told my mother I was scared of walking home from school by myself. I was ten and starting to get attention from boys. But my mother said I'd be fine because I had good instincts: I knew who to stay away from. Fast-forward to high school, where there were more times than I could count where I said "no thanks" or "maybe next time" to peers who ended up in trouble for you-name-it. And now, as a cardiologist, my intuition had earned me a reputation for accurate diagnostics. More experienced colleagues often came to me for consults on a patient. I couldn't figure out how they missed certain indicators, but I knew why. They didn't focus on the right questions; they didn't put all the pieces together. They lacked intuition.

"Okay, Shiloh. I hear what you're saying: You need intuition to customize the *experience*?"

"We call them sessions."

"Right. But what I still don't understand is what types of things you do during these sessions. Admittedly, I thought it all led to sex, but I'm realizing now that I'm wrong. So, what do you do, and what does it lead to? In other words, why do these men come to you?"

"It's simple. Most of these men just want somebody else to be in control. They spend their days managing people, businesses, circumstances—exercising large amounts of control. Then, they often go home to a partner who needs them to take care of the leaky gutter, the misbehaving kid, the renovation bill that's due next month, and oh, honey, can you also spend time exciting me with foreplay? They're tired. They're mostly tired of being in control, so they want someone else to carry that burden. Their whole life is one cumbersome to-do list, and they just want someone else "to do" for them."

"I get that. I do." *More than you know, Shiloh.* "So, you whip them? Or stick items in places?" I asked slowly with a wince, thinking about Andrew.

"Sometimes, although, I'm not into kink anymore. I like the psychological subservient stuff. For example, I had one client who asked me to tie him in a corner and ignore him for an entire session. He would sit completely naked on a stool, I'd tie a phone cord around his wrists behind his back, and he wasn't allowed to speak. I realized quickly, without him saying anything, that this must have something to do with his mother. Side note, Dr. Wells: It's always the mother." she smirked. I coiled.

"Anyway," she continued, "he would purposely act out, even though he knew not to. So, I would punish him."

"Punish him, how?" I asked.

"In this case, I'd whip him across the chest and tell him all the reasons he was being a bad boy."

I startled. "And how did he respond?"

"Excitedly, if you know what I mean."

"No, I don't, actually," I replied. "You said you don't have sex, that it's not about sex."

She clicked her tongue. "Everything is about sex, Dr. Wells. Just because I don't have sex with my clients doesn't mean they don't get aroused."

"Right," I answered slowly.

"Dr. Wells," Shiloh interrupted my thought. "Can I ask you a question?"

I raised my eyebrows in affirmation.

"Why are you asking me these questions?"

I hesitated. I knew Shiloh would sniff out an excuse. "Because Andrew asked me if you were available. For hire, I assume."

Shiloh laughed. "I've been expecting that."

"You were? Why? How?"

"You didn't find it strange that he came in with Jed the other day? Like he has nothing better to do than follow him into a free clinic? I knew he was going to ask you something, and I suspected it would be related to the night he came in."

"I didn't put it together until he approached me."

"So, what did you tell him?"

"I told him to ask you himself," I said.

"But there must have been a reason he came to you first. What does he want you to do for him?"

"He wants medical supervision," I answered directly.

"Can you be more specific?"

"He said he wanted me around in case something goes awry. A discreet insurance plan, if you will. He mentioned erotic asphyxiation."

"Oh, no, I'm not into that," Shiloh answered quickly. "But he's not either."

"What do you mean?"

"He has never been with a professional," she said easily. "That was obvious the night he came in. He's never had someone who can help him identify what he really wants, what he really needs."

"And what is that?"

"He needs a Mistress."

"A mistress?" I challenged.

"Not a mistress, as in a girlfriend on the side," Shiloh clarified. "A Mistress is a female Master. She has complete domination over her sub."

I scoffed, speechless. "I don't even know what that means. But how do you know this?"

"The same way you know that when someone comes in complaining about their back, the problem might actually be their heart. Experience. That, and he wouldn't make eye contact with me."

"All right. I think I've learned enough for one night. Thanks for being so open, Shiloh. I appreciate the education." I pushed off the counter.

"So, you're going to tell him I'm available, right?" she asked casually, blowing off dust from her fingernail tips.

"No, I—*no*," I answered with narrowed eyes.

"Why not?"

"Because I'm not a fucking pimp, Shiloh," I exasperated. "I would never do that to you."

"*To* me? You wouldn't be doing anything to me. You'd be doing it *for* me."

"You want to do this?"

"Yes. And quite honestly, you should want me to. It could be good for the clinic."

"For the clinic? I don't think this has anything to do with the clinic."

"But it could. Think about it. We need to hold the sessions somewhere. Why not the clinic?"

I laughed with repulsion. "I think this conversation has gone off the rails."

"We could split the money," she said seriously. "Someone like Andrew would pay $500 per session. Perhaps more. That's not even counting the gifts. And you know he has a lot of friends."

"I don't need the money, Shiloh."

"No. But the clinic does."

"Excuse me?" I asked defensively.

"I'm sorry," she softened. "But that's why we're having the dinner, right? A dinner on a budget? To woo the people who could donate to the clinic?"

"Yes, it's a fundraising dinner," I retorted. "So that the clinic can continue to offer services. It's not a dinner to find sexual patrons."

"We didn't find them. They found us," she played. "And that's exactly what we'd be doing—offering services."

I tipped my head as if she said something ridiculous.

"Look, I know it's not an EKG, but this clinic is supposed to offer help for heart, mind, and body, right?"

I stared, unamused.

"Why not, you know, *expand* that offering?" she said.

"For one, it's illegal," I said.

"Illegal? Says who?"

"Says the law. Money for sex is illegal."

"Who's having sex?"

She stumped me.

"For sexual favors, or whatever," I corrected.

"Who's giving favors? This is a service. Services are a legal charge. Even dominatrix services."

"Really?" I asked warily.

"Yes. You can verify it with Mara. Guess how she said most dommes screw up and get in trouble?"

I lifted my index fingers and thumbs to indicate *how*? But also, I was trying to figure out why Shiloh and Mara were conversing about such.

"Taxes. They don't pay the taxes on their income," she said.

"You're kidding me."

She stared seriously.

"And why were you and Mara talking about this?"

"Because I want in," Mara answered.

I pivoted quickly to see Mara standing behind me holding a stack of files against her satiny, black blouse; her shiny hair swung over one shoulder.

"Mara, what are you doing here?" I accused.

"I work here," she teased elegantly, her full lips in a pursing smile.

"I don't understand. *You* want to be a dominatrix?" I asked, flabbergasted.

"I didn't say that."

"How do you want *in*? You want to watch? Assist?"

"Not exactly," she answered while filing folders alphabetically.

"Okay, can you both please just speak directly! I'm not a goddamn decoder!" I lost my patience.

"I apologize, Dr. Wells," Mara turned around and stood obediently.

Shiloh cleared her throat. "The truth is that we have been talking about starting a side business. A dominatrix service, obviously, to make some extra money. I would lead with the services. Mara would manage the business end. I'm not good with taxes and all that," she shrugged. "Kat would apprentice until she could be on her own."

"Hold it—Kat?" I flustered. "*Kat?*"

"Yes," Mara answered. "Kat needs the money."

"The same Kat who barely speaks five words a day is going to apprentice to be a dominatrix?" My head was spinning.

"She needs the money," Mara repeated calmly.

"Can't we give her a raise at the clinic? More hours?" I asked.

"I'm afraid not," Mara answered. "She's working the maximum hours allowed." Mara didn't have to say out loud the other answer: The clinic couldn't afford to give her a raise. In fact, the clinic was just shy of having to lay off someone if things didn't turn around financially.

"She has a second job," Shiloh added. "An overnight shift stocking shelves. It's hard to manage those hours with her daughter."

My mouth dropped open. "Kat has a daughter?"

"Mmm-hmm," Shiloh answered. "Six years old. Cutest thing you'll ever see. Long black ringlets."

I felt foolish not to know this. I had worked with these women for six months and didn't know Kat had a daughter. How much of these women's lives had I not learned? And why had I not learned? Was I that self-absorbed? That busy? Or were these details just not relevant to me? Likely, it was a combination of all these points. But I couldn't help but feel a little left out, and I made it a point to pay more attention to the details of my staff's lives.

"Just so I'm clear," I addressed them both, rubbing my temple. "You have discussed starting a business—a dominatrix service—with Shiloh as Lead Domme, as you call it, and Kat as the apprentice? Mara," I directed at her. "You would manage what exactly? Collecting money? Filing taxes?"

"All of that, correct," Mara answered.

"Because Kat needs the money. Mara needs, I don't know—to stay busier? And Shiloh, you just miss the good old days?" I muddled.

"It's a little more than just missing leather and ticklers, Dr. Wells," Shiloh said mildly defensive. "Aside from the money, there is something very powerful about having someone fully submit themselves to you. I'm sure you can relate."

I scoffed, but then I thought about the first time I performed a cardiac catheterization. The patient was a young athlete who had a heart attack after pushing himself at the gym. I remembered the fear, the focus, and then the massive elation when I saw his arteries free up. It was euphoric to have his fate entirely in my hands, and it gave a high that could last all day.

"So, you like the power? The control," I asked more as a statement.

"We're all a little sick, Dr. Wells." Shiloh answered with a smart smile.

CHAPTER TWENTY

The Evening Under the Stars had arrived.

The transformation of the clinic's rear parking lot was mesmerizing. Beau and I pulled up to a glittery dinner deck that looked like it had served patrons for years. A long, rustic wood table with candles and simple, yet elegant place settings adorned the table, while lights and greenery thread throughout Tobias's pergola-type construct. Smells of oregano and lamb wafted from the tableside rotisserie.

The team was standing to greet us, anxiously awaiting our reaction, like kids seating their parents for their puppet show.

"Wow," I marveled.

"It's like Bucks County and Old Europe had a baby," Beau awed.

"That's exactly what we were going for," Irena said, pleased. "Rustic meets elegant charm."

"You nailed it. I don't know how you pulled this off on the budget you had," I said impressively.

"Most of it is rented or borrowed. Except for what I built," Tobias shrugged modestly. His barreled chest puffed proudly and his taut buttoned up shirt struggled to envelop his colossal frame.

"It's magnificent. Truly. Let's toast before the guests arrive," I said, holding up my glass of champagne. "To a very special and talented team."

As we sipped the champagne, we eyed each other, each gaze silently communicating different agendas. While the team had worked together to make this event a culinary success, a duplicitous subteam had planned a way to make this night a financial success in more ways than one.

The execution of our plans would either be a lifeline or a dead pulse, and only one thing was certain: Tonight was the clinic's defibrillator.

"Jed, can I have this dance?" I asked.

"It would be my honor," he charmed.

The table had been cleared and moved aside to allow for an intimately lit dance floor. Violins and Bublé-type music complemented our full bellies and boozy limbs.

"Have you enjoyed tonight?" I asked, swaying to Jed's strong lead. He danced like a gentleman, proper and commanding.

"This has been wonderful, Dr. Wells," he grinned. "I've gotta be honest, I didn't know what to expect attending a dinner at a clinic—I came out of respect for you, of course—but you'd never know that we weren't in a backyard in Tuscany."

"I'm glad," I smiled. I cleared my throat lightly. "I have a question for you, Jed."

"Sssh," he shushed softly. "I love this song. I remember dancing to this song on the Aegean Sea. The night was much like tonight. Sky full of stars, warm with a slight breeze, food and wine…." He closed his eyes and danced to his own beat, almost unaware that he had a partner. I wondered about Jed. He seemed a person very content to be alone, yet never alone.

The song ended. He opened his eyes and entered our moment again.

"Sorry, Dr. Wells. Please, go ahead. What did you want to ask me?"

The plan was to survey Jed about Andrew. I needed insurance on the type of person Andrew was. I also wanted to gauge Jed's interest in the "special services" the ladies wanted to offer. But the nostalgic look in Jed's face pared back my intentions and I ignored my contempt for nostalgia.

"Who were you dancing with?" I asked. "On the Aegean? And just now?" I had a feeling it must have been someone Jed loved very deeply.

He snorted. "That was a long time ago."

"Memories have a way of creeping in though, don't they? To feel like the present?"

Jed smiled somberly, and I thought I almost saw a glaze in his eyes. I panicked; I've never done well with other people crying. Luckily, he turned on the business switch.

"What were you going to ask me, Dr. Wells? You need another donation is my guess?"

I narrowed my eyes. "How bold of you."

"Well, I've been invited to many dinners, Doc. The food is never free."

"Actually, this dinner is to show our appreciation of your already very generous donation. My question is about Andrew."

"Oh," he bellowed, as if I said something hysterical. "What do you want to know about him?"

"Can he be trusted?"

"With what?" he asked curiously.

"Let's just say—hypothetically—that I was willing to entertain my last conversation with him further."

He raised his eyebrows.

"And that maybe Shiloh was interested in offering, let's call them, *special services.*"

He snickered.

"But that they come with a hefty price tag and some stipulations. One of the stipulations being secrecy and indemnification of the clinic and any of its employees should something go awry."

"The clinic? What does the clinic have to do with anything?"

"Because—hypothetically—the special services could be offered at the clinic."

He guffawed. "Where?! In an exam room?"

"In the basement. We have a large basement with a separate back entrance that could be retrofitted for these services." The ladies had talked me into this plan and had shockingly already recruited Tobias for the renovation.

"Well, well. Aren't you surprising, Dr. Wells," he chuckled. "I knew I wasn't wrong about you. I'm not wrong about anyone."

"What does that mean?"

"You acted indignant when Andrew approached you. Like you were above this kind of *dirty* business. But something in my gut told me that we were built similarly."

I stared at him suspiciously.

"Doc, you are a beautiful woman. And you're a brilliant doctor. No one can argue with that. But there is something beneath all that prettiness."

I didn't know what Jed was talking about. And when did he start calling me just "Doc," I flouted. But I assumed he thought I was interested in performing the services, as well; as if there was a dominatrix inside my lab coat just waiting to use my stethoscope as a whip.

"*I'm* not interested in offering special services, just to be clear. My motive is the money. I need it for the clinic."

"That's what I wasn't wrong about."

"That the clinic needed money? Isn't that a given of any nonprofit?"

"No, Doc. It's not just about the money."

"Excuse me? What do you think it's for then?" I asked, offended.

"How do you think I became so successful, Dr. Wells?" he asked. "I grew up in Kensington to two Irish immigrants. My dad was a drunk and my mother laundered clothes to barter for food. When you grow up like that, failure is never an option. I have a feeling it isn't for you, either."

I scoffed. I had the inclination to push off and tell Jed that he had some fucking nerve, but for the first time in my life, I felt understood. And not judged for it.

"That's not it," I said, deflecting.

"You sure? Listen, I'm not trying to detract from the noble cause of this clinic; I watched my mother die of cancer without access to good health care. That's partly why I'm here."

I softened. "I'm sorry about your mother."

"Cancer took my wife as well," he said.

"I'm so sorry. That's who you were dancing with," I reflected, feeling crude for every assumption I ever made about Jed.

He brushed off my comment.

"Back to you," he said with a determined smile. "Tell me, Dr. Wells, if the clinic failed, wouldn't it punch you in the gut that They were right?"

"That who was right?"

"Anyone who ever thought that you couldn't."

There wasn't enough room on a sheet of paper for the tally marks of all the times someone suggested I couldn't do it. I couldn't make it out of Castle Hill, couldn't go to college, couldn't become a doctor, couldn't have a successful career and family, couldn't keep up with an affluent crowd, or couldn't have a fancy table full of fancy food.

And though Jed was probably right, I couldn't let him know it.

"I appreciate that you shared your story with me, Jed," I said sincerely, and I meant it, but I had to bring this circle back to where it started. "Right now, I can't focus on *why* I need the clinic to succeed, I can only focus on *how*," I said passionately. "And all I want to know from you is whether Andrew can be trusted."

He smiled thoughtfully, then must have calculated that I wasn't in the mood to share my story with him tonight. "He can be trusted. If there's one thing Andrew knows, it's how to keep a secret. His whole life is a facade protecting his secrets."

"What about you?"

"What about me?" he asked with a smug grin.

"Are you interested in *special services*?"

He chuckled. "Not of that kind. But I am interested in something you have."

I tipped my head. "More pills?"

"Mara."

CHAPTER TWENTY-ONE

"He wants to date you," I said glibly. We had scheduled a light day following our dinner, so the clinic was quieter than normal.

"Is that code for something?" Mara asked.

"No. He just wants your company. Wants to take you to restaurants and benefits and such," I said.

"I'm versed in the concept of dating," Mara replied. "But I'm accustomed to a man asking me directly for a date, not asking through my employer."

This next part was going to need careful delivery. "He doesn't want to date for love."

"What does that mean, exactly?" she asked with an elevated tone.

"He just wants company."

"What kind of company?"

"The kind with no attachments," I answered.

"He wants a prostitute," she said. Her flinty gaze narrowed.

"He wants company. There would be no sex," I added.

"So you agreed?"

"Of course not! I don't have the right to accept his offer. I contemplated even bringing it up to you," I ruffled.

She eased. "How much would he pay?"

I looked up sharply. "You're considering this?"

"I'm curious."

"Five hundred dollars."

"Per date?" she asked.

"Per hour," I answered.

Mara blinked quickly, digesting the potential. "Jed Terry will pay $500 an hour to have dinner with me? Why?"

"The way he put it: He wants a companion when he wants one and no companion when he doesn't. He doesn't want to have to charm or coo, and he doesn't want to have to call the next day."

"I'm sure there are plenty of *services* that could accommodate that," Mara said. "That feels like the very definition of an escort or a prostitute."

"He wants more than a pretty thing on his arm or a warm body in bed. He wants an intellectual conversation at a restaurant and someone to enjoy the theater with him. He wants someone who can keep up with his crowd of people, not raise eyebrows."

"His crowd?" she piqued.

"Yes. I got the impression you'd be attending social events with him."

She nodded her head slowly in thought, and I wondered if being with his crowd was an alluring or disturbing element of his proposal.

"He wants an hourly girlfriend, then," she contemplated.

"Basically. He's lonely but he doesn't want to be in love. And he certainly doesn't want anyone to fall in love with him, which I understand tends to be the case."

She macerated the proposal. "I'll do it," she said confidently. "But I don't want any of the money. It all goes straight to the clinic as a donation."

I scoffed. "Mara, that's insane. You should have a cut, or why else would you agree to this?"

"Because it's exactly the opportunity I've been waiting for."

There is a medical term called collateral circulation.

This occurs when the heart's main arteries fail, usually due to blockage, and the blood finds circulation via another path, building nearby minor vessels. Some people have very little collateral circulation, while others have a reliable supply of blood through vessels that have swollen to act like small arteries. In rare cases, these swollen vessels might supply the heart with just enough blood to survive a heart attack.

After Mara calculated the extra income could exceed $20,000—just in the first month—I wagered that if collateral circulation could save someone's life, then there was no reason collateral compensation couldn't save the clinic.

I couldn't believe how simply the plan came together. It was as if everyone made a wish and tossed a penny into the fountain, and each wish came true at the same time.

I needed to bring money into the clinic without sacrificing any more of my time: Beau's patience was thinning by the day, and the twins were getting old enough to notice how long mommy was gone.

Shiloh wanted to add some color back to her rather black-and-white life. As she put it, vanilla was great; there's a reason it's the classic winner. But ordering different flavors with different toppings occasionally was not a bad thing. Oh, and bringing a grown man to his whimpering knees was a satisfying occupational hazard.

Kat needed the money, that seemed obvious now. But I had yet to figure out Kat's full story and I was eager to learn it.

Andrew had been prospecting the perfect domme for some time and inadvertently found her at the clinic. Bonus was that he thought I could offer some medical supervision during dangerous sessions, but Shiloh convinced me that wouldn't be necessary. I chose to trust her.

Jed Terry's penny toss had a wish I hadn't foreseen: an escort in Mara. Though he was content with the nonsexual agreement, it still made me wonder: *Why all the Viagra?*

Mara had been waiting for this opportunity, as she called it: a taste of the lifestyle she once enjoyed by way of a noncommittal relationship. I was sure there were other motives for Mara, but they had yet to unfold.

And Tobias. Who would have guessed he'd be pulled into this? When I asked him why he was getting involved, he replied simply, "Because they need my help." *They* being Mara, Shiloh, and Kat, to whom Tobias had become protective of in a brotherly way.

Which led me to Irena. Irena was the only one who hadn't been wrangled into this sub-service of the clinic. Tobias and I agreed that she would never approve, and that it was best to keep her focused on "front end" clinic services. And though Irena and I were never the type of friends who painted each other's toenails while telling secrets, she was as close to family as I'd ever known and I had never felt the need to keep something from her. But I had to agree with

Tobias that it was best Irena stay focused on the routine clinic services. Doylestown was changing Irena, and not necessarily for the worse. Though I was the one who pulled her to the suburbs reluctantly, Irena was the one who acclimated easiest. I even suspected she was dating a local chicken farmer who brought eggs to the clinic twice a week, but I hadn't inquired. Such was the nature of our relationship; I'd find out when it made sense to find out and no sooner than that.

And so, the rooms were being prepped. The staff was gearing up. The patients were booking. And they were all waiting for the doctor to arrive to begin operating.

CHAPTER TWENTY-TWO

She wore a black leather corset with fishnet stockings, and her red hair gave the illusion of a dragon tipping its head backward and breathing an elegant swirl of fire that lingered around her head.

It was Go Time. Tonight was my late-appointment shift at the clinic, so it was arranged that Mara would manage the desk while I tended to appointments. The schedule was stacked in a way that I wouldn't need a medical assistant, which would allow for Kat to be downstairs with Shiloh. Irena had just left, having completed the day shift, and Tobias was wandering around somewhere, preparing for his duty of letting the "other" patients in through the back door.

No pun intended.

"Hello, Doctor," Shiloh said, gauging. It was agreed that for this to work, our relationships had to take new form when we stepped downstairs—into the Dungeon. I would be known simply as the Doctor. Not Dr. Wells, but certainly not Faith; there was still a hierarchy. And since the Doctor only came to check in, it was imperative Shiloh stay in character. Even so, when I walked downstairs to find her organizing her tools in a lit glass case, I was taken back.

"Shiloh," I greeted. "You look good in black." And she did. It was hard to look away from her. Her skin looked milky against thick eyeliner and crimson lipstick, the type of skin that was better untanned. Her creamy arms were lean and muscular, but her hips were full. The leather corset trussed her waist so tight that it seemed to spill its contents out of the top and bottom; her silhouette resembling the number eight.

She tipped her head and continued neatly spacing her tools perfectly apart, like a valet would organize a duke's silverware before dining.

"What's this, then?" I asked, walking over and running my finger along an A-shaped wooden structure with a leather-wrapped straight beam on top. It still smelled new, like chemicals and grain.

"That's a horse," she answered, polishing the handle of something that looked like a paddle.

"I see. And this?" I asked, walking toward a large X-shaped stand, also wrapped in leather, secured to a frame that was bolted into the polished concrete floor.

"That's a cross," she answered, amused.

"Mmm-hmm," I mumbled. "I recognize that, at least," I smiled, pointing to a table similar to those in the exam rooms. In fact, I was sure the medical supply store was where she ordered it from; most of the equipment for that matter. Behind the table, displayed in neat rows on the eggplant-painted wall, were various instruments: whips, cuffs, and leather tools I couldn't identify.

"And that," I shrugged, pointing to a sterilizing autoclave. "This room is starting to feel familiar now," I teased.

"I remember the first time I walked into a dungeon," Shiloh said easily. "I was seventeen."

"Seventeen?" I interrupted, alarmed. Shiloh was still in her mid-20s, but I hadn't realized she started domming so young.

She smiled. "Yes. I wouldn't become a domme for several years. But my older cousin, whom I adored, had dragged me to her dungeon. We were hanging out that night—going to the movies, I think—and she had to drop by "work" to pick up money. She told me to stay outside but I insisted on coming in with her; I was curious. I had an idea of what she did, though she never shared details. I followed her in, and while she was in another room, I heard a man cry out. It startled me at first, but I realized it was a cry of pleasure. I walked closer to the room and peeked in through a window, just like that one, only smaller," she said, pointing to the three-foot, one-way window film that Tobias had cleverly sourced from an old police station. I didn't see the point in it, but Shiloh said it would allow me to "supervise" without entering the room, thereby ensuring discretion and anonymity, which I was learning was the name of the game.

"Anyway," Shiloh continued, "I saw a man strapped to the cross. He was wearing only a chastity belt of sorts; it had locks on it. And the domme was writing on his body. I couldn't tell what she was writing. But the man was clearly enjoying the experience. He let out a small groan of pleasure, and before he even finished the groan, the domme scorched him across the thighs with a leather whip she held in her left hand." Shiloh demonstrated the whipping, which made us both flinch.

"It terrified me," she laughed in remembrance. "And the man hollered in pain, but a satisfied look settled over his face, and I realized that he had groaned on purpose. He was instigating the pain."

I winced, picturing a grown man strapped to a contraption such as the eight-foot leather wrapped cross standing arm's length from me.

"Too much?" she asked, sensing my discomfort.

"No, go on," I endured.

She snickered at my bravery. "You're definitely not a domme, Doctor. Not that you don't have it in you, but I can tell it's not your thing."

"And yet, here I am building a dungeon in the basement of my clinic," I countered.

"Well, you're a practitioner offering a service. You must have the proper room and staff, right?"

I shrugged pathetically. It didn't really matter now. I had committed to the plan and I didn't have a compelling reason not to stay committed at this point. "Are you going to finish your story? I'm interested now."

"Where was I? Right, so the domme, whose name was Domina Red, was writing on the man. Turns out he had a ballpoint pen fetish. I'll spare you further detail on that, but...."

I secretly longed for the details, but I feigned indifference.

She continued without pause. "Red wrote slowly and intentionally, and from time to time she whipped him if he made a sound. I could not keep my eyes off her, the way she controlled this man. She was attentive, but not giving. She was performing a service for him, yet the man was trying to please her, obey her. It seemed that he came to please her more than she was expected to please him. The dichotomy was fascinating."

I found it fascinating, too. I was still trying to wrap my head around the psychology of this relationship between a domme and the subservient. I was keen on the fact that my perception of dominatrix was driven by Hollywood sensationalism, and that the practice was much more complex.

I supposed the misperception was similar to how I once viewed practicing medicine. My childhood fantasies of running into a hospital with my white coat flapping in the wind to save a patient's life were a stark contrast to what practicing medicine on a daily basis entailed. Regularly, my days were filled with dull, crammed appointments; writing 'scripts, advising people to exercise and eat well, then seeing them six months later to find that they had clearly done neither of those things, which led to me writing them more 'scripts. Paperwork piled onto paperwork. There were great moments, of course, but practicing cardiology was not quite how it was portrayed in the movies, running into good-looking doctors on the elevator and cutting arteries during surgery to the background sounds of intense theme music.

The truth was, I had come to enjoy my time at the clinic much more than my time at the practice or hospital. At least at the clinic, my hands were less tied. The patients were more grateful. The staff was more intimate. And though I still found myself on the outside of inside jokes, I belonged in a way a mother belongs with her children.

"So, you became interested after that experience?" I brought myself back to Shiloh. "But you said it would take several years before you would participate?"

"Yes. My cousin wouldn't let me have any part of it until I was a legal adult, which was the responsible thing to do," she said. "But she also wanted me to go to college. No one in my family had gone to college, and that was very important to her."

"I remember from your application that you did go to college. You majored in psychology, if I recall correctly?"

"Yes! Good memory, Dr. Wells."

"It's Doctor in the dungeon, remember?" I corrected amusingly.

"Right. Well, yes, Doctor. Since I was a girl, I have wondered how people felt. And it wasn't just people. I'd study animals and bugs, and wonder, 'Did they feel pain?' 'Did they love their mothers?' 'What made them cry? Ache? Long?' Psychology seemed a natural choice."

"It suits you. You're very good with people. Your empathy is deep."

"Thanks. I went to college, but it was expensive. My parents made just enough money to make getting loans difficult but paying for college impossible. My dad was a plumber—good years, bad years—and my mom worked at a flower shop. By my sophomore year, I didn't know how I was going to pay for my next semester. That's when I approached my cousin about domming. I knew it could help pay for college."

I nodded in understanding. "And that was it for you? You had found your 'thing?'"

"Not exactly," she guffawed. "It was helpful, that's for sure. It did pay for my college and much more. And I learned a lot during those two years. But they closed down their dungeon; Domina Red moved, I think. Anyway, a couple years ago, a friend approached me about doing it with her. She was one of the only people who knew I had dommed with my cousin. She desperately needed the money, and I needed a job, so...."

"And you liked it as much the second time around?" I asked.

"I liked it more," she answered thoughtfully. "I had matured. When I did it in college, I would just take on whichever client my cousin and Red threw at me, and I had to do some pretty shitty things that I wasn't into. But on my own, I could be more selective of my clients. I interviewed them. I only took the ones I found interesting. And I liked helping them."

"Helping them how?" I asked.

"Everybody wants one thing above all else, Doctor."

I raised my eyebrows in expectation.

"They want to feel accepted. Acceptance of someone is the ultimate act of love."

"It's unconditional," I acknowledged.

"That's right. You asked me before why these men—or women—why they come for these services? Is it to be humiliated? Whipped? Flogged? No. They come because they have a deep need to be accepted. All of them. The weird fetishes, the strange desires, the curious needs. And if someone accepts those needs, they feel loved. They're coming to be loved."

"Wow. I never thought of it that way."

"Most people don't. And admittedly, it's not always that way. Some dominatrix services are kinky and cruel and lure the wrong crowd. But I run mine differently. We'll run ours differently."

I smiled. I had agreed to allow the dominatrix services to transpire in the basement of the clinic. I had even agreed to supervise, if medically necessary. And I was doing it because selfishly the money would keep the clinic afloat, but also because it seemed it would help these women in distinct ways, as well. I felt a sense of gratitude for Shiloh's discretion in keeping the services palatable, if one will.

"And you and Mara worked out how to manage new clients?" I asked. This was a big concern of mine and they knew it. I had to trust that any new clients would be properly vetted out and that the identity of my clinic and myself was to remain anonymous until the new client could be trusted.

"Of course."

"Run through it for me again," I instructed.

She snickered. I had made them recite the process several times already. "Our existing clients are not allowed to give prospects anything other than my phone number. The phone number is different every week, as you know." I nodded. Shiloh was to get a new burner phone each week and text the new phone number to the list of existing clients. The text would say something benign, so that any recipient of it could easily explain it away as a scam. But it would always contain the code word: Budapest. The clients would use that new number to call or text for appointments that week, never to personal phone numbers and certainly never to the clinic.

"I'll arrange an interview with the prospective client," she continued while polishing the leather of the horse. "They'll be instructed to park on the street, in front of Cal's pizza shop." Cal's was less than one block from the clinic, but near dozens of other retailers and merchants. One would have to guess that it could be anywhere in Doylestown they were going.

"From there," she said, "I'll verify their identity and tell them to wait for their escort."

In swooped Tobias, a.k.a "The Escort."

Tobias would meet the new client and lay down the ground rules: Payment first, no touching unless instructed, and no second chances. If anyone got out of line, Tobias would escort them out. For good. And no one wanted to be escorted out by a nearly seven-foot Greek giant with fists the size of melons.

I smiled at the thought. "Tobias will bring them quietly to the dungeon?"

"Yes," she smirked. "Tobias will give them the glasses you saw." I recalled seeing the blackout glasses they would use as a blinder. "Then he'll put them in his car, drive them around the block a couple times, and escort them downstairs once he's convinced that he's messed with their sense of direction."

"I meant to ask you this before, but why not just do the interview at Cal's? Or a coffee shop or something?"

"Because Doctor," she specified. "I have to establish dominance from the beginning, and I can't easily do that in street clothes at a pizza shop."

I nodded my head in agreement.

"Besides, they have to see what they're paying for," she pet her hair back behind her ear suggestively.

"And they'll pay, from what I understand," I said. "Substantially." Mara had run through some of the preliminary income estimates and I was blown away.

The sound of a can toppling over startled us, and we instinctively looked toward the door. Kat appeared in the doorway.

She was wearing a kimono.

Shiloh and I gasped at the same time. "Kat?!"

She nodded obediently but wordlessly as she brushed by, the tail of her thigh-high kimono fanning behind her. Shiloh and I watched with parted mouths as she inspected the post, similar to a coat rack, that held gnarls of rope of different thickness.

I realized that I had been anticipating seeing Kat as a domina-trix; I was curious to see both of their *dramatis personae*, but I had wondered more about how Kat would go from meek to pique, and the manifestation was magnificent. Her hair was pulled up into a neat bun with two ornate gold pins intersecting, giving the illusion that the pins held the bun in place. Her face resembled a porcelain doll— simple complexion, painted eye, and taut, puckered lips the color of fresh blood. But it was hard to focus on Kat's face or hair when one's eye fixed on her kimono, gold with red and black swirls of nature. The robe rested high enough on her thighs that with the slightest motion of her arm, one was teased with the bottom peek of her buttocks. A knee-high laced up leather sandal completed the look.

"Kat, you look—" I searched for a worthy word. "You look arresting."

"Arresting?" Shiloh chuckled. "Like a cardiac arrest? Did she make your heart stop, Doctor?" she teased. Kat offered a small smile of gratitude.

"Yes. To be honest, I think it did skip a beat," I marveled. "Where did you get that robe?"

"It was my mother's," Kat answered plainly, while coiling a rope between her elbow and the V of her thumb and index finger. She secured the neat wreath with a skillful knot that made it cinch. She moved onto the next rope.

"Will those ropes do, Kat?" Shiloh asked passively. Shiloh had moved on to cleaning the glass case around her now polished tools.

Kat nodded.

"Your mother? Was she Japanese?" I asked, still trying to grasp this transformed woman who stood before me, manipulating rope like a seasoned cowboy.

"Her mother was."

"So, your mother was half-Japanese," I confirmed. Kat's unique look made more sense now; her small ballerina-type frame and her reverent face with dark, almond-shaped eyes and straight nose. Yet her hair was still a strange shade of brown, like rust and espresso, and it had an inconsistent wave to it, which must have come from her paternal side.

She nodded.

"And that was her robe?" I pried.

She nodded. Extracting information from Kat was like squeezing the truth from a patient about her diet, and I wondered how Shiloh and Mara knew so much about her.

I decided to be daring. "Your mother has passed, I assume?"

Kat nodded.

"Did she wear that kimono?"

"Her mother's mother did," she answered.

"In Japan?"

She nodded, then finally offered, "She was a Geisha. One of the last true Geisha." And the pieces of Kat's story began falling into place.

"It's beautiful," I said sincerely. "It's obviously shorter than a traditional Geisha kimono. Did you have it altered?"

She nodded at Shiloh with a proud smile.

"I helped her," Shiloh winked.

I wondered if her mother would've approved of Kat altering a family heirloom for use in a dominatrix dungeon, but it was none of my business.

"Perhaps you'll pass it to your daughter one day," I smiled. I had yet to meet Kat's daughter, though I learned that Kat was a single mom who was six years and nine months sober, nine months longer than the age of her daughter. I didn't know how Kat found addiction, but I did know why she found recovery. And thanks to the Massenet Foundation, I also knew how she came to find an education and steady employment.

"She'll get the longer robe when she graduates college."

I squinted admirably at Kat's determination to see her daughter go to college so that she could know a future that perhaps was out of reach for herself. I remembered the ache of knowing that if I wanted to forge a different path than the one predisposed for me, I had to come with heavy machinery to clear the debris. It's easier to follow the path known. It's even easier to believe it's the only path available to you. It takes something more substantial than just a desire to carve out a new path. It takes fortitude. It takes grit.

"Not a moment sooner," I validated. Kat stopped toiling rope and stared seriously at me. A moment of kinship waved between us.

"I better get back to the clinic," I said, moving toward the door. I paused before leaving.

"What's your name, by the way?" I asked Kat. I meant her Domme name. Shiloh had shared that hers is Mistress Raven.

"Lady Ayano," Kat answered.

"Ayano." I rolled it on my tongue. "What does it mean?"

"It means colorful woven silk."

I smiled, assuming the name was inspired by the kimono she wore.

I was wrong.

CHAPTER TWENTY-THREE

As I shifted from room to room performing follow-ups and minor routine office visits, Mistress Raven and Lady Ayano were on my mind.

Just a level below where I was checking someone's swollen glands, Andrew was in Raven's claws. A colleague of Andrew's was scheduled next. In fact, we were booked solid for the next month and a half. We now held two appointment books: one for the clinic and one for the dungeon. Shiloh, being tech-savvy, had made the dungeon's appointments only viewable to certain logins: mine, Shiloh's, Mara's, and Kat's. When Irena logged in, she saw only the clinic's appointments. It took some maneuvering and clever planning on Shiloh's part, and I was impressed with the efficiency.

And now, I found myself rushing through appointments in hopes of having enough time in between to make sure everything was fine downstairs. Stripped down, it meant that I was curious as hell.

I could tell Mara was curious, too. I'd find her lingering toward the back of the clinic, finding reasons to go outside briefly to put a bag of something on the landing or rearrange the porch decor. Just feet away was a separate back entrance that led to a soundproof and well-ventilated space. As impressive as Shiloh's computer work had been, Tobias's craftsmanship of the dungeon was expert. During construction, Shiloh went down with him to point out what should be here, what should be there, and a few days later, an apparition of deep purple walls, a polished concrete floor, recessed fluorescent lighting, lit glass cases, neat rows of hooks on the walls, and a finished ceiling was revealed. The effect was clinically seductive, disturbingly warm.

The team had been as resourceful in building the dungeon as they had been coordinating the benefit dinner. But even with their budgeted execution, the clinic had to front more money than it could afford. The clinic was bleeding profusely, and I could only apply pressure long enough. It needed a money transfusion. I couldn't afford the idea of losing the clinic.

Fortunately, Jed and Andrew had a surprising number of friends who stuffed the bookings and were willing to pay significantly for an early appointment. When we told someone that the waitlist was four weeks out, they would offer to pay double, whatever it took, to come before then. It didn't take long for some patrons to agree to pay $1,500 per hour. I shook my head and was wide-eyed when Mara informed me of some of the hourly rates.

"Is that normal?" I gaped at Shiloh. "To pay $1,500 an hour?"

"No. I've never made more than $300. But Jed and Andrew have fat-pocketed friends. And the fact that a doctor is on premise doesn't just make them feel safe; it makes them feel that there's some validity to it."

Suddenly, my heart thudded in my ears. *How much do they know about The Doctor?* I alarmed. It was assumed they wouldn't know about me unless a problem arose that would require me to command, but could I trust that my anonymity was secure? If these men came to know about me, I must make it a point to know *more* about them.

"Do we have cameras downstairs?" I asked.

"No," Mara answered quizzically.

"Could Tobias install some?"

"I could ask him," Mara said, jotting a note to remind herself of the task.

"You want cameras?" Shiloh asked. "For protection? Or for collateral?"

"Both," I replied.

"Then you'll want them done professionally," she said. "I know someone, and she'd do it for a good price."

"Call her. I want it all. Every angle and full audio."

Two weeks later, Kate Salters showed up to lace the dungeon with high-tech cameras that you couldn't find if you tried. She even synced the cameras to an application on my phone so that I could view the reel at all times.

"Oh, I appreciate it, but I'm sure I won't need to see live footage. I only need the cameras in the event that something happens," I had told her confidently.

"Just in case," Kate smiled.

Right now, I found it enticingly difficult not to check the app.

I entered the front reception area between appointments. It had been a little more than an hour since Andrew first descended the stairs to the dungeon.

Mara sat in Shiloh's place. She was playing receptionist during these "after hour" appointments.

"Patient in exam room 1 will need a follow up in two weeks," I said, handing her a folder. "Room 3 is good to go. Tell her to call if anything changes."

Mara took the chart and placed it neatly beside the keyboard. "Our 7:30 p.m. appointment canceled. There's a patient in room 2. One more due in at 7:45 p.m.," she spoke robotically.

The cancellation meant that we'd have fifteen minutes between appointments, and I'd surmised the same thought was circling in our minds, hesitant to funnel out.

"Come to my office after rooms 1 and 3 have left," I invited.

She perked her eyebrow. "Of course."

Moments later, Mara glided in, her tight pencil skirt close to her long, slender legs; her gold jewelry shimmering in the harsh fluorescent lighting.

Wordlessly, I pulled up the camera app on my phone and tilted it for both of us to see. It was as alarmingly clear as any high-def TV.

We jumped as the audio booted and a loud bark! jolted through the speakers.

"Oh my," Mara gasped, hand to her chest.

On all fours, wearing nothing but a collar, was Andrew Yale. Attached to the collar was a long, leather leash resting in Shiloh's (Mistress Raven's) black fingernail-painted clutch. She held the leather strand midway, leaving three feet of leash on both sides.

"Good boy," Shiloh congratulated firmly. "Sit."

Andrew Yale sat on his haunches like a dog, his erection pointing outward.

"Stand."

Andrew stood on hands and knees.

"Bark," Shiloh commanded with soft authority.

Andrew barked, only this time it was followed by a cold snap across his buttocks; Shiloh was using the remaining half of the leash as a whip.

"The command to speak is '*Speak!*'" she scolded powerfully.

Andrew silenced, but his still-erect manhood indicated that he had not been deflated.

Kat (Lady Ayano) idled nearby, appearing equally ready to be at the Mistress's command, the perfect Maiko.

"How are you ever going to learn, you bad, *bad* dog," Shiloh contemplated. "You whore of a dog. You dirty, shameful, pathetic dog. Perhaps you need more discipline."

Andrew's body tensed excitedly, and if he had a tail, I suspect it would've wagged.

"Or perhaps that collar is too loose," Shiloh straddled Andrew's back and pulsed her hands around his neck, then she pulled his head up by his hair and slipped one finger into the collar and tugged it tightly. She held it tight for only a moment—maybe three seconds—but Andrew's body began heaving with pleasure. His inhales and exhales waved with anticipation. I realized what Shiloh was doing. She was using the dog collar to simulate the erotic asphyxiation Andrew desired, but linking it to what she deduced was his true need: A Mistress.

"Huh," I awed at the genius of her technique.

Mara closed her mouth and cleared her throat. "Quite the experience," she said, re-poised.

We looked at each other diffidently, like two might look at each other after cheating on a test. We should have stopped watching and gone back to work, but, well, the patients could wait another minute.

Shiloh stood directly in front of Andrew, his face intentionally an inch from between her legs. "Sit."

Andrew hesitated a millisecond, and Shiloh cracked her whip along his welted backside again.

"Sit, *now!*"

Andrew immediately obeyed.

"Lady Ayano," Shiloh said smoothly, "grab rope. We need to tie this pup up; he needs to learn a lesson. He needs to learn the *sit* command better."

Kat obediently fetched a swag of quarter-inch thick green rope.

"Now, you dirty mutt, *Stay.*" Shiloh turned around; Andrew's face now nearly nuzzled between her plump buttocks. Andrew sniffed excitedly. She swiveled as if a bee had stung her and whipped him swiftly. "Bad dog!"

Andrew put his head down in shame, but once again, he had not deflated—quite the opposite.

"Where are your manners?" Shiloh rebuked.

She slowly began walking toward Kat. The camera view split: one view followed Shiloh while the other fixed on Andrew. I mentally commended Kate Salters's remarkable technical work.

Andrew stayed put, following his master with his pitiful eyes. She pivoted calmly. "There's only one thing the command 'come' means, right?" Shiloh let the word "*come*" linger seductively as she spoke.

Andrew remained silent, a response I expected he had learned.

"*Come.*" Again, the word sounded as if there were multiple "M's."

On all fours (nearly fives), Andrew obeyed, panting eagerly.

"*Stay,*" she commanded when he had nearly reached her. The camera went back to a single view as the three people occupied one frame.

"Now, *sit,*" Shiloh said slowly and vehemently.

Andrew complied, then Shiloh stuck her high heel between his legs, purposely allowing her shin to graze his *third leg*, and kicked them open wide. He let out a lusty moan.

Shiloh nodded to Kat, and Kat knelt with the rope next to Andrew's bended right thigh. As if rehearsed for this precise moment, Kat began wrapping her rope around his leg, connecting the web with elaborate twists at certain junctures, then wrapping the rope in strands of two from the right thigh, around Andrew's haunches, to the left thigh, where she mimicked the weave. The practice was methodical and mesmerizing, like someone pulling taffy, and I wondered how Shiloh stayed in character, standing authoritatively uninterested in front of Andrew. Mara and I had tilted our heads to watch Kat snake the rope through one loop, around one twist, into a sequenced knot, then back to a fluid strand.

Both legs were now tangled in the rope with his thighs bound to his calves and his ankles bound to each other, but Andrew's erection stood untouched in the snarl of green rope. The effect made it seem like the only zucchini in a patch, reaching for the sun, ripe for the picking.

Tap, tap. Mara and I jumped.

"Hey," Beau stood in my office doorway.

"Hey!" I said too excitedly.

"You ladies okay?" Beau chuckled; his dimples recessed. "Whatcha watching there?"

"Oh," I quickly slept my phone. "Nothing. A video a colleague sent about a patient." He knew not to push further; HIPAA was HIPAA.

"I stopped by to see if you wanted to get a drink after work. Tiff offered to sit at the house for a bit," he said. Tiff was our college-aged neighbor who on occasion offered to watch the sleeping kids while she did her homework. "There's someone waiting out front, by the way." He motioned toward the reception area.

"Of course, excuse me," Mara exited punctually.

I let out a sigh that brought me back to my senses.

"Yes. I have one more patient. Can you wait twenty minutes? Or better yet, get a head start and find us a place at the bar. Order me a drink when I text you?" Our regular establishment was only half a block from the clinic.

"You got it," he winked.

I fluffed my shirt repeatedly, airing out perspiration from my blouse.

A strong drink was exactly what I needed.

I walked slowly to meet Beau.

A tornado of thoughts twirled inside of me, stirring everything up in its path. I had not anticipated Beau stopping by. Nor had I anticipated watching part of a session on my phone with Mara.

Perhaps most surprising of all: I had not anticipated the way my body responded to watching Shiloh and Kat (as Mistress Raven and Lady Ayano) heeling Andrew Yale like a sex-sick pup. I thought I'd be somewhat benign about it; that, if anything, it would be psychologically satisfying to my curiosity. I supposed there might even be a small tingle of arousal, like watching an inappropriate movie scene.

But there was more than that. I experienced something that I hadn't felt since I watched TV shows with fancy tables full of food. Or since being in college and watching peers ease into programs because their fathers played golf with Professor so-and-so and their mothers served on the board of some elite institution. It was a feeling like cud. I would push it down, but it would come back up for further processing.

I was jealous.

And as I paced one foot in front of the other, I swallowed the feeling back down with resentment. I was never proud to be jealous. "Jealousy is like a green parasite, Faith," my mother would say. "It will infect you slowly; as you feed it, it makes you weak." I remember looking at my belly when she would say that, picturing a green worm swimming through the slosh. I'd resolve to stop feeding it right then and there. But like a bad hangover, I'd forget about the green parasite, and the next time I saw something I wanted, I would find myself back in the cycle of jealousy and ambition. And in fairness, I reasoned, jealousy was a strong motivator for my success.

Perhaps over the past several years, I had felt it less because I was at the top of my game. I had finally accomplished everything I had set out to do. I had squashed that green bug with my ambitions to become a wife, a mother, a revered doctor, and a thriving free-clinic owner (at least to those who didn't peek at my financials).

Yet, tonight, I saw something I didn't have and I wanted. I wanted to feel as free about sex as Shiloh did. I wanted to know my sexuality in an adamant way, rather than feeling like sex was a task and that "getting in the mood" was a chore. I wanted to own my sexuality, and I wanted mine and Beau's bedroom to feel as galvanized as the dungeon.

My pace picked up as I neared the bar. I wondered if tonight we could start practicing.

CHAPTER TWENTY-FOUR

"Good morning, Irena," I greeted as I entered the clinic the next morning.

It was my day off from the practice, so I had three consults on the schedule before I had to head to the hospital for follow-ups and paperwork, then back to the clinic for our "other" appointments. Somewhere between the hospital and our next round of puppy-whipping (if that's what was on the agenda), I had to make an appearance at home for after-school cuddles and homework help.

"Good morning," Irena observed warily.

"What?" I asked expectantly.

"I don't know. *What?*" she asked, tilting her head and raising her thickly penciled brows. I noticed her hair was different. Did she put highlights in it?

"You did something to your hair," I said glibly as I checked the schedule.

"I love when you deflect, Faith," she replied. "It might be my favorite quality about you."

Dammit if Irena wasn't the only person in the world who could read my face the minute that I walked in the door.

"What could I be deflecting from? It's Thursday." I answered defensively. "Morning," I added.

The clinic was still quiet. Patients weren't scheduled for thirty minutes. Shiloh was due in soon, but Mara and Kat were on the later schedule. Tobias was, well, wherever Tobias was.

"What did you do last night?" she probed, still with a hand on her cocked hip. Her chest and forearms were tanned deeper than her normal bronzed Greek.

"Did you take up sailing or something?" I asked, avoiding eye contact.

She clicked her tongue and stared at me.

"Say what you want to say," I proffered.

"Something has happened. You have a different vibe."

I shook my head as if her assessment was ridiculous.

"Are you pregnant again?"

"God no," I answered quickly. Another baby would put me over the edge and she knew it.

"You and Beau doing okay?"

"Yes, why?" I asked defensively. Did Irena have a lens into my brain?

It was as if she could watch the reel from last night. If you asked both Beau and I separately if we had a good night, we'd likely agree: Yes. After walking home tipsy and rushing the sitter off, Beau was content. And textbook-wise, I was, too. But though the choreography of the night was on cue, there was something lodged between our movements, something that had never been there before. Something that wedged itself between us, blocking the connection that was required to reach that fiery temperature of the dungeon. That thing was Life.

Mortgages, jobs, kids, flailing businesses: the things that built resentment in a relationship. I was understanding more every day what Shiloh meant about why people come to the dungeon for services. It was easy. It was an escape. It had no strings or responsibilities of Life. I remembered a time when it seemed that way for me and Beau—when we were younger and our independent choices didn't impact the other's so greatly. I wondered if it was possible to ever get there again.

"So, you're not…like…seeing anyone else, right?" Irena asked carefully.

"No!" I replied adamantly.

"Okay, good," she put her hands up in surrender. "I had to ask, but I'm glad the answer is no."

"Beau and I are good."

"Okay," she said as she gathered paperwork.

"We are," I said more convincingly.

"*Okay*," she said adamantly.

I stared at her expecting a challenge, but she just kept on about her business. "I think he's getting impatient with me," I relented. "With my schedule."

"Uh-huh."

"What do you mean, 'Uh-huh'? You agree with him?"

"I don't agree or disagree, Faith. It makes no difference to me where you spend your time. But I'm not surprised Beau's feeling that way. I don't know how you have time to eat, let alone be a mother and wife. Do you even sleep?"

"Not since med school," I scoffed.

"He probably misses you, is all."

"Misses me?"

"Yes," she clucked. "I've seen it a million times. Children and careers take over a relationship, and it's difficult to carve out time for each other."

"Well, we went on a date last night," I said.

"That's good," she said. "Make that a habit. Sex, too. My parents drove each other nuts, but they loved each other madly. I heard my mother tell my aunt once, 'Have sex every day. And if you can't, at least kiss real hard.'"

I laughed at her heavily accented imitation, but her words put salt on a wound I knew was open. I couldn't recall the last time Beau and I "kissed real hard."

"Just make sure Beau knows he comes first," Irena concluded, as if it were the easiest thing in the world.

"He knows he comes first," I said defensively. "And Matthew and Juliet. They are the reason I am doing all of this," I waved my hand at the ceiling.

"I know," she said with a reassuring smile. "And I'm sure your family knows that, too. What you're experiencing is normal. You guys will be fine. It's just a busy time in your lives."

"How are you an expert on every damn thing, Irena?" I sighed with a smirk. She had never been married and didn't have kids, yet always knew the perfect thing to say.

"It's in my DNA to know everything," she chuckled.

"In my next life, maybe I'll be Greek," I winked.

"I think you do just fine as you are," she said as she grazed my physique with a look: *You're really going to complain about that?* I smiled at my friend, who had become the older sister I never had.

"I may not have told you as much lately, but your management of the clinic, Irena, is really admirable. We're grabbing more positive attention than I know what to do with."

She shrugged a *thank you*.

"I can't stand my partners at the practice, but at least I have you guys so it balances out," I joked.

She snorted in agreement.

"And I'm excited about some of the fundraising efforts Mara is engaged in; it will be very good for the clinic," I kept layering. Irena nodded her approval. Irena believed that Mara was working with Jed Terry to raise money at benefit dinners and social events. In fact, Mara was escorting Jed. But for the accounting books, the income Mara generated would be labeled "donations."

"Good things are happening," she nudged my shoulder with her pencil. "I mean, would you ever have imagined we'd be here?"

"No," I laughed.

"You should be proud, Faith. Look at what you've done," she boasted.

Yes, *look at what I've done.*

CHAPTER TWENTY-FIVE

"How long has she been doing this?" I asked Mara, who was standing next to me with the tip of her red-manicured finger on her chin; her long, shiny arms crossed softly.

"Two hours," she replied without turning her head.

"How long will this go on?"

She shook her head unknowingly, eyes still fixed. "Depends. She's taken up to six hours."

"You're serious?"

"Her sessions generate the highest income. There's a four-week wait list to get on her books."

"What?" I asked with a gasp.

"They take hours; one session can generate over $5,000."

"I'll be damned," I remarked.

"Many of whom are women," Mara smirked satisfactorily.

"*Women*?"

She nodded silently.

"Who would've thought," I awed.

We continued watching as Kat—Lady Ayano—bound a specimen of a man into a cross-legged position with his arms tight behind his back, yogi-like. The wheat-colored ropes looked brilliant against his richly dark, glistening skin. Beads of sweat ran down his muscled arms as they twisted behind him tightly. His sand dollar-sized nipples puckered between the gaps of the intricate web; his bulging chest chivalric. Straight down his back, a thick braid was intertwined with red rope, giving the illusion of a large vein running down his spine. Near his groin were clusters of knots; the organ between his legs exposed potently.

"It's beautiful," I relented.

"I could watch it all day," Mara agreed.

"Where did she learn it?"

"Her mother, I believe. It's called Kinbaku-bi," Mara said elegantly, and I wondered how she could make everything sound like something you wanted to eat. "It is a Japanese style of bondage."

I made a mental note to look up Kinbaku-bi on the Internet. I was anxious to learn more about what I was witnessing. Kat was purposeful in her appliqué. It reminded me of watching Beau paint. He mixed colors for so long that I would get bored and walk away, only to come back fifteen minutes later to the same hue of blue, at least to my eye. But for him, the shade of blue had to be exactly the way his mind envisioned the color of the sky, or the ribbon, or the gem. Kat was as thoughtful as she weaved her way around this statuesque body, as if she already knew the end result; she just had to figure out how to get there.

"Do they talk?" I asked.

"Almost never."

The doctor in me kicked in. "Do they hydrate? They must stay hydrated."

Mara broke stare and grinned at me. "Yes, Doctor. They hydrate. In fact, that, too, is beautiful. Lady Ayano tips back their head and streams water from above. Sometimes it drizzles out of the sides of their mouth. Sometimes she will drip it in a straight line down their chest or back. They find it incredibly erotic, as if the water is the reward. She teases them with it." Mara once again watched as Kat stood back and pondered her next tether.

"Sometimes," she continued, "she will take ice cubes and rub them soothingly in places. Other times, torturously."

"Torturously?" I asked curiously.

"Yes. She'll find a sensitive spot—between toes, belly button, or around their, uh, you know," she implied by waving her hand near her lap area. "And she'll keep the ice there until they're whining with pain."

"Ouch," I smirked.

I noticed that Mara used Kat's domme name, which I had never heard her use before. I wondered if there was a subconscious validity to Kat's position as a dominatrix; it certainly appeared she found her niche. She worked independently now, no longer needing Shiloh for every session. Although, they still teamed up for certain clients, a good thing for the clinic because it brought in double income.

"How are we doing, by the way?" I asked Mara. "Financially."

"We are doing very well," she replied confidently. "Invoices are at Net 30. We're caught up," she clarified. "We made the down payment for the imaging machine the clinic needs, and it won't be long before the savings account has ample reserve."

"Good," I said matter-of-factly, but I was more impressed than I let on. Several months ago, the clinic was scrapping to make payroll; now we were easily affording expensive equipment and socking away money for a rainy day. The apprehension of a failing clinic had faded with the help of some very unlikely patients.

"And the team? How are they doing?" I asked, knowing Mara would have a better pulse on their condition than I would.

"They're content. Quite content," she answered confidently. "The money is especially helpful to Kat."

"How so?" I asked.

"As you know, Kat doesn't have family in the area," she said. I nodded, but I didn't have that information about Kat; she respected authority too much to confide in me.

"Since her mother died?" I guessed.

"Yes. Her father died when she was a baby. Her mother raised her the best she could. Her mother's death is what led to her challenging years." Mara said "challenging years" as though they were delicate, and I surmised that she was referring to Kat's years of drug abuse. "She doesn't share a lot of details, but from what I understand, she ended up in foster care after her mother passed. There were some difficult times, but when she got pregnant with Ena, she changed her lifestyle and never looked back. It is very important to her to give her daughter a different life than she had. That's why this extra income is so valuable to her. She was able to put Ena in dance class and piano lessons. She's been able to afford a two-bedroom apartment so that Ena could have her own room. You should have seen how proud she was to surprise Ena with unicorn-themed bedding."

"I'm glad," I smiled, touched. I remembered a time my mom brought home a radio for my bedroom. I was in seventh grade, and

I cherished it as if she had brought home a chest full of diamonds; probably more. I was glad that Kat was able to offer her daughter that same kind of joy. I reflected on how interesting it was that two people—Kat and I—could come from such similar circumstances yet follow two very different paths, only to end up in the same place.

"Kat's daughter—Ena—where does she go when Kat is here?" I asked, more invested in their welfare.

"You don't know?" she looked at me, surprised.

"I don't really ask those kinds of questions," I simpered defensively. "I can barely keep details about my own life straight."

"Fair enough. Ena is usually with Tobias."

"Tobias?" I asked, shocked.

"Yes. Kat brought Ena to the clinic one night before starting a session. A friend was supposed to come by to pick her up, but she never came. Kat panicked that she would have to cancel the session, but Tobias stepped in and offered to stay with Ena. They spent three hours at the picnic table while Tobias taught her how to play chess. Now, they do homework, play chess, and have dinner while Kat manages her sessions."

"I had no idea," I said.

"I'm surprised you haven't seen them around," she said.

"I guess I haven't noticed," I said easily, but I regretted that I hadn't met Kat's daughter when she was around the clinic so often. I supposed it was practical for Tobias to keep her out of the areas I would tend to be, but I decided I'd make it a point to meet her.

"Excuse me, I must get ready," Mara interrupted my thoughts.

"That's right. You have a date tonight," I replied.

She nodded a confirmation.

"How is that going? With Jed? Is he holding up his end of the deal?" I asked, meaning: *Is he behaving*?

She nodded again, and I realized Mara would not be one to complain even if he wasn't. I would have to probe.

"Mara, you have the power here. You know that, right?"

She shifted; eyes staring at Kat.

"Mara, you say when you're done and that's it. It's done. You don't owe me anything. I need you to really hear that."

"I do. But I have a plan and I need to see it through."

"A plan?" I asked, confused.

"It's time for me to go, Dr. Wells," she said politely and walked toward the stairs.

I gazed back through the one-way window toward Kat. There was much more intention to Kat's knitted work of body art than met the eye, and I realized there was more to Mara's work as well. What was this plan?

I'd have to run some diagnostics to figure it out, and I knew just where to turn.

The thing I couldn't figure out about Jed was why he was always so goddamn happy. A lollipop was lodged in his cheek when I walked into an exam room at the practice.

"Dr. Wells," he said airily, pulling the lollipop out with a loud smack.

"Are you here for your tetanus shot, Jed?" I asked playfully.

"Maybe. Does it still go in the behind?" he grinned.

I rolled my eyes. I was not going to entertain that question.

"How have you been feeling?" I asked seriously as I strapped the blood pressure cuff around his bicep and put the ear tips of my stethoscope into my ears.

"Never been better, Doc."

The cuff released with a loud hiss. "Your blood pressure is good: 118 over 68."

He beamed, lollipop clicking against his teeth. "Did Mara tell you?" he inquired.

I shook my head as I typed notes into his chart. The charting system was much more sophisticated here at the practice than the clinic's paper charts. I was looking forward to having a similar electronic system at the clinic as our next purchase thanks to our extra "donations."

"We're going away," he said.

"Oh?" I was surprised Mara hadn't mentioned something as significant as a vacation with Jed.

"Mediterranean mostly, Spain and France. Maybe Morocco. Maybe Greece," he said with the ease of someone who can just "figure it out when he gets there." But I knew Mara did not have that kind of luxury. For one, she didn't have the paid vacation days to gallivant around the Mediterranean. Despite myself, I wondered how much money this type of "date" would cost Jed.

"Sounds nice."

"You ever been?"

I chuckled. "No. I haven't been outside of the United States, believe it or not. I've never even left the East Coast. Florida is as far as I've gotten." I winced for a moment picturing Beau begging me to take a vacation to Hawaii or France. My go-to response: "After *this*, or after *that*." I wondered when "after" would ever be.

"What a damn shame, Dr. Wells!" he chagrined. "You have to get out more. Get away from work. Anyone ever tell you that?"

No, never, I thought sarcastically. "You're probably right, Jed," I amused. "Let's talk about your blood work—"

"I know, I know," he interrupted. "My sugars are high again."

I grinned. "And your cholesterol."

"Well, it's Bourbon season," he shrugged. "And you know what goes well with Bourbon? A nice spice-rubbed steak. I can't get enough of the one down the street," he pointed east with his lollipop.

"Uh-huh. Could it also be those things?" I smiled, nodding toward his candy.

He looked at it quizzically. "Nah," he said, popping it back in his mouth. "I have a sweet tooth, what can I say? Which brings me back to Mara."

I perplexed picturing Mara as "sweet," but I was glad he brought her up again because I had been anxious to probe about their arrangement. Mara was tight-lipped, but I sensed some resolve in her that I could not pinpoint. I was hoping Jed could shed some light on it.

"It seems your time with Mara is well spent," I punned.

"The trip," he ignored my comment. "What d'ya say, Doc? Can she have the time off?"

I deflected. "I'm going to up your cholesterol medication. We'll do blood work again in three months. In the meantime, watch the sugar. And eat more vegetables."

"And Mara? The trip?"

"I'll talk to her about it," I said, putting my stuff in order to conclude our exam.

"She doesn't want to ask for that much time off. She's afraid she'll lose her job," he said.

I peeved slightly that Jed was meddling in my relationship with Mara, at the same time wondering about how much Mara confided in Jed.

"I said I'll talk to her about it, and I will," I smiled conclusively.

"Okay, then," he dazzled, popping the lollipop back in his cheek.

I waited for him to ask the question that always comes at the end of our appointments, but he just kept twirling his candy.

"Aren't you going to ask?" I finally jested.

"Ask what?"

"For Viagra," I challenged.

"Nope. Don't need it anymore," he gestured proudly.

"You don't need it physically? You are able to get a natural erection?" I asked in a professional manner. If Jed's erectile dysfunction had reversed, and it was possible for the lucky few, it was something worth noting. Then I realized there was nothing in his notes about it in the first place, so perhaps that meant I was asking out of curiosity?

"I think it's the yoga. Or the tea. I don't know, but Voilà!" He gestured his lollipop in the air like a magic wand.

"So, you've started doing yoga?" I asked. It was hard to picture Jed being serious long enough to complete a yoga session.

"Yup," he gloated. "And I meditate."

I smiled in an effort to stifle my shock. "Well, whatever it is, that's wonderful."

It dawned on me that I knew someone else who religiously practiced yoga and meditation: Mara. They obviously were spending more time together than the books showed; I wondered how much more.

"I'll see you in three months for your follow-up, then," I concluded pleasantly.

He winked.

CHAPTER TWENTY-SIX

"Will you be home for dinner tonight?" Beau asked as I gulped the last of my coffee before heading to the hospital.

"I hope to be," I answered sympathetically. It was always my intention to get home for dinner, but I couldn't control who might code or need an extra consult. Medicine was unpredictable, and though doctors fully appreciated that facet, doctor's families had a hard time understanding it. They wanted Mommy home for dinner. But in my case, Mommy needed to work so that there was dinner to have.

"Okay then," Beau said. He grabbed the paper and folded it to the sports section. His muscular forearms peeked out of his light blue linen shirt, and his tousled just-woke-up hair looked like he purposely styled it. He could still tug at my heartstrings by doing nothing at all.

"I'll do my best. I promise," I offered.

"Mmm-hmm," he hummed through a swig of coffee.

"I *will*."

"Yup," he placated.

I hated his disappointed face, but I couldn't help that it also stoked resentment in me. Did he think it was easy for me to manage so much to provide this life for us? I wished I could take the kids to art classes and playdates instead of tending to dying patients and a straggling clinic. (Admittedly, that wasn't entirely true, but he didn't need to know that. Ever.)

"What do you want me to do, Beau?"

"Nothing, Faith. It's okay. Just go to work," he said with a semblance of defensiveness.

"I hate when you do that."

"Do *what*?"

"Hold my job against me."

"I'm not doing that, Faith," he sipped calmly. Dammit, I hated how he could stay so calm and polite.

"It feels like you are."

"How?" he scoffed.

"Because you set me up for failure."

"Not today, Faith," he exasperated as he grabbed his coffee and walked to the sink to rinse it out. Clearly, he was not in the mood to entertain this conversation, which seemed to creep up at least once a month. But I was.

"You do, Beau. You do it with questions like, 'Are you going to be home for dinner?' and 'Are you going to make it to Juliet's library day?' You know I'd love to do those things, but I have too much going on!"

"To no one's fault but your own," he said under his breath while loading breakfast dishes into the dishwasher.

"What was that?" I sneered.

"Nothing, Faith. Please, I don't want to fight," he said tiredly.

I didn't want to fight either. I wanted to be the wife who could make him happy—make it home for dinner and tug that Brad Pitt hair up to the bedroom for a steamy shower together. But I didn't know how to find the energy, much less the time. I knew I had to figure out how to, though. Whenever we did eventually have a date night or bedroom time, we had a glorious week of getting along and being on the same page. But the connection wanes, and we are left with the sediment of resentment at the bottom of the glass, waiting for the glass to fill again with sweet wine. We both wait for the other to fill the glass, gingerly stepping around and over it, until either it breaks, or we get lucky and one of us fills it.

Today I couldn't fill it.

"I'm sorry I'm not the wife you dreamed of, Beau. I'm sorry that I have to work so that we can enjoy this beautiful home in this expensive town."

"No, don't do that," he said.

"Do *what*?" I mimicked his earlier reply.

"Don't act like you do it all so that we can have a big house and nice cars," he said.

"Well, I do," I argued. "If I didn't work, we might still be living in that two-bedroom apartment, and the kids wouldn't be going to a preschool that costs more than most of my semesters in med school."

"Even if that were true—and it's not, because I am perfectly capable of providing for this family, too, in case you forgot—we'd be perfectly fine," he said passionately.

"No, we'd be broke, Beau!" I shouted.

"I'd rather be broke and together than rich and only see my wife fifteen minutes a day!" he shouted back.

"You've never been poor, Beau! You have no idea what you are talking about!" I said from a place that stung.

He sighed. He knew he hit a chord. "Faith, let's not get off track here."

"Look, I'm sorry that I chose a demanding career and my schedule changes by the minute, but you knew that when you married me. So, I don't get why you act surprised about the fact that I might not make it home for dinner."

"I didn't act surprised. I may have acted disappointed is all, and I'm sorry for that. In fact, I'm sorry for a lot of things, too," he said, revving up. It was obvious Beau wasn't ready to concede.

I braced myself; I knew what was coming.

"I'm sorry, Faith, that I'd love to see my beautiful wife more often. I'd like to have a glass of wine on the porch with you and talk about our day like we used to. I'm sorry that the kids don't even bother asking where you are because they know the answer: Work. But most of all, I'm sorry that I agreed to open that goddamned clinic. Because I can handle the practice and the hospital shifts. But then, you added in a third job that was supposed to be "once in a while," and instead it has become nearly every day!"

I opened my mouth in protest, but I had nothing.

"You said from the beginning," he continued, knowing he had the upper hand, "that Irena would run the clinic. That you'd only be there once, maybe twice a week. Of course, I knew it would require more time in the beginning, but it has been almost a year now, Faith. A year of you creeping into bed late or coming home too exhausted to even talk."

"Not every night, Beau! I was home last Friday by five o'clock!"

"Last Friday? Do you even hear yourself? Your retort is that you made it home *once* in the past two weeks for dinner?" He threw the dish towel on the counter. "Well, thank you for gracing us with that night, Faith. Really, you shouldn't have."

"What you're doing is not fair, Beau. It's not my fault that I have to work!"

"Do you, though?!" he yelled. "Do you really need to work *so* much? Or do you choose to? You don't have to take the extra shifts when your partners go away, or work every day off at the clinic, but you do because you always have to be the hardest worker. You always have to be the best. You have to prove that you can do it all. So, you take that extra on-call shift, and you allow your partners to go golfing and boating with their families while your family pines for your attention!"

"Who's pining, Beau?!" I squealed. "The kids never say anything! You're the only one who complains."

"The kids don't say anything? Are you fucking kidding me? They're four years old!"

"You know how hard it was for me to get where I am, Beau," I tried to calm the tone. "And I'm sorry I can't do it all, but I am trying. I can't make everyone happy."

"No, just the people at work," he said icily.

I exhaled sharply. I saw the conclusion to this conversation: I was failing as a wife and mother.

We stood staring at each other, a torrent of frustrated emotions twirling between us. For a quick moment I wondered what I would have wanted Beau to say. Did I want him to say, "We understand that you have to work every day and night. We are fine. We don't need that much of you." Of course, I didn't. I knew I worked too much. I knew that the kids were at ages where it mattered for mommy to be around. I knew that Beau was trying harder than I was—showing up at the clinic for date nights and trying to stay up late to wait for me.

I knew that he was more patient than most husbands would be. And I knew I was walking a tightrope whose threads were breaking one by one. I knew it.

But…I had to work. "I have to go," I said resignedly.

We didn't move. I could almost hear his thoughts: *Of course you do.*

I picked up my purse and walked toward the door, leaving the only man I've ever loved or trusted disappointed. Again.

As I droned through the day, I sulked about my conversation with Beau.

I had the pressures of an already overly demanding job, plus the clinic, plus I was supposed to be Supermom and wife. It felt like an impossible list of things to be consistently great at being. And while I couldn't discount the fact that Beau put his career on hold so that mine could thrive, it felt unfair that he could develop such strong feelings about how much more *I* needed to do. I was giving all I had, for God's sake.

But grinding inside was the guilt that Beau was right. I knew that I could manage being around more if it wasn't for the clinic. And I knew that I was at the clinic more often than I needed to be because of what was happening in the dungeon. The truth was, I could easily schedule my clinic appointments and consults for one day a week, but I allowed for them to be spread out so that I could keep an eye on the happenings downstairs. I got in the habit of dropping by the clinic any time I didn't have appointments elsewhere—during lunch, before work, after work, days off.

Even Irena noticed, asking why I was spending so much time at the clinic. "I've got this, Faith. Go home. Be with your family. You don't always have to come check in on things," she said to me regularly.

"I know. I was just stopping by on my way home," I'd tell her. Which wasn't true. Irena would leave and I would linger to watch what was taking place in Raven's talons or Ayano's bondages. But even that was unnecessary. Mara was fully in control of the downstairs operation. She took great care in understanding each day's patrons, anticipating their needs, and conferring with me about possible risks. Andrew Yale, for example, was whining more and more for Shiloh to tighten his collar. And there were times I wondered if Shiloh contemplated granting his wish. (It seemed the relationship did go both ways.) I had warned Mara to keep an eye on Andrew and Shiloh; they were getting too comfortable.

And maybe that's why I felt the need to be around more often. Though things seemed to be running smoothly, I had a hovering feeling of unrest. What might go wrong? Who might need me? What more can I do? I felt like if I wasn't everywhere, at all times, things might go sideways.

Meanwhile, I grudgingly acknowledged that if I put as much priority into making sure things ran as smoothly at home, or at least in my marriage, I might not have a routine blow up with Beau that left me feeling like I had accomplished the one thing I tried to avoid at all costs: Failure. And as much as I tried to rationalize my actions, I knew my prioritization gauge was tilted. I took for granted that Beau would forgive my shortcomings, so I consistently let him down to be reliable for my colleagues.

The result was that my family was getting used to operating without me, and if I didn't find a way to make myself more present, I was afraid Beau would not need me to operate at all.

CHAPTER TWENTY-SEVEN

It was hard to believe that someone would want this for any reason other than to perhaps lose weight, but as I peered through the one-way glass into the dungeon, I couldn't peel my eyes off Kerry being wrapped from head to toe in plastic wrap.

"Do you like Christmas?" Shiloh asked blankly as she tugged the Costco-sized plastic wrap taut around his thick torso, then passed it to Kat, who mimicked the other side. Their method was slow and careful, layering evenly and thoughtfully with a plan.

"Yeth ma'am," Kerry replied in a lispy little-boy voice.

Shiloh didn't react. She continued to bind Kerry's plumpness to a pole as though securing casing around a sausage.

"Tell me your favorite thing about Christmas," Shiloh commanded gently.

"I like the tree," he giggled.

I winced reflexively. There was something unsettling about his voice. And his giggle. I was sure there was some psychological reason for his child voice that Shiloh found intriguing, but I found it off-putting. This was not a session I cared to watch, except that the plastic wrap was interesting, and it kept my begrudging interest.

Also, Mara was coming down, and I needed to talk to her. Oddly enough, the two of us standing at this window had become somewhat of a regular meeting spot, and even more odd was the surprising amount of business we discussed here.

"Mummification," Mara said as she took her place beside me. We stared through the window in tandem, like two CIA agents sitting on a bench to share secrets.

"That's what this is called?" I asked.

She nodded.

"I guess it makes sense. They're wrapping him like a mummy," I observed.

"It's more common than one would think. I've been told," Mara said with a dignified snicker. "This man has been here four times. By the second session, he started speaking like a child and demonstrating a fascination with Christmas."

"Christmas, really? Any idea why?"

"You know Shiloh—she's been trying to figure it out. She thinks he was traumatized at some point in his childhood, but not after he experienced some great moments, most likely having to do with Christmas."

I blinked fast as memories of my mother sitting in the pew at Christmas Mass fluttered behind my eyes, and I was stupefied to have a parallel sentiment as a man being wrapped in plastic wrap. "Well, to each his own, I guess," I said as more of a question.

Mara snorted softly. "As Irena would say."

"I saw Jed the other day," I changed the subject casually.

"Mmm-hmm?" she replied.

"He says you want to go away with him?"

She inhaled heavily. "He wants me to go away with him, but I told him I have a lot to do here. Four weeks to be away is too much."

"Four weeks? I've never taken four weeks off from anything," I laughed.

"You should, Doctor," she reprimanded.

"Why does it feel like everyone is telling me to take a vacation?" I joked defensively. "Anyway, I would agree that four weeks away is a long time. We can make it work if we have to, but to be fair to the staff, it would not be paid time off. Although, I assume Jed would be paying for this trip? And I don't mean travel expenses, obviously."

She cleared her throat as if she had something to tell me, but didn't want to. "I think he was hoping I would go willingly. Not as business."

"What?" I gasped and turned to look at her for the first time. Was Mara getting emotionally attached to Jed? Was a non-business relationship forming? I couldn't believe it, given what I knew about both of their non-committal wishes.

"There's no need to worry. I have everything under control," she said confidently.

"You've said that a couple times now, Mara," I glared. "I have a feeling there's something you're not telling me." She stayed silent. If there was anything Mara was not, it was a liar. She also was not generously forthcoming, but if I asked her a direct question, she would give me a direct answer.

"What exactly is your agenda with Jed?"

She hesitated, "We have someone in common."

"In common?" I asked suspiciously. "*Who*?"

"Someone I used to know."

"So you and Jed have a friend in common?"

"Not a friend," she interrupted briskly.

"Okay, an acquaintance in common," I corrected cautiously. "So what? Why the need to 'have everything under control' or 'have a plan' for a shared acquaintance?"

"Because I'm hoping to run into him again," she answered soberly.

"Wait, you haven't seen this person yet? Does Jed know you have this acquaintance in common?"

"No."

"Why haven't you told him?"

"Because I don't want him to know."

"Mara, you have to give me more to work with," I exasperated. "You and Jed have an acquaintance in common, which is imploring you to spend more time with him because you're hoping to run into this person?" I laid out carefully. "But you don't want Jed to know that you know this man?"

She didn't reply.

I continued with my examination. "Why do you need Jed? Why don't you just reach out to your old 'acquaintance?'" I was careful not to call him a friend.

"Because I can't reach out to him," she said nervously.

"And why can't you?" I asked slowly, sensing that I was close to drawing out the truth.

She closed her eyes and took a shallow breath, then turned to look me in the eyes. "Because he has a restraining order on me."

I numbed, my mouth gaping. "Your ex," I concluded.

She looked back through the window; her breathing had accelerated slightly.

"Jed knows your ex, and you're hoping you'll run into him while being with Jed because you can't purposefully run into him on your own," I determined.

"You are good at diagnostics, Doctor," she anxiously smiled.

I stared back through the window, running the equation through my mind. The pieces of information tumbled like a sticky ball through a cotton field, gathering questions as it rolled. Had Mara had this plan all along? Did she recognize Jed as her ex's acquaintance from the beginning? Was that her motivation to accept Jed's offer to be his, well, escort, if we could be honest about it? How long had Mara been waiting for this chance to confront her ex? And the most important question of all: What did she plan to do when she did run into him?

"Mara," I said with a slight panic. "What do you plan to do when you run into your ex?"

She didn't move.

"Mara," I nudged.

"I don't know yet," she relented. "I just want him to see my face. To remember the face of the woman he beat, he hurt, he humiliated. He might have broken my hip and my femur, but he didn't break me." Her voice was like iron as it caught, but I knew she wouldn't get emotional. Not in front of me at least; I was not the type of person to hug someone if she cried, and she knew that because she was the same way.

"Mara," I said firmly. "You can't do anything dangerous."

She stared ahead.

"Mara, listen to me," I took hold of her shoulder and turned her to look at me. "It's not worth it. He's not worth it. Look how tall you're standing now."

"I know," Mara sighed dejectedly. "But I just want him to see my face. I want him to see how happy I am now. I want him to know he didn't win."

I could relate. I could also sense that this conversation had hit its max.

We both turned back to the window.

"How long will he stay like that?" I lightened the mood as we watched Shiloh and Kat string Christmas lights around a now fully mummified Kerry.

"Until they're done with him," she bantered.

"What are they doing to him now?"

"Looks like they're putting decorations on him."

Kerry flinched, and Shiloh reprimanded him by poking the ornament harder into his skin. Kerry stopped complaining, but his arousal to the pain poked out of a special hole from the plastic wrap; Shiloh carefully hung a star from it.

"This is humiliating," I observed.

"That's the idea," Mara concurred.

"I guess I'm just too cheap to understand the idea of paying for someone to humiliate me," I said. "Not that I'm judging; I just don't get it is all."

"I suppose it's not that different than people paying for a psychiatrist. Everyone has issues they have to deal with in one way or the other. This is his therapy; he feels better when he leaves than he did when he got here."

"True," I had to agree. "But nobody's wrapping me in plastic wrap, no matter how bad I need therapy," I laughed.

"Maybe not plastic wrap," she insinuated.

"Not a leash either."

"Mmm, no?"

"You think I'd enjoy being walked on a leash and barking like a dog?" I exasperated.

"No, Doctor," she humored with an elegant laugh. "I don't see you barking like a dog. But I do wonder how you unwind. Do you have an outlet? Do you ever just, I don't know, give in? Let someone else take control?"

"Of course I do. Beau is in charge of everything in the house. I'm basically a visitor," I chortled.

"By choice," she amused. "I have a feeling that's a job you wouldn't want control of."

I frowned.

"I hope that doesn't offend you," she clarified. "You're a wonderful mother. Domesticity isn't for everyone, and that's okay."

"Well, I'm still not getting on a leash," I joked to end the conversation. "Let's get back to work."

"Of course," Mara obeyed as she followed me back upstairs to the clinic.

Mara was right about one thing: I did feel the need to control my surroundings. I always had, I realized, as I recalled my checklists and calendars in preparation for second grade. Perhaps, I acknowledged, that as a child if I didn't do it, who would? I was never good at letting other people control my destiny and a sinking sensation thrummed in my chest: Was I losing control of Mara?

I didn't know. But I did know something felt abnormal, like seeing a spike on an EKG. Was it the sign of a heart attack or something benign?

I would have to wait for more symptoms to manifest.

"I must say, Dr. Wells, I'm impressed with what you've done with the clinic in such a short time," Lisa Dolin commented; her impressive (but not obnoxious) diamonds dripping from her ears.

I tipped my head. "It's all in a day's work, right?"

"No, Faith, it's not in a day's work," she chided smartly. "A day's work is what shows in your personal taxes. The Angel Clinic's taxes are reflective of a different kind of work, a work of passion. Trust me, I've done taxes for twenty-five years for some of the richest people in Philadelphia. I know the difference."

I smiled, but I wished I could accept the compliment wholly. Lisa, who was one of the most brilliant tax minds of Philadelphia, and who had only taken me on as a client through the recommendation of Jed Terry, also had become a close personal acquaintance, one I admired greatly. For Lisa to believe that the clinic's success was entirely due to passionate fundraising and clean income made me pulse a little. But then again, *who was to say the "fundraising" we were doing at the clinic wasn't passionate*? I weighed in my mind. I'd take that compliment, after all.

"So, the books look good?" I asked.

"They're impeccable. Your office manager is thorough."

"I lucked out with Mara. She's as sharp as they come," I said. I didn't add that she was a former tax attorney; her story wasn't mine to tell.

"And beautiful. God, the way she speaks is mesmerizing."

"I know," I laughed. "I just want to hear her swear once. Just once."

"Yeah, but it would sound unnatural," Lisa laughed as she gathered signed papers into a folder. "I went to catholic school, I might have mentioned, and I remember one time I heard a nun say 'dammit.' It scared the shit out of me. Some people shouldn't swear."

"I guess you're right," I agreed.

"You're doing good work here, Faith," she said, her bleach-blonde hair resting on her shoulders.

"Yeah, well," I deflected.

"What do you mean, 'Yeah, well?'" she flouted. "The Angel Clinic's first year of taxes, albeit there were only three months of revenue, were not promising. I was worried. The grant was blown and you were overextended in helping patients who couldn't afford to pay. Then you talked about the equipment you were going to purchase and the procedures you were hoping to offer. I thought: *No way.*"

"I always knew you believed in me," I joked.

She snorted an apology. "Rooting for you and believing in you are two different things. I always let the numbers tell the story, and let's be honest—your numbers sucked."

I shrugged while sipping an iced tea.

"But a year later, your clinic is thriving," she amended. "It's unbelievable. And you've become a full-scale cardiac care facility. It's really pissing off some of the practices," she laughed. "Do your colleagues complain about the revenue you're taking from the practice?"

Lisa was probably one of the few who understood that hospitals and practices were businesses first, health facilities second, no matter what they claimed. Doctors prioritize their patients' health, of course. But doctor's wishes and opinions get tangled in a messy network of administrators, run by boards, run by the shackles of federal and state funding, and insurance and pharma conglomerates. Doctors were encouraged continuously (to the point of harassment) to bring in income. So they did. Because if they didn't, they didn't get paid. It was exhausting and unromantic. At least, at the clinic, the private funding allowed me to disregard all the bullshit and be the kind of doctor I dreamed of being when I entered med school.

I brought myself back to Lisa's question: "The partners at my practice complain about everything. You know that Lisa. At first, it was, *Is the clinic going to take too much of my time?* and I proved it wouldn't. Then it was, *Would I call in pro-bono favors from them all the time?* and I didn't. Now it's, *Why are patients going there instead of here?*"

"I'll bet," she smiled proudly. "Like I said, you've created a solid reputation, Faith. People trust you. Women trust you."

I blushed a smile.

"And your numbers are proving that you are as good at business as you are at medicine. Which is rare, you must surely know. Do you know how many truly independent practices or clinics exist anymore? Almost none. They're all part of a network and for good reason. It's too expensive to do alone. But you've done it. I don't know how. But damn, girl! Cheers to you."

I lifted my glass, clinked hers gently, and sipped the sweet taste of "making it happen," as my mother would say.

"The question now," Lisa said as she set her glass back down, "is where do you see yourself a year from now?"

I looked at her quizzically. I hadn't thought much about it, though I knew I had been putting off addressing the inevitable question: Was our current "donation" income sustainable?

"I suspect some of our donations will ebb," I answered. "We'll have to find new donors to contribute to the clinic. But the ladies have a good handle on it. I'm sure they'll figure out a new angle."

"That will be tricky," she conceded. "If JT Enterprises stops their hefty donations, that would be a substantial blow to your revenue."

I grimaced. I didn't want to be dependent on Jed Terry's "donations." Or Andrew Yale's. Or any of the now-regular donors.

"Well, for now, I can count on those donations."

"For now," she agreed. "But I'd start thinking of ways to diversify."

If only Lisa knew to which degree I had diversified, I mused. But I knew what she meant, and it didn't involve dungeons. I did need to talk to Mara about an eventual exit strategy, as well as how to sustain the clinic after that much-needed income waned.

"That will be my top priority this year," I said.

"Good," she grinned. "I believe you."

At least I had finally earned Lisa's faith, which was reassuring. Because it seemed that everyone else needed more Faith than I could offer.

CHAPTER TWENTY-EIGHT

When I was ten, my mother took me to a festival in Fairmount Park. I remember this day clearly because it was the first time I had cotton candy. I also remember how beautiful my mother looked on that day. Her jet-black hair was shiny in the sun and she wore a striped romper that matched the awnings of the booths.

As we shared the cotton candy, we stopped to watch a man on a unicycle juggling bowling pins. First, he tossed two pins, teetering on the unicycle. Then a helper tossed another pin into the mix. He handled it easily. Then another pin, and another, until six or so pins were tumbling between his two hands.

"How does he do that?" I marveled.

"Practice, I guess," my mother replied.

"Yeah, but how does he always catch them?" I couldn't comprehend.

She shrugged while taking an airy bite of the cotton candy.

"What happens if he drops one?" I suddenly feared.

"Then he drops one," she answered.

"But then does he lose?"

"Lose what?" she asked.

"I don't know. Lose his job?"

She laughed at me, and I smiled reflexively, though I was serious with my question.

"Oh Faith, my overachiever," she squeezed my shoulder with one arm. "If he drops a pin, then he just picks it up and starts again."

"Oh, right," I grinned. But the concept was disconcerting. He had practiced and worked for who-knew-how-long to demonstrate his adeptness in keeping those pins in the air. The thought of him dropping one in front of a crowd ignited anxiety in my chest. How could one feel so at ease, I wondered of my mother, about him just dropping one and starting over? Didn't she know how humiliating it would be for him to fail in front of all these people? All these people who relied on him to keep those pins in the air?

I worried about this until only the sticky, stained paper cone of the cotton candy remained.

I woke up to the hair-raising screech of the alarm clock.

"Why haven't we invested in one of those alarms that play music or nature sounds?" I groaned and rolled over to find an empty space in the bed beside me. *Where was Beau*?

I lazed into the bathroom, brushed my teeth, and grabbed a robe. It was my day off. An actual day off. I could have filled it easily, but I thought I'd surprise Beau with a peace offering of spending the day with him, wherever he was.

"Hey," I said sweetly when I found him in his studio, painting.

He looked behind him, paintbrush in hand, and grinned a quick nod. "Morning."

"What's this piece called?" I asked, sauntering over to his canvas.

"I don't have a name for it yet."

"I like the colors. That's a very deep purple," I commented, then quickly realized it was a similar midnight purple as the dungeon's walls. My stomach roiled a little; I tried not to let my mind mix thoughts of the dungeon when outside of the dungeon.

"Aren't you going to be late for work?" he asked, glancing at his watch.

"Actually," I said charmingly, "I'm not going to work today."

He lifted his eyebrows. "Really? Why not?"

"Because it's my day off," I said.

"I know, but you usually go to the clinic on your days off."

"Well, not today," I smiled. "I thought maybe we could go to lunch or, I don't know, pick out tile for the sunroom."

He grinned nervously. "I wish you would've told me sooner that you had the day off."

"You sound disappointed," I pouted.

"No, well…Yes, I am. But not because you took the day off, but because I don't have the day off. I scheduled something at the Princeton gallery."

"Oh," I answered, surprised. Beau hadn't worked with the gallery in Princeton since I was pregnant with the twins. In fact, he hadn't worked with any galleries. He had worked on a few commission pieces, but not entire works. "So, you're submitting new pieces?"

"I submitted a portfolio to Jean last month. He's interested. I'm going up to have coffee with him today."

He submitted a portfolio? Where did this portfolio come from? How had I not noticed that he had a whole new collection of paintings? Even more disturbing: Why hadn't he shared them with me? A pang in my heart jabbed as I remembered an easier time of sitting on the couch with a glass of wine while he presented his pieces to me. I'd joke about the person's facial expression, and he would patiently teach me how to read art, though we'd agree it would never live inside me like it did him. Art touched his heart, but it didn't go much past my brain. Though who's to say which organ is more vital?

"Well, that's great," I encouraged with as much pep as I could muster. I was deflated, but I knew I couldn't ask him to cancel his plans for me. "How about I take the kids to school so you can get a head start then?" I offered.

"You're gonna take the kids to school?" he snorted quizzically.

"Yes," I answered sharply. "Jesus, I'm capable of taking the kids to school, Beau."

"I know you're capable, but—" he hesitated.

"*But...?*" I gestured.

He sighed. "Nothing. Okay, great. They just got switched to Miss Dill's classroom because Mrs. Newton's on maternity."

"Yeah, I know," I said. (I didn't know.)

"Their lunches are—," he said.

"I can take care of it," I said.

"Right, I know," he grunted. "But I already did it. They're in the fridge."

"Oh, okay."

"I guess I'll go shower then," he said warily.

"Great, I've got this," I smiled.

How hard could it be?

Hard. Fucking hard, is how I would define taking the kids to school.

It wasn't the part where Juliet's brush got stuck in her hair and I had to cut a wad of locks out to release it.

It wasn't the part where Matthew slammed his finger in the pantry door while grabbing a granola bar for breakfast while I tended to Juliet's hair.

It wasn't the part where I forgot their lunches and had to turn back around to get them (while telling the kids that Mommy forgot her wallet so they wouldn't tell Beau I forgot the damn lunches).

It wasn't the part where I had to ask someone how to get to Miss Dill's classroom, or the part where I couldn't have chosen Miss Dill out of a lineup of ten teachers.

It wasn't the part where the other moms awed, "Faith! Wow, it's great to see you! I'm so used to seeing Beau, I had to do a double take!" ("*Keep your eyes off my dimples*" is what I wanted to say back to those condescending cookie-bakers as I smiled politely.)

Those parts I could shimmy off.

Hard was the part where I stopped in the hallway to look at the classroom pictures of "Weekend Fun." I searched for the twin's drawings—past the photos of stick figures of families fishing and making sandcastles—until I found Juliet's drawing. It was a chicken scratch image of a girl, a swing, and a larger figure. The caption read: *Daddy pushing me on a swing* (in her teacher's handwriting). *Okay,* I thought. Then, Matthew's photo—much more articulate than Juliet's, he clearly took after Beau with art—had an image of two people playing what looked like Jenga. The caption read: *I love when Daddy plays games with me!*

I scanned the other photos. Moms, moms, moms.

I walked to my car with slackened shoulders and the desire to trip a mom carrying a tray of cupcakes. I got into the car and stared blindly out the window.

Where have I been? I choked down the heaviness.

Then: *Where was I going?*

My car drove itself to Philadelphia.

It wanted to drive to the clinic to keep a pulse on the happenings and touch base with Irena. It wanted to spend extra time at the practice catching up on paperwork. But it drove itself straight down Route 611 toward the turnpike, and when it reached the option of going east or west to Philly, it had gone too far to turn back.

I ignored phone calls coming in from the hospital, from patients, from unknown numbers. I ignored the persistence of being constantly available and relented to the power of just not giving a shit. I knew it wouldn't last, but I'd enjoy it while it did.

By the time I reached West Crystal Street, my coffee was gone, my mind was empty, and for once, I didn't have a plan. I slowed in front of my mother's apartment building. I wondered when it became my mother's apartment and no longer mine. Someone had painted the red bricks a strange shade of cream, making it look like a giant chunk of cheese, I grimaced. I thought about going in. I thought about the smell of the hallways; metallic, stale, and airless. I pictured the wooden railing that led to her apartment whose top had been held so many times that the stain had worn off. I remembered the last time I was in the apartment sifting through old photos and high-stepping over garbage. And then I remembered Bobby Clay. I took a deep breath.

I almost couldn't picture his face anymore—a blur of boring features surrounded by clean-cut brown hair and an expensive suit. But my blood could still burn thinking about the way he strung my mother like a marionette doll, then cut the strings so easily when she stopped dancing. And those syrupy eyes—the eyes that ogled at me when I was young, the eyes my mother kept away from me, and the eyes that dug into me the day I saw him at my mother's apartment. I despised those eyes and sitting outside of my mother's apartment made me remember how much I despised him.

Some feelings you can't shake no matter how much time has passed; repulsion was one of them. Though I didn't know much about Bobby Clay beyond my antipathy for him, he ruined my mother's life. And by ruining hers, he also ruined mine. My mother wasn't a lot of things, but she was at least mine until he showed up. She didn't bake cookies and she drank too much, but she was all I had. And he took her. He took her with his money, with his promises, and then he took her with drugs.

I let out an angry sigh as I stared at the front door of the apartment building, a double door whose hinges were always squeaky. Mike, a maintenance man, used to come around from time to time and spray the hinges with WD-40, and I loved how easily the doors moved after that. I looked over at the two locust trees flanking the sides of the building. I used to sit in the locust tree closest to the other apartment building and read my books and watch as people walked in and out of the building. Sometimes, I would fantasize that the man with the hat was my father or that the heavy-set woman carrying a canvas tote was my aunt. I would never know, since my mother wouldn't talk of such things, and I learned to stop asking. Over the years though, bits and pieces had sputtered out by accident. My mother was from "everywhere" around Philadelphia, she would say, and her mother had passed away when she was a teenager. Around the time that she lost her mother, she must have met my father, who I believed was not from the area because she said that "he always hated this town" and had "gone back to where he belonged." As far as I knew, I had no aunts or uncles and therefore, no cousins.

It dawned on me that my mother was as lonely as I was. Perhaps that's what led her to the drinking. Or, perhaps that was already programmed in her genes. I could relate to wanting an escape from reality because that's what I found in books and school. The difference was that my mother's escape kept her trapped, and my escape set me free.

A familiar ache took hold as the presence of a mother I longed to understand felt close enough to touch. I wanted her to be so many things she was not. I wanted her to stay home more, cook a meal with me, go to Mass every Sunday, not just on Christmas. But she wasn't built that way. *Why couldn't I understand that?*

I took a deep breath as a realization crept into me like a fumy gas, slowly taking over: Maybe understanding my mother wasn't the right thing to seek. Maybe acceptance would do. My mother's foundation was made of sand, and when you mixed alcohol with sand, it turned into mud. My mother was an alcoholic. And a drug addict. And a lot of things that my childhood anecdotes were incapable of understanding. But my adult-self could have compassion for how hard it must have been for her. I didn't know what haunted my mother and I wished I had more answers than questions, but I knew that she loved me. She loved me the best that she could.

Tears threatened and I angrily panted them away.

I pictured my mother's beautiful face, the glowing smile that Beau painted onto canvas and that now collected dust in a box somewhere in the attic. Maybe it was time to pull out that portrait and change the narrative of my mother so that I could tell my kids of a woman who was hard-working and laughed like a wind chime. One who hid a piece of my favorite pie at work until her shift was over to bring it home to me. One who told me good grades were important and shrieked with joy when I got into college, even though she dropped out of high school. One who took me to Christmas Mass and smiled through the halo of candles as we held hands listening to the choir. One who was my everything, even when we had nearly nothing.

A car honked behind me, and I jumped, my reflections drying up to throw my hands in the air. *What*? The driver pointed to the handicap sign, where I had been idling. I stuck my hand out of the car window to wave an apology and drove off.

As my car pivoted back into the moving lane, I decided that it was time to change my narrative as a mother, too. Beau's words, *"I'd rather be poor and together..."* rang in my ears. I remembered telling Matthew and Juliet, as I held their just born bodies to my chest, that I would give them *everything*. I was determined to give them a fancy table full of food, a prominent name, inheritances, and connections— all the things I didn't have growing up. But if I boiled it down, it wasn't any of those things that I needed as a child. It was only one thing: It was my mom.

I was going to bake some cookies when I got home.

CHAPTER TWENTY-NINE

I didn't make cookies.

Instead, I tended to my ignored phone calls on my way home, which led me back to the hospital for an emergency consult. But still, I had it in my mind that I would be home to make cookies before the kids came home from school.

So, I was surprised to find Beau on the back patio having coffee with one of the twin's friend's mothers (I assumed). An attractive one. Cookies and fruit were laid out for the kids, who were busy on the play set.

"Oh, hi Honey!" Beau got up to greet me with a kiss on the cheek, as I gazed upon the duo with a cautious smile.

"I didn't expect anyone to be home," I said politely. "Hi, I'm Faith," I offered to Beau's guest, who wore an intentional ponytail; one that was not just thrown in a holder, but one that required manipulation to make bumpless sides and a perfect swoop.

"The kids had a half day," Beau said obliviously, but his guest was quick to reciprocate my greeting. Too quick, I felt.

"I'm Carly. Beau has told me so much about you, Faith! I'm glad to finally meet you!" She got up to stand beside me, like an ally.

"Has he? Good things, I hope."

"Of course, good things. Only good things!" she replied enthusiastically. "Your kids are so cute. And polite. Oh my God, when Matthew says, 'Yes, Ma'am,' I just melt."

I smiled a *thank you*, but I wasn't biting Carly's reel of instant friendship. Beau sat back down with a cookie in hand. I couldn't tell if I was glad or annoyed that Beau seemed uninterested in our interaction.

"Sorry, Carly, but remind me, is your daughter in the twins' class? I'm surprised we haven't met before," I added so that she knew I paid attention to the mothers at the school.

"We just moved here last month," she said.

"Oh? From where?"

"Not far. Jersey. Haddonfield," she smiled. Her teeth were perfect.

"Mommy!" Matthew ran over to give me a big hug. Juliet, our social butterfly, was still occupied on the playset with Carly's daughter.

"Hi Matthew!" I hugged him vigorously. "How was your day?"

"Good!" he said out of breath from playing. "Daddy, can I have another cookie please?" he directed to Beau.

Beau lifted the plate for Matthew to grab another cookie. He held the platter to me. "Here, babe, you should try one. Carly made them. They're delicious."

I smiled, hoping that it looked genuine enough to hide my begrudging feelings that *Carly* made cookies today. *I* was supposed to make cookies today. I suddenly felt self-conscious about the frozen cookie dough I bought and placed in the freezer before coming outside. Carly's cookies were probably made from scratch.

"Oh, I had a big lunch," I declined nicely. "They look delicious though. I'll have one later."

"They're from a box mix," Carly said quietly, leaning into me as if we were sharing a secret. "They're not that great," she conceded. I suddenly felt a little better about Carly. And my frozen cookie dough.

I laughed politely. "I'm sure they're wonderful."

"Beau said you're a doctor?" Carly asked.

"Yes."

"That's so admirable," she sighed. "I wish I had something as great to say about what I do."

"Do you work outside of the home, Carly?"

"Yes and no. I sell jewelry," she said as if it were not worth mentioning.

"That's nice. What kind of jewelry?" I asked. I was beginning to feel the tides of inadequacy shifting.

"Not the kind you'd wear," she laughed. Then, as though she was afraid she might have offended me, "Not that you wouldn't look great in it! Just—it's kinda cheap jewelry. You probably like the real stuff."

"I like anything that sparkles," I said affably. Carly wasn't so bad after all. But I still didn't like that Beau was chomping on his third cookie.

The kids swept toward us. "Mommy! I'm hungry!" Carly's daughter whined.

"We're going home right now, sweetheart," Carly said.

"I'm sure we have something inside," I offered, hoping desperately that she would decline.

"Thank you," she said. "But we really have to go anyway."

Phew.

"Thanks for the cookies, Carly," Beau said as he held the squealing twins over each shoulder.

"Of course," she swatted her hand. "Thanks for letting Riley play. This is her first playdate in Doylestown. I really appreciate it."

I saw Carly and her daughter out, then went inside. The twins had gone somewhere in the house to play, and Beau was pushing the screen of his watch repeatedly.

"Hey, mind if I go for a run since you're home early?" he asked. "I need the steps after all those cookies."

The damn cookies.

"Carly was nice," I avoided his question. I was interested in how the playdate came to be.

"I guess," he said, his watched beeped as he pressed.

"I didn't realize the kids had a half day. Their teacher didn't mention it when I dropped them off," I said.

"It's no problem. I had planned to pick them up, anyway," he replied indifferently.

"Did you and Carly have this playdate planned because of the half day?" I probed.

"No," he grinned. "I mean, kind of. Yesterday, when the kids ran out from school, they begged us to play together. Carly suggested they play today."

"You didn't mention it this morning," I said.

"I didn't think to," he said, twiddling with his watch again.

"But you knew I had the day off," I said.

He looked up from his watch. "I'm sorry. I didn't know we had plans. Do we have plans?"

"No," I roused. "I just thought you would've mentioned it. I wasn't expecting to come home to a woman in my backyard hanging out with my husband."

He stopped fidgeting with his watch and looked at me with a smile. "Are you jealous, Faith?" he mocked. He put both hands on the counter, seemingly entertained; his triceps flexed impressively.

"No," I huffed.

"I think you are," he said. This time, with a proud tone to it. Truth was, though Beau was good-looking—dimples to die for, shiny eyes, always-golden skin that curved around his sculpted body —I was rarely confronted with opportunities to be jealous. Stares and glances didn't faze me, but seeing Beau with another woman was jarring. My instincts told me that today's playdate—and Carly—were completely benign, but I still didn't like it.

"I'm not jealous. I'm, I don't know, surprised. It doesn't matter," I said, though I couldn't hide that it *did* matter from my tone, and I wondered why I didn't tell Beau that it bothered me to see him with another woman. Even if it was a playdate. I knew he wanted to hear that, but I couldn't bring myself to say it.

"Okay," he said, unconvinced.

"I'm *not*. Carly seems nice, if not a little boring."

He chuckled. "Boring? What makes you say that?"

"I don't know. Just a feeling I get about her. She was practically drooling that I was a doctor. She seems like the type who wakes up dreaming about ways to claw out of her life."

"Maybe," he said.

"She sells jewelry," I said condescendingly.

"Is that a bad thing?"

"No," I replied quickly, realizing how snobbish I sounded. "She just seemed like she wished she did more. That's all I was saying. Maybe she wished she had prioritized a different career path."

"I didn't get that impression. She has a Master's in computer science. She worked for one of the big tech giants. Can't remember which one. She was working on her PhD, then she had kids and decided it was too much to pursue," he said.

"You learned quite a bit about her," I said glaringly, but this time my jealousy didn't seem to amuse Beau.

"What do you mean?" he asked in a careful tone. "Two adults talking while their kids play is normal, and 'what you do' is basic conversation."

"I just don't get why she sought *you* out for a playdate," I admitted.

"She didn't seek me out," he said incredibly. "The kids wanted to play. That's it."

"But she brought cookies and juice boxes and—"

"That's what people do, Faith!" he interrupted.

"And her perfect ponytail—" I kept on.

"Her what?! I can't believe we're having this conversation. She came over for a playdate. She brought cookies because it's polite. I don't care to defend her, or anything else, for that matter," he said as he pushed off the counter with an incredulous shove.

"I'm not asking you to defend anything. I was just making observations," I countered.

"I'm going for a run," he said as he brushed past me, a cold breeze trailed behind him.

I stared at the empty kitchen, willing my pulse to slow down. I could hear the twins playing two rooms over, oblivious to the conversation Beau and I just had. I sighed. Why did Carly's presence bother me so much? And why did I feel the need to belittle her? Since when did I have the audacity to judge another woman's circumstance so harshly? Making fun of her profession?

I chortled out loud. *Me*, of all people, poking at a woman's way to make a living, when women are whipping and cuffing men for money under *my* employ?

I shook my head and walked outside to clear the cookies. I knew my rancor had nothing to do with Carly and everything to do with me. Though I tried to convince Beau that Carly was jealous of me, it was obvious that I was jealous of her. She was the wife and mother—today, at least—that I yearned to be.

That Beau probably wanted.

Later that night, I tried to make up for my small tantrum earlier in the day.

After reading two separate books to the twins and tucking them into bed, I entered our bedroom with the intention of re-claiming my territory.

But Beau was already asleep.

CHAPTER THIRTY

"Dr. Wells, it's Kat," she said in a desperate voice. "You need to come in. And hurry!"

I jumped out of bed and rushed down the stairs. "Kat, what's going on?" I asked calmly as I nudged on my sneakers and grabbed a cardigan to slip over my tank top. I got in the car and roared toward the clinic.

"It's Andrew Yale," she said meekly. "He's not moving."

"Is he breathing?" I asked pointedly.

"Yes, shallowly."

"What's his BP?"

"Eighty-five over fifty-five."

"And his pulse?"

"One-thirty."

"Okay," I processed. Hypotensive and tachycardic.

"And he's clammy and almost incoherent," she continued.

My chest sunk.

"Is he in pain?"

"Yes. Mostly his chest and arm, his left arm," she said, knowing full well what that meant.

"Call an ambulance."

"We can't," she panicked softly.

"You have to, Kat," I said calmly. "He is likely having a massive heart attack and could die soon if we don't get him to the hospital."

"Dr. Wells, he's naked and tied up. And—" she stopped.

"And what?" I said.

"And we can't move him. He can't walk himself. We can't let the paramedics—"

"I know," I interrupted frustratingly. I knew what she wanted to say. We couldn't let the paramedics down into the dungeon. It would ruin the clinic. Then, my heart sunk. It would ruin me. *Fuck*, I repined.

"Go get Tobias. He'll help get Andrew upstairs. I'm going to call an ambulance now... I'm almost there. But get Tobias! Knock his door down if you have to."

"Shiloh already is, Dr. Wells," she obeyed.

Click.

"Goddammit!" I hit my steering wheel, a minute away from the clinic.

Maybe I didn't need to call an ambulance. Maybe I should wait just a few minutes to get inside to properly assess the situation. *Time is muscle*, my mind relayed. If Andrew Yale was having a heart attack, every minute of his oxygen-deprived heart could lead to permanent death of the most important muscle in his body. Not to mention that— *fuck*! I shrugged the thought away, but it still materialized—if Andrew Yale had a heart attack and died on the floor of the dungeon, I would have a lot more to worry about than losing the clinic or my medical license. I could lose everything.

I called 911 as my tires screeched into the back parking lot.

Tobias was carrying Andrew Yale effortlessly out the lower back door of the dungeon toward the upper back door of the clinic. Andrew hung limply over Tobias's shoulder like a wounded soldier.

I could hear the sirens of the ambulance in the distance and knew they would reach us in mere minutes.

"Get him inside quickly," I hollered, leaving the car door open and my ignition running.

Tobias laid him on the table of room 3, ironically, the same exam table I first met Andrew on. I instructed Shiloh, who had thrown on a sweatshirt and sweatpants over her black leather corset, to wait outside for the ambulance.

"Andrew, it's Dr. Wells. I'm just going to listen to your heart. You're okay, Andrew," I assured him, slinging one end of my stethoscope into my ears and the diaphragm to his chest. He opened his eyes warily and groaned in terrifying pain.

Kat was grabbing the EKG machine and wheeling it over. I heard the ambulance sirens get closer as Kat and I furiously dotted Andrew's chest with electrodes.

"Kat, I need nitroglycerine tabs from the emergency pharmacy cabinet," I redirected her. "Here's the key. Tobias, get me a heat pack."

They both nodded and veered off in opposite directions.

"Andrew. Stay with me," I said calmly as I grabbed a pair of sterile gloves to start an IV line. "I'm going to put an IV into your arm," I advised, tightening the tourniquet and tapping for a bulge. I hadn't run a line since med school, and dammit, I couldn't find a vein. They were flat.

Tobias returned with the heat, and I placed it on Andrew's arm to help get the IV in place. "You're doing great, Andrew," I said while I continued working for a vein.

Andrew's neck had a red imprint of a chain collar, and his forearms and thighs were covered in welts from Kat's ropes. Tobias had managed to get his boxer shorts on before hauling him upstairs at least, I shuddered.

Finally, I got a vein.

Andrew's eyes lilted back and his head heavily swayed to one side. I slapped his face repeatedly with gentle force. "Andrew, stay with me!" He semifocused back to meet my eyes, panting, wincing in pain.

I could hear the gurney in the hallway and men's voices. I grabbed the EKG tape from the machine. The peaks and valleys told me what I already knew: Andrew was in cardiogenic shock.

Kat came running in. "These?" she asked, out of breath.

I grabbed the nitrates and stuck one small, white pill under Andrew's tongue.

The paramedics swept in, ushered by Shiloh.

"He's having an ST elevation MI," I advised. "I gave him one sublingual nitro. Get him straight to Doylestown Hospital. I'll call ahead so you can bypass the ED and go directly to the cath lab."

The younger paramedic started untangling a portable EKG machine.

"You can do that in the ambulance!" I reprimanded the young medic.

"But it's procedure—," he said.

"I already have the EKG! I am a physician and I am in charge here!" I outranked and shoved the tracing into his hands. "Just get him to the hospital."

He relented to the chain of authority and put the EKG machine aside. They lifted Andrew onto the gurney. Andrew moaned in pain.

"Hit him with morphine when you get him in the ambulance," I instructed.

"But—," the older paramedic (but not by much) protested.

"*Hit him with morphine,*" I said determinately. My tone reminded him that my training in med school and to become a specialist in my field far outweighed his judgment in this matter.

"Of course, Doctor," he said. He nodded to the younger paramedic, and they wheeled Andrew down the hallway and out the back door.

I followed toward my car, which was still running, and I called the hospital to instruct that Andrew was to bypass the ED and go straight to the cath lab upon arrival. Then, I called Dr. Moran, the cardiologist on-call, to advise of Andrew's status. I offered to assist in the case so that I could keep a close eye on Andrew.

As I swerved into the reserved parking lot of the hospital, I let out long sigh.

You better make it, Andrew Yale, I silently pleaded. *It's not just your life that depends on it.*

CHAPTER THIRTY-ONE

Two things happened the night of Andrew's heart attack.
One: He survived.

Two: I prayed for the first time since I was young.

I left the hospital after Andrew's stents were placed and he was wheeled into a recovery room in the cardiac wing. His parents showed up while he was in the cath lab, adorned in Dolce and diamonds, even in the middle of the night, and crowded the hospital with their overbearing presence.

I quietly snuck out before having to field their questions, throwing my gown, gloves, and mask in the bin with a weighty drop. Everything felt like it was dropping, and even at 1 a.m., I knew I had a long day ahead trying to pick up the fallen pieces.

I got in my car and drove around in a tired stupor, employing my car's direction with my subconscious like a Ouija board.

That was too damn close, I rebuked as I ran through the possible outcomes of Andrew going into cardiac arrest in the dungeon. If he hadn't made it to the hospital and pulled through this heart attack, I couldn't imagine the ramifications. I pictured an ambulance having to come down to retrieve his body, the police following, taping off the dungeon like a crime scene. I'd have been called in for questioning, as would the ladies. *Oh,* I shuddered, picturing Kat trying to keep her composure during questioning; she would buckle and fold faster than a levered ironing board. And the police's questioning would not have been the worst of it: How would I ever explain this to Beau?

Dear God, I rubbed my forehead. Before starting this side business, I anticipated certain risks. The possibility of someone threatening to expose me was one I anticipated, which was remedied with the video footage I had. I anticipated clients getting pushy, maybe even out of line, but Tobias was around for brut. I even anticipated minor medical needs, solicitation of drugs, or requests for kinky medical services. But someone having a heart attack in the dungeon? I supposed I knew it was possible, but I thought the risk was low enough to avoid.

I stopped the car to think. I looked up, fingers to my temple, to realize I was lolling in front of Our Lady of Mount Carmel Church. The hazy lights of the streetlamps cast a calming bloom on the quiet street, which mirrored the ambiance that radiated from the lit church. Across the street, the full moon illuminated the Prayer Garden.

I put my car in park and walked toward the flower-lined path that led to the shrine of the Virgin Mary. The click of my heels echoed as I made my way closer, each step wondering what it was walking toward.

I stood limply in front of the glowing statue of Mary, her comforting smile lighting on me as she held baby Jesus, and I felt a well of emotions bubble in my throat. I choked them back.

"Bet you're wondering why I'm here?" I asked Her frustratingly.

She answered with a placating smile.

"I don't pray anymore," I told Her. "I stopped praying a long time ago."

She remained silent, naturally.

"I prayed so hard when I was little," I said with more resentment than expected. "I wanted to be good, so that things would get better for us."

The bubble that had been lodged in my throat shot up to my eyes and burst. A tear fell. Then two. Then a stream of them silently melted down my face.

"But things didn't get better," I croaked. "Even though I prayed so hard I thought my rosary beads would snap." I looked up at the sky and let out a weepy laugh, remembering my childish prayers, but my smile stifled quickly. I realized I hadn't moved, but neither had She, I glared tiredly. My legs throbbed from standing.

"And then Bobby? The cocaine?" I asked, frustrated to say his name out loud. "That's when I stopped praying, just so you know," I reprimanded.

But that wasn't true, I realized. I might have put the rosary beads down and replaced them with a stethoscope and the concrete answers of science, but I still pleaded in my heart every day. And if a heartfelt supplication isn't a prayer, then what is? And if I tallied up the things I'd asked for—*please* become a doctor so that I could make a better life for me and my family, *please* get pregnant so I could be the mother I always wanted to have, *please* have a table full of fancy food with people around it so I wouldn't be so lonely—the marks would indicate that my prayers were actually answered.

But that's the thing with prayers, or pleas, or bartering, or negotiations. If you get, you must give. Otherwise, the relationship wobbles.

I thought of Beau and my heart sunk, collapsing with my tears. I hadn't been fair to him, and I knew it.

I'm sorry, Faith, that I'd love to see my beautiful wife more often.

I'd like to have a glass of wine on the porch with you and talk about our day like we used to.

Beau's words echoed between my sobs.

He probably misses you, is all, Irena's voice chimed in my head.

I looked up at Mary tearfully. "I can't believe it. I've tried my whole life not to be like my mother, and I did the one thing I loathed her the most for."

Mary stared.

"I made him lonely," I said. I grabbed at my chest as I realized how unavailable I had become. Over the years, whatever parts of me I had allowed Beau into had slowly closed back up until I was only available on the surface.

"Did I fuck up?" I whined, then quickly to make up for the profanity, "Sorry." There was a baby there, after all (and not just any baby), I shamed blasphemously. Though, in my defense, this conversation was mother-to-Mother.

"Is it too late?" I asked Mary. "Am I too late to do things differently?"

Mary stared.

"I don't want to be too late," I cried. "I want to do better. I just don't know how."

Then a thought that had sat in my heart for years, but had never materialized in my head, formed: *What if I'm not enough?*

A pain so sharp that I could have mistaken it for a heart attack stabbed my ribs as I remembered trying to be enough for my mother—a good enough daughter to spend more time with, a good enough Catholic to take to church more often, a good enough doctor to fix her heart. The pain of not being enough for her hurt me to the core, and I wondered if it had blocked the part of my heart that would allow anyone else to hurt it so deeply.

Beau only wanted one thing: He wanted me. And it wasn't just about wanting more of my time or attention—he wanted *me*. For the first time, I understood that difference. I swallowed heavy.

Maybe it was time to put a stent in my own heart.

"I have to forgive her," I cried.

Like in a movie where the clouds part and a ray of light escapes, my chest broke open and let out a lifetime of pain. I dropped to my knees and wept as my body cleansed the fears I had buried deep. With each sob, my heart gained space as it let go of what was clogging it, until finally, I felt: I had room.

"She was taking up space, Mary," I choked. "My mother. I have to let her go. So that I can let him in."

She stared at me as though saying, "Yes, dear. I think you've finally figured it out." Or at least, that's what my exhausted, deluded mind heard her saying. Images of my mother swam in the glossy film of my eyes.

Finally, I stood. My body felt weary, but renewed.

"I couldn't fix my mother," I whimpered with resolve. "But I can fix me."

I inhaled a stuffy breath and blotted my swollen eyes. I couldn't remember the last time I cried myself into a puffy face, I surmised pathetically. I looked around, grateful for the protective shrubs hugging me in from the outside world.

There was only one thing I wanted to tell Mary; one thing that screamed at me every day, but that I pulled the shades down to dismiss it. One thing that once I looked at, I'd have to face.

"I miss her."

"Beau," I shook him awake.

He sat up, alarmed. "Faith, what's wrong? Is it the kids?"

"No. The kids are fine," I said. I kneeled on the side of the bed next to him.

He put his arms on my shoulders and guided me up to him. "You're shaking, Faith. Come here," he pulled me close. "What happened?"

I couldn't stop the torrent of tears, which alarmed Beau more.

"Faith, what happened?" he asked urgently. "You have to tell me right now."

I wanted to tell Beau everything, but I knew that I couldn't; I wouldn't. I didn't know what I planned to tell Beau—not about tonight, but about everything. But tonight, I didn't want to talk about anything. I just wanted to curl into Beau and let him wrap his arms around my worries.

"Just don't give up on me, Beau," I cried. "I'm going to change."

"Change what? I don't want you to change."

"I already did. I let her go, Beau. I forgave her," I cried.

He didn't need any more words. He knew who I forgave, and he let out a sigh and held me tight. I breathed in Beau's bare skin; his muscular arms embracing me. Then as quickly as they came, my tears dried up. I felt a euphoria of relief.

"I'm sorry, Beau. I'm so sorry."

"No," he pulled me from his embrace gently to look at my face. "You don't ever have to be sorry to me, Faith."

"I do. I didn't let you in—not all the way—but not because I wouldn't. Because I couldn't. But I can now."

He held me at bay, studying my face. I looked down at his body that was striped from the moonlight shining through the blinds. A surge of arousal mixed with the euphoria and I felt it taking over my body. I grabbed at the drawstring of his sweatpants and looked up at him expectantly.

"What are you doing?" he asked warily, but clearly, he had felt the shift of energy, too, as I saw the bulge in his pants grow.

"I'm yours, Beau. All the way. You can have whatever you want of me," I said yearningly.

Beau stared for a moment like one stares at a meal they've been waiting for, contemplating how to take the first bite. Then, he grabbed the back of my hair with one strong hand, put his other hand firmly around my buttocks, and nearly threw me down on the bed with a lusty thud.

He pinned my arms above my head and towered above me, forcefully pressed against my parted legs. "Whatever I want?" he asked headily, his face inches from mine. I could not recall a time in my life I was so filled with desire.

I answered by craning up and biting his lip. As if I had unlocked the chains of a tethered dragon, Beau came undone. He ripped off my pants and dropped off his only article of clothing.

And I'll be damned if I didn't let Beau in. All the way.

Afterward, we laid together, stroking each other tenderly. The heady smell of Beau's body drove me further into him. A whole new level of intimacy had formed that I didn't know existed until tonight.

Tonight, something had changed. A transfer of power, a surrender to a battle we didn't know we were having. On the surface, Beau wanted more of my time and I wanted more of everything. Underneath it all, I just needed Beau to take control, and Beau needed me to finally let him.

"Beau?" I asked.

"Mmm-hmm?" he breathed into my hair.

"Will you help me with something?"

"Anything."

"Will you help me get the portrait of my mother out of the attic and hang it at the clinic?"

I could sense his eyes opening, even though I couldn't see them. He turned me toward him. "Yes," he said simply, but he knew there was nothing simple about the request.

I reached forward and kissed him softly. It was a tender moment that quickly heated up, and we found ourselves wrestling into another knot of passion.

Who knew that my night would go from having a "come to Jesus" moment to having a "come to Beau" moment?

And maybe I had finally come to exactly where I needed to be.

CHAPTER THIRTY-TWO

Though I got little sleep, I felt rejuvenated from an enlightening night with Beau.

In fact, when the alarm went off only two hours after we had relented to sleep, I contemplated calling in sick and nudging Beau for another round. I smiled at the new sensation (*Had I ever been the one to initiate?*) before the weight of the day ahead burst my coitus bubble.

"Do you have to go?" Beau asked drowsily. I looked over at him; he even had dimples when he slept.

I turned to kiss his ear and whispered, "I'll be home for dinner tonight. And dessert."

I felt his cheek recess. God, *I wanted him now*, I realized, and it completely threw me.

I clicked my tongue that I couldn't stay in bed and sauntered off to face the aftermath of last night's events. My heart raced as I anticipated confronting Andrew. What had he said to his doctors, my colleagues, about last night? To his parents? *Ugh*, the weight of the potential trouble I was in sat heavily in me. Luckily, today was my shift at the hospital, which would make dropping in to see Andrew Yale seem natural.

He was sitting up eating a pudding cup when I walked into his room.

"Andrew, good morning," I smiled as I walked toward the computer cart to review his chart, or pretend to review his chart; I had been checking on it nonstop since I awoke.

"Hey Doctor," he said sheepishly, as if he were in trouble.

"Dr. Wells, if you don't mind," I corrected softly.

"Right, sorry," he said, spoon in one hand, empty cup in the other.

"You had quite the night last night," I reflected. "How are you feeling today?"

"I feel okay, I guess," he answered. "Tired. And this is sore," he nodded toward his wrist where arterial access was obtained for his cardiac catheterization.

"That's all normal. And yes, you'll be sore."

I checked his vitals and listened to his heart, making notes as I worked. A silence hung while we contemplated how to address last night's incident.

"I—" he started.

"Andrew—" I said at the same time.

We both grinned.

"Andrew," I took lead. "What happened last night can't happen again."

"Well, I don't plan to have back-to-back heart attacks, Dr. Wells," he joked.

"I mean, it can't happen again. Any of it."

His face fell as if I'd told him his puppy "didn't make it."

"What are you saying?"

"I'm saying that it's over. The dungeon. The collars, the whips, the everything." I hushed, looking around to ensure that a nurse hadn't snuck in.

"But *why*?" he whined. "Me having a heart attack had nothing to do with, you know, *that*. I eat too much bacon, for God's sake."

I irked when patients diagnosed their heart condition better than I did.

"That might be true, but the fact still remains that I can't have that type of liability at my clinic anymore. Last night, my heart stopped almost as soon as yours did. I could lose my license, Andrew," I half-scolded.

He scoffed. "No, come on. You're not doing anything. Anything like that," he clarified. "You know what I mean."

"But I am doing something. I'm letting it happen. I'm the ultimate escalation point. It's happening in my clinic, on my property, and if donations were traced far enough, the trail is clear. They lead to me."

"Well, when you put it that way…But you're not actually doing anything illegal," he lawyered. "Maybe the donation part, but we could fix that."

"The legality isn't my concern. The ethics is," I confirmed. "I am a doctor who took an oath to do no harm."

"You're not doing harm. You're doing good! Look how happy your clients are!"

"That's what I told myself at first, but it's dangerous. I have a feeling you and Shiloh went too far last night," I alluded to the asphyxiation and he knew it.

He sighed. "Every business has its hiccups. We'll reel it in."

"No, I'm reeling it in, Andrew," I said authoritatively.

"What about Shiloh?"

"What about her?"

"Can I still see her?"

"I'm not Shiloh's keeper," I scoffed. "You'll have to ask Shiloh."

"But she won't have anywhere to, you know, see me," he intimated.

"Andrew, I have a feeling you could solve that problem pretty quickly."

"Yeah, but we wouldn't have you," he pouted. "I could have died last night if you hadn't come."

I smiled. "I'll still come if you call, Andrew." Then, an idea materialized. "You can rely on me to help with any situation that goes awry. Discreetly. As you are aware, the medical records at the clinic are not part of the larger network. I keep them private."

"Yeah?" he perked.

"Yes. And maybe my clinic can rely on your help in return."

He caught on. "I'm sure Mom and Dad won't object to me abdicating your clinic into the Yale Family Trust donation portfolio long-term, especially after last night. You saved my life."

I nodded satisfactorily. "Speaking of Mom and Dad. What did you tell them about last night?"

"I told them that I was in town to meet Jed when I suddenly felt unwell. I thought I was coming down with the flu, so I stopped in to see you. The staff was cleaning up for the night, and they were kind enough to call you in since they recognized me. I passed out while waiting for you, you came and did your doctor magic, I left in an ambulance, and well, now I'm here."

"And they didn't have any questions?"

"No," he shrugged, then winced in pain. I looked up at his stats instinctively.

"You need to rest," I said. "When you're well, we can finish catching up."

He nodded, settling back into his resting position.

I stared at him, calculating how to feel about Andrew Yale. Before he limped into my clinic (I winced remembering how we met, he on his side and me with forceps and lube dealing with his posterior emergency), the naughtiest thing I had done was smuggle Viagra samples to Jed.

But somehow, Andrew had wormed his way into all of our lives, and though maybe I should have been, I wasn't sorry for it. I recalled how I didn't understand why Jed took to Andrew; I found him to be an aloof trust fund man-boy. But eventually I understood. Andrew grew on you like a stray cat you hesitated to feed but later allowed to sleep in your bed; harmless, if not a bit selfish and depraved.

"I can say this, Andrew. It's been real," I said with a wink.

It had been real.

This past year and a half, I set up a real clinic with a real vision. I cultivated a real family in the women who worked for me. I offered real services to people with real needs.

And last night was the realest I had ever felt with Beau. It had taken me over three decades to find it, but I had finally experienced real intimacy. Real vulnerability. Real desire. Real connection.

And it was real nice.

That afternoon at the clinic was like walking into the classroom after the class misbehaved for the substitute.

I first saw Tobias when I pulled up in the back of the clinic. He was watering the flowers; his six-toed cat watching him with a sassy scowl.

"Hey, Doctor Wells," he said gingerly.

"Tobias, hi. I'm glad you're here," I said, the beep of my car doors locking behind me.

He stood at attention, but his eyes diverted from one direction to the other as if searching for an escape route.

"I wanted to thank you for helping out last night," I said.

He shrugged as if to say it was nothing.

"I need you to rent a storage unit and start transferring the furniture and equipment from downstairs to it."

His eyes widened, but he nodded obediently. "Right now?"

I smiled. Tobias: the perfect accomplice. God, I wished I could clone him.

"No, not now," I said. "Tonight."

"After the appointments?"

"No, instead of the appointments," I said resolutely. And like a dutiful soldier, Tobias needed no further clarification.

I placed a hand on his shoulder and stared at him briefly with gratitude before heading into the clinic.

"How's Andrew?" Shiloh asked as I set my bag down in my office. Kat hurried herself out of sight, practically hiding her face behind a folder as she walked down the hall.

"He's good," I answered flatly.

She nodded with trepidation, fearful that a lengthy interrogation was coming. But it wasn't. I had thought about how I was going to handle the staff and had come to a quick conclusion, as a doctor must do. There would be no drama in dissolving our side hustle. There didn't need to be a long, thought-through process to end it; it just needed to end. So, I decided to forego the play-by-play of "how did it happen?" and skip right to "can't let it happen again."

"Where's Irena?" I asked.

"In room 1," she answered.

"Okay," I said, opening the system to today's schedule. I was hoping to breeze through my two consults and hurry Irena out of the clinic. I was aware that Shiloh was still standing with a frozen stare.

"I don't want to know what took place last night," I finally said.

She let out a sigh that sounded like a mixture of relief and shame.

"Did you clear tonight's schedule?" I asked. She knew I meant the "other" schedule.

"Yes," she said. "Except for one interview."

"Excuse me?" I challenged. I turned my head from the screen.

"I'm sorry, Dr. Wells, but Mara made me keep him on the schedule. He's a new client. Someone Jed Terry personally referred."

"I don't care who referred him, to be frank. I asked you to clear the schedule so that we could have a meeting. Shiloh, I think you know what the meeting is about."

Her shoulders slackened. "I think I have an idea."

"Now is not the time to be taking new clients. Tonight of all nights, especially. I have to be home by seven for dinner."

She looked at me quizzically. Being home for dinner was not a priority she was accustomed to hearing me say. I wasn't accustomed to it, either.

I shrugged. "I do; I promised Beau. Cancel the new client, please. Send Mara to me if she has a concern about it."

She puffed and twirled her earring but didn't move.

"Anything else, Shiloh?"

"It's just that—" she bit her lip. "Mara was pretty adamant. The appointment just came through this morning, and when she saw who it was for, she told me I couldn't cancel it under any circumstance."

I narrowed my eyes in disbelief.

"And then she left," Shiloh added.

"Mara left? This morning? And hasn't been back?"

She nodded.

"Did she say where she was going?"

"No," she shifted to her other hip. "I've been calling and texting her all day. I'm a little worried, if you want to know the truth."

I furrowed my brow trying to process why Mara would have left so abruptly. It was very uncharacteristic of her. And the fact that she hadn't answered any of Shiloh's messages concerned me; they were quite close.

"It doesn't make sense," I stewed.

"I know. It was very odd. Even the call was weird. The man almost made it a point to give me his full name. I'm used to our clients giving some predictable pseudonym such as 'Wolf Master' or 'Blade.'"

"What was his name?" I asked; maybe I could ask Jed about him and get a clue as to why Mara might be so interested in this new client.

"Bobby," she answered. "Bobby Clay."

Don't look for zebras they teach you in med school. It meant that if you heard hoof beats while generating a differential diagnosis—or weighing the probability of one disease versus another—not to search for a zebra because it was likely a horse. Most diagnoses are simple, but if you're always looking for the zebra, you might miss the horse.

Of all the men I feared might expose me, never did I anticipate Bobby Clay to be one of them. I felt as if the room stole the air out of my lungs.

"Are you okay?" Shiloh asked. "You're pale, Dr. Wells."

"I need a minute, Shiloh," I managed to bleat out.

"I'll go get you some coffee," she said cautiously.

I choked in a breath after she left. The room seemed smaller as my eyes tried to adjust to the swirling thoughts.

Think, think, think, I implored. But my palms were sweaty and a squeeze in my throat made the air thick. There was only one reason Mara would have had such a reaction to Bobby Clay calling for an appointment. How could I not have connected the dots earlier? Then I realized there weren't many dots to connect. All I knew of Mara's ex was that he was an attorney. There are thousands of attorneys in the Philadelphia region. How could I have guessed? I could've asked Mara more questions, I supposed. But that wasn't my style. I was never one to probe in personal affairs; I didn't find the value in it. Maybe I should have.

My stomach turned as I contemplated my next move. In what sick universe was Bobby Clay the same person who destroyed Mara's and my mother's life— and now could ruin mine?

I had to find Mara, but I didn't know where to start. Wait, yes, I did. I grabbed my phone and texted:

Jed, it's Faith Wells. Are you with Mara?

Swirly dots, then:

No, Doc. Why?

So, Mara didn't run to Jed. Of course, she wouldn't have because Jed referred Bobby Clay. But still, I needed to talk to him. How much did Bobby know about the clinic? About me? About Mara? Hopefully, Jed had followed referral protocol, which was to only give Shiloh's phone number, this week's burner number. So, it was possible Bobby knew nothing else. But then, why the full name?

I replied to Jed:

Can we meet for coffee?

Immediately:

Sure, Doc. When and where?

I thought about a location, then:

Biscotti. Can you be there in 20?

Thumbs up confirmed.

Shiloh entered with a cup of coffee as I gathered my things together.

"Shiloh, can you ask Irena to stay late tonight?"

She held the cup of coffee protectively as I flung around looking for my keys.

"Irena?" she asked, confused. "You want Irena to stay late?"

I looked at her exasperatingly. I didn't have time to explain to Shiloh. "Yes. I need her to take my appointments. I have to run out."

"I can see that," she said. "But what about our meeting?"

"I'll worry about that later," I sighed. "I'll be back."

I swept past her, then turned around. "If Mara calls you back, tell her I need her urgently. *Urgently*, Shiloh."

Her brow furrowed as she nodded.

I turned to leave, then pivoted again. "Oh, and don't cancel that interview tonight. Keep it on the schedule."

I left the clinic and walked toward Biscotti, my mind racing as fast as my heels.

CHAPTER THIRTY-THREE

The door chimed open and a warm scent of butter and sugar closed around me.

The air in a coffee shop was much different than the air in which I worked. My air was cold and clinical, a constant feed of metallic filtration. Biscotti's air was thick and warm; flavors and scents that seeped into you. A dichotomy of how I felt, and how I wanted to feel, I thought as I took a chair at a free-standing table by the window.

I checked my phone. Mara hadn't replied to my text. *Where could she be?* I tapped my foot in the air waiting for Jed to join me. I checked my watch and huffed impatiently. I realized how seldom in life I waited for anything; I seemed to be the person someone was always waiting for. I didn't like the feeling, and it made me think of Beau.

Shit, I couldn't miss dinner with Beau. I looked at my watch again. Three o'clock. I had four hours to talk to Jed, find Mara, have a meeting, and make a plan to deal with Bobby Clay's impending interview.

"Fuck," I gritted through my teeth quietly.

"Hey, I thought that was you, Faith!"

I turned around to see Anna from the Massenet Foundation approaching, her beautiful golden-streaked hair floating effortlessly, like she took a minute where most would take an hour to have hair that good. But I didn't have time for small talk.

"Hi Anna, how are you?" I forced a smile, then glanced back toward the door.

As though she could sense that I wasn't there for leisure, she gracefully said, "I'm well, Faith. Thanks. I came over to tell you that I received the clinic's financials for the grant allocations, but we can talk about that some other time," she shooed. "Can I have Jared pack up some biscotti for you to take back to the clinic?"

I looked at her surprised. I didn't know Anna owned Biscotti, or did I? I guess I never thought to ask. I was really beginning to not like the part of me who didn't ask or care about anyone's business, in this case, literally.

"Is this your place?" I asked.

"Yeah," she smiled. "My husband ran it at first, then I ran it for a time, but now we focus mostly on the foundation. My sister-in-law runs Biscotti, and I come in to stalk her from time to time."

I chuckled nervously, both because I was anxiously waiting for Jed to appear, but also because in the midst of my personal crisis that involved a dominatrix giving patients heart attacks, a missing escort-of-sorts, and now a demon from my past coming back to haunt me, I felt inept in the company of a woman who ran a charitable foundation and a cozy, glowing coffee shop where the only dark thing that probably ever happened was the dark roast itself. It didn't help that Anna was drop-dead gorgeous either. And genuinely kind. My irritation mounted.

"It's nice," I said. "The shop. And I'm sure my staff would love some biscotti."

The door chimed and Jed entered. I had hoped this would be the queue for Anna to leave, but she had already put her arms out to welcome Jed.

"Hey doll!" Jed exclaimed, kissing one of Anna's perfect cheekbones, then the other.

"How are you, Jed?" she welcomed him familiarly.

"Never better. Can you ask Jared to make my usual?" he glanced at me. "Doc, you're not having anything to drink?"

"I'm good, thanks," I said. I was running off straight adrenaline and could've used the caffeine, but I also was running out of time, I was reminded as I glanced at my watch.

"I hate to be rude, but I have to get back for some appointments at the clinic," I said.

"Of course," Anna grinned. "I'll have Jared package up some biscotti and bring some coffee."

"My usual," Jed clarified.

"Your usual, Jed," she teased. "Good to see you, Faith."

"You too, Anna. Thanks again."

Jed sat down cheerily, looking around the shop as if he was searching for anyone he knew.

"Jed, we have a problem," I said quietly.

"Is this about Andrew?" he replied, barely making eye contact. "Because you don't have to worry about him. He's not gonna say a thing."

A twenty-something-year-old guy with a perfectly stylish beard showed up with two coffees and a box of biscotti.

"Thanks Jared!" Jed beamed.

Back to the issue at hand: "It's not about Andrew, although, that is going to change things. It really shook me up."

He sipped his latte loudly. "What's it about then?"

"Bobby Clay," I spewed.

"Oh, yeah," he chortled. "What about him?"

"I understand you sent him to Shiloh," I said.

He shrugged. "He has deep pockets and he loves women. Kind of an asshole, to be honest. Never really liked the guy, but he heard through the grapevine that I knew of a service he might be interested in. I thought he'd be a good fit for Shiloh; she loves the odd ones."

"She likes odd, not vulgar," I repulsed.

"I don't know if he's vulgar," he downplayed. "I don't know him all that well, but he's very successful. Seems to have some strong connections."

"I know," I said.

"So, you know him?" He asked, amused.

"I know of him," I replied indifferently. I didn't want Jed to know how I knew him, yet. Maybe ever. Right now, I just needed to know what Bobby knew of me.

"Did you follow the referral process?" I asked.

"Of course I did," he replied, sipping his coffee and acting disinterested again. "I only gave him Shiloh's number. The one she sends each week," he said in a low voice. "I'm surprised he gave her his full name. Amateur."

Sadist, I corrected in my head.

"Is that why you asked me to meet you here, Doc? To talk about a referral?"

I sighed. "No. I can't find Mara."

That caught his attention. "What do you mean?" He looked directly at me for the first time.

My suspicions were confirmed. Jed cared for Mara; otherwise, he would've regarded Mara's whereabouts as a non-issue.

"She left the clinic this morning and we haven't heard from her since. We've been calling and texting. I thought maybe you'd know where she was."

He stared in thought, hand on his coffee. "I haven't seen her since last night."

Last night? I glared at him with interest. Nothing was on the books about last night. I fought my instinct to not pry and instead decided to practice asking about someone's personal life.

"So, you spend time together?" I asked. "Off the books."

He flipped his hands up slightly and confessed, "If it's about the money—"

"No, Jed," I interrupted. "It's not about the money. I trust all of that will work its way out; it always does. I'm asking because maybe you'll know where to find her?"

"I know where she likes to go to think."

"Okay," I said encouragingly. "Where?"

"Peace Valley Park. There's a bench on the lake. She sits there to process." I had a feeling Jed had been there with her more than once, and I deduced that their relationship was much more than seeing each other "off the books." Had they found love despite themselves?

Whatever. I didn't have time for that. Literally, I was running out of time because I had to be home for dinner.

"I'll drive," I said.

"Do you want to go alone?" Jed asked as we pulled up to a parking spot overlooking Lake Galena. Mara was in the distance sitting on a bench with a shawl wrapped around her.

I looked at Jed. He was staring at Mara, obviously concerned.

"If you don't mind," I said, unbuckling.

I crossed the grassy landing toward Mara. She didn't move, even though I knew she heard me approach. I sat next to her.

"Do you remember when you told me about your ex?" I said, staring at the soft peaks of the lake. The afternoon sun was ebbing and a soft glow sat on top of the water.

Mara didn't speak, but she blinked heavily.

"There was something I wanted to tell you that day, too," I continued. "I wanted to tell you about my mother. She was so beautiful, Mara. Long, jet black hair and these indescribably blue eyes. When she was sober, which wasn't very often, her eyes looked as shiny as sapphires."

She smiled barely, and if she were to speak, I'd guess she'd say what everyone used to say: "Just like yours."

"Anyway, I never knew my father. Of course, I went through years of wanting to, but then I just kind of, I don't know, didn't want to anymore. I was too busy managing my mother, her drinking and her whereabouts," I exhaled. "We grew up poor, and I mean really poor, but I kept busy with school. I loved learning; I felt like it was a superpower that made me stronger every day. Also, it was where I wasn't alone. I had a teacher, Mrs. Neiran, who sort of took me under her wings. She helped me get into college. She had the most amazing shoes," I smiled in remembrance.

Mara smiled warmly, but there was something troubling in her eyes.

"I practically lived at school and the library," I continued anyway. "I was obsessed with becoming a doctor so that I could fix my mother. I really believed that once I became a doctor, I could easily fix her. Just snap my fingers and we'd be this happy little duo who went to restaurants and shopped on the weekends," I recalled dogmatically. "But two things happened that made me realize it wouldn't work that way. One, I began to understand what addiction really was and how it couldn't be fixed with a snap of a doctor's fingers. And two," I paused.

She waited patiently.

"Two was Bobby Clay," I said.

She billowed a loud whimper and looked at me with tears in her eyes. She was even beautiful when she cried.

"Bobby's your ex," I confirmed.

She nodded, her face a rich shade of caramel from the waning sun.

"He was my mother's ex, as well," I said somberly.

Mara stared at her hands; a heavy tear dropped on them. I let her process in silence, then finally she looked at me sorrowfully. "I know."

I was jarred. "What?"

"I know Bobby was your mother's ex," she said.

My mouth dropped as I tried to make sense of what Mara repeated. "How did you know?" I asked scornfully.

"I'm so sorry, Faith," she blubbered.

"How did you know?" I asked again with vigor.

"I wanted to tell you—" she appealed.

"Mara, how did you *know* that Bobby was my mother's ex?" I cried. I didn't realize, but angry tears had filled my eyes.

"Because I started seeing Bobby shortly after she passed away," she answered.

I paused. So, Mara started seeing Bobby after my mother passed away? Perhaps Bobby mentioned my mother in passing, which was hard to believe. Or, perhaps Mara had met my mother before she died. "Did you know my mother, too?" I asked.

"No," she answered quickly. "I didn't know your mother personally."

"Then how did you know about her?" I asked confused. "Bobby said something?"

"Well, yes, of course. Not at first, but eventually," she answered as if it should have been a given. But I was confused. I thought Bobby kept my mother a secret. "Faith, surely, you know that—" she stopped herself.

"Know what?"

"Bobby was obsessed with your mother," she said gravely.

"*What*?" I barked.

"He cared about her deeply," she said, realizing I didn't know this bit of information.

"No he didn't," I rejected.

"It seemed that way to me, at least," she said earnestly.

I shook my head. My mind was still trying to reconcile that not only was Bobby my mother's *and* Mara's ex, but that Mara knew all along. And now, the most disconcerting information of all: That Bobby might actually have cared for my mother.

"I had known Bobby from the firm for many years," Mara tried to explain. "He was very upset when your mother died. I tried to comfort him. That's how we ended up in a relationship," she looked up at the lake, her hands making knots of her shawl.

I didn't know how to respond.

"Of course, it didn't happen quite that way. Everything with Bobby is gradual until—until it's not," she said with a sigh. "You see, I had just made junior partner at the firm. My two boys had left for college. Bobby and I were both working late at the firm one night and he suggested we get a drink. I knew I shouldn't have accepted, but the truth was, even though I had accomplished all I had set out to do, I was lonely, Faith. And Bobby," she laughed pathetically, "Bobby was captivating, to put it lightly. He had this way of sucking you in, and you couldn't see anything else around you while you were with him."

She paused and we both stared out at the lake. I detestably acknowledged that perhaps that's how my mother felt in Bobby's presence.

"It didn't take long for things to turn into a high-speed roller-coaster ride," she continued. "Our affair was passionate and intense, but while I fell madly in love with him, he never regarded me as more than a replacement of your mother. And a bad replacement, at that. He was cruelly obsessed with her. He would ask me to talk like her, laugh like her, dress like her," she shook her head disgracefully.

I rubbed my fingers against my forehead as Mara's words transmitted out like a foreign voice through a radio.

"When I refused to do drugs with him, our relationship turned physical," Mara said with her head down.

I sighed. I recalled Mara telling me about her ex—though I didn't know it was Bobby at that time—and how he had become abusive. The abuse is what led to her fractured hip and femur. It also led to her setting his Shore house on fire. The links from that story and this one were beginning to make a chain.

"I turned into someone I wouldn't even recognize today, Faith," Mara said with her head down. "To this day, I don't know why I stayed. I thought about leaving him every day that I woke up and every night that I went to bed. But I didn't. I was in too deep."

I closed my eyes. I wondered if my mother ever had those feelings. My anger began to dissipate into something that resembled empathy.

"My boys, who were in college, knew that I was in an abusive relationship," Mara said ashamedly. "They tried to talk me into leaving him, but I wouldn't. So, they followed us one night. They pinned Bobby against a wall and told him that they were taking their mother, and if he ever came near me again, they'd kill him."

"That was brave of them," I said, sympathizing with her sons' desperateness to stop a man who was sucking the soul out of their mother. I remembered the weight of the statue of Saint Francis in my hands.

"I know," her scratchy voice cried. "But I went home with Bobby that night. Not my boys!" She crouched over as if in pain and sobbed into her knees. "I chose him over my boys," she howled. It was unnerving to see Mara fall from grace, and as much as I wanted to be bitter, I felt compassion.

"Have you reached out to them?" I asked.

"I called them before I went away," she said, referring to prison. "But they didn't take my call. I couldn't bring myself to contact them after my release. I have betrayed them," she said in a low, regretful voice.

We sat in silence for a moment, sniffling through our thoughts. There was still one link of the chain that didn't make sense.

"Why did you come to the clinic? Why did you find me?" I asked.

"I got out of prison and I had nothing. I had lost my boys, I had lost my career, and I had lost my dignity. The only thing I could think about was revenge. But he took that from me, as well. I couldn't go near him because of the restraining order. So, I tried to think of somewhere he would find me. And I wagered that he would eventually make his way to your clinic."

"Why?" I suddenly felt violated. "What would he want with me?"

Mara chuckled. "You're a spitting image of your mother."

My heart wrenched.

"I always thought it odd that he knew when you graduated med school and where you started your fellowship. He even knew when you got married. It seemed that he could hold onto your mother by holding onto you."

"I feel sick to my stomach," I said as a sour taste filled my mouth. The thought that Bobby kept tabs on me breached my sense of security and my heart raced with familiar angst.

Mara rubbed her palm with her thumb. "Once I started working at the clinic and came to know you, Faith, I realized I had made a mistake. I wanted to tell you everything, but I couldn't find the right words, and eventually, enough time had passed that I thought maybe I was crazy to think that Bobby would ever come. And I was relieved because I couldn't wish that upon you. Then, when you approached me about Jed, I realized I could formulate a new plan that wouldn't involve you. Jed would take me to Bobby."

"That's what you meant when you said you had a plan," I said.

"Yes. For months, I waited for Jed to take me somewhere Bobby might be. I was going to confront him, maybe embarrass him somehow. But I never ran into him. It seemed that even though Jed and Bobby shared acquaintances, they didn't run in the same circles. Meanwhile, Jed and I became quite close, and I started feeling a conscience about involving Jed, as well. Truthfully, Faith, my resolve to confront Bobby started fading. Being at the clinic and being with Jed made me feel like I was becoming whole again."

I had felt that burn of revenge, as well as the calm of releasing it.

"You could have told me, Mara," I said.

"I know," she said sincerely. A tear streaked down her right cheek. "I'm so sorry, Faith. I never meant to hurt you."

I sighed heavily. I believed Mara. Before she knew me, I was just a name. And after she knew me, I became someone she wanted to protect. I could be angry at Mara, fire her, reprimand her, but what good would that do?

"So, why are you here?" I asked. "Why didn't you let Shiloh cancel Bobby's appointment and put him in the past for good?"

"Because I realized something," she said. "He called and left his name. His full name. He did that on purpose, Faith. He's either doing it to get your attention or my attention. He's baiting one of us."

She had the same hunch that I had; Bobby knew something. Maybe he only knew about Mara. Maybe he knew about me. Maybe he had been planning how to pin us both for some time. I didn't know. But I knew one thing: It was time to stop Bobby Clay.

An idea sprung, a plan too perfect.

"Mara, you can't go to the clinic tonight," I said. "He's not worth it. You'll risk everything just being in the same room as him," I alluded to her restraining order. "But you can still get revenge. Remember when you told me that if you had just let other people in, stopped trying to fix everything yourself, you could have avoided going to prison?"

She nodded. "The cameras."

"That's right, Mara," I smiled cunningly. "The cameras."

CHAPTER THIRTY-FOUR

The sun was setting as I pulled into the clinic's back parking lot. I looked at my watch: 5:45 p.m. I could do this.

I walked in briskly and went straight to Shiloh without stopping at my office.

"Dr. Wells," she startled.

"Shiloh, I found Mara," I said.

She sighed relief.

"We have a situation that needs to be dealt with, but I don't have much time. Where's Irena?" For once I asked not because I was hoping she'd be gone, but because I hoped she'd be available.

"In room 2 with Kat. It's our last appointment."

"And Tobias?"

"Probably upstairs in his apartment."

"Okay, I know this sounds crazy, but I'm going to run down the street to the costume store. I will be fifteen minutes. When I get back, I need you, Kat, and Tobias ready to meet."

"Will Mara be joining?" she asked hopefully.

"No, not tonight. But ask Irena to stick around until I get back. I need to talk to her."

She nodded compliantly.

I made it to the costume store just before its 6:00 p.m. closing time. "I'll be quick!" I promised the clerk as he directed me to exactly what I was seeking. I checked out in less than five minutes, hurried back, and even had time to swoop into the bakery for half dozen chocolate dipped strawberries and some cupcakes. I left a sizable tip to hurry out before waiting for my change; time was counting down.

Irena was waiting outside as I briskly walked up. She was sitting on a chair with her arms and legs folded; her bag was on her arm ready to go. She looked at her watch, which made me instinctively look at mine: 6:14 p.m.

"You wanted to see me?" she asked impatiently. "Is that the emergency you needed me to stay late for?" She nodded toward my costume and bakery bags.

"No," I said, putting down the bags as I took the seat beside her. "I had another emergency I needed to tend to."

"At the hospital?"

"No."

"With a patient?"

"No."

"What's going on, Faith? I've been working since 6:00 a.m. And I don't mean to give you an attitude, but I'm fucking tired. So, what can I do for you before I go home and beg Josh to draw me a long, hot bath instead of the other plans we had tonight?"

I slackened. "I'm sorry, Irena. I've been selfish." In more ways than one, I realized. Were Irena and Josh, the chicken farmer, living together? Had I been such a poor friend not to know that?

"I need your advice," I said, regretting now that I needed even more from her. "You're the only person who knows about certain parts of my life."

She softened. "What's going on?"

"You remember how my mom was really strung out the last few years of her life?"

She nodded.

"But it got really bad toward the end?"

"Because of that douchebag," she said.

"Right. Well, let's just say that I found out that douchebag hurt another person I loved."

She raised her eyebrows. "Who?"

I hesitated. I wanted to tell her, but I was afraid it wasn't my secret to tell. But I also knew that Irena would not be able to give me informed advice if she didn't know, so I confided in her. "Mara."

She gaped, unfolded her arms, and leaned forward. "What? You're telling me the man who practically killed your mom hurt Mara, too?"

"Ever wonder where her limp came from?" I alluded.

She gasped. "Woah," she shook her head, trying to fit the pieces together.

"And here's the thing: Let's just say that hypothetically, I had an opportunity to get back at him."

She perked up. "Really? How?" Then, she waved me off. "No, never mind. I don't want to know. Would it get you in trouble?"

"No, it's nothing illegal. It won't hurt him physically. In fact, it's something he's asking for."

"Would you get caught?"

"No. I don't think so."

"Then I'd say, let that dog lie in the bed he made," she said, her South Philly street accent peeking through her words.

I sighed apprehensively. Even though Irena was giving me the confirmation I needed, I still felt anxious about carrying out my plan. But what choice did I have? If Bobby knew about the dungeon, he might try to expose me or Mara, and I couldn't let that happen.

"Do I tell Beau about any of this?" I asked.

"That's the first time you've ever asked me that," she amused. "When did you develop a conscience about letting Beau in on that part of your life?"

"I'm trying to be a better wife," I said and eyeballed the bags.

"By putting on a costume for Beau tonight and smothering yourself in cake?" she laughed mockingly.

"No," I answered. *But why hadn't I thought of that?* "I'm bring-ing home dessert. I'm trying to make it home for dinner more often. I'm trying to make it home more often at all, really," I shrugged. "The costume is for something else."

"That will mean a lot to Beau," she said seriously. "I'm glad to hear that."

"So, would you tell him?" I asked. "About anything?" My ques-tion was laced with ulterior motives. Her answer would help me define whether I would ever tell her or Beau about the dungeon.

She thought for a minute. "That's up to you, but I'd say if you're not breaking a vow, breaking a law, or breaking a heart, you might be better off leaving it where it is. Sometimes telling a secret is just a transfer of burden."

She was right. Of course, she was right. Irena was good at relationships. Any time I had ever taken her advice, it was the right call; she was the reason Beau and I got together in the first place.

I looked at my watch: 6:26 p.m. I had to hustle.

"So, we have a plan?" I stared expectantly at Kat, Shiloh, and Tobias.

"Yes, I understand what to do," Shiloh answered gloomily.

"Me, too," Kat said.

Tobias nodded as he leaned against the door jamb.

"I sense that you're upset?" I asked, reading their dejectedness. Before laying out tonight's plan, I told them that this session would be the clinic's last.

"Certainly not at you," Shiloh spoke first. "But it's sad to see our work coming to an end. We had such a good thing going. But all good things come to an end, right?"

Kat smiled at her sympathetically in agreement.

"This clinic survived because of your work," I said.

They all smiled.

"And I learned *a lot* about something I never thought I would have!" I laughed.

We all shared a chuckle.

"But Shiloh, I'm serious about starting your own business. You can have all of the equipment downstairs; Tobias will put it in storage until you figure out a new location. I'm sure Andrew Yale has resources you could pursue."

"Hmmm. I am fond of that pup," she smiled. "But no. I think I'll try to do it on my own. Or maybe it's time for me to find something else to do. I don't know. I'll think about it."

"Okay then," I said with approval. "Kat," I redirected. "I can't tell you how many times I sat at that window for longer than I had time for to watch your rope work."

She smiled meekly.

"I really think there's an opportunity to make your work into some kind of photo art. I can picture an entire gallery filled with images of those beautiful bodies wrapped in colorful ropes. My husband has worked with a very talented photographer. I could put you in touch; maybe you can work something out?"

She answered with a proud grin. "Okay."

I looked at my watch. "I gotta run. It's almost dinner time."

They all hastened into action. Tobias held the door for the ladies, but before Shiloh followed Kat out of my office, I stopped her with one hand and held up the costume bag.

"Shiloh, one more thing. Would you consider wearing this tonight?"

CHAPTER THIRTY-FIVE

I walked into the house at exactly 7:00 p.m.

"I'm home!" I hollered boastfully as I shuffled my shoes off and put my purse in its place. The house was quiet and somewhat dimmed, and a burst of familiar smells filled it. Beau had made chicken soup, I smiled.

I entered the kitchen. The table was set for four and the good china was laid out, even for the twins. A bottle of wine and a fresh loaf of bread were breathing in the middle of the spread.

It looked like the fanciest damn table that ever existed.

"Oh, hi!" I heard Beau descend the stairs. "You're home!"

I smiled at him sincerely. "This is lovely."

He came close and kissed my cheek. "It's just some chicken soup," he said as he took the box from my hands.

"What's this?" he asked eagerly.

"It's just dessert," I mimicked.

But we knew the soup and the dessert were not "just" anything. We knew they were everything. They meant we cared. They meant we were trying. And they meant that we were going to be okay.

The twins bumped down the stairs. "Mommy! You're home!"

I scooped them up for a giggly cuddle, then they guided me to the table. "Daddy let us set the table!"

I winked at Beau, who was pouring our wine. God, he looked sexy tonight. Did he get a haircut today? I noticed.

We ate dinner and shared loud laughs. I kept searching for words to explain how this night felt: *Warm.* Everything felt warm. From time to time, a short-lived thought would flash into my brain about what might be happening down in the dungeon, but I sent the thoughts away quickly. No more ruined moments from him, from her, from anyone, I told myself. I was done with that.

These are my people, and this is our table.

That night, after we tucked the kids into bed and took a hot shower together, I let Beau take control of the night again. This time, he had even more confidence. He had been thinking about what to do with me, I could tell.

It was just what the doctor ordered.

CHAPTER THIRTY-SIX

Istrolled into the clinic the next day without a care in the world, and I wondered if the odd feeling I had was what people called "letting go."

I didn't contemplate looking at the video of last night's session with Bobby Clay, but after Beau fell asleep, I crept into the bathroom and couldn't resist checking my text messages. Two simple lines from Shiloh gave me all the information I needed:

Spring cleaning at the clinic is complete.

We finished the tasks on the list, even the dirty one.

And though I was filled with this new sensation to not give a damn, I was still human and therefore curious as hell. I hoped he squealed like a pig.

I saw Irena first.

"Good morning," I said.

I expected her to wave good morning and go about her duties as she usually did, but she said, "Ah," and walked toward me. She cocked a hip to stop directly in front of me.

"Good morning," she said hastily as a preamble. "Listen, Faith. I don't know what's going on here today, but Mara is a goddamned mess. She looks like she has the flu or something. I told her to go sit in your office for a minute. Shiloh is the total opposite: frenetic and bouncing like a bunny."

I narrowed my eyes. I couldn't picture either of those scenes.

"Kat is—well, Kat's always Kat; I never know how she is."

I opened my mouth to comment, but she cut me off.

"No, don't tell me. I have a feeling this has to do with whatever you were talking about last night and I don't want to know. I just want you to go take care of your staff-gone-crazy and get this place back to normal."

I nodded.

"I'll take your next two appointments," she said firmly before pivoting to walk back toward the exam rooms. Then, she stopped and turned around. "You had a good night though, huh?" she smiled.

Typical Irena. She could always read my face. "I don't know what you're talking about," I said coyly.

She chuckled. "Right. You have that look of accomplishment. The same look you used to get after a complex surgery or a good vacation. When you used to take them," she added sarcastically.

I opened my mouth to comment, but again she cut me off. I didn't know what shifted in the universe to have my two closest people shush me lately, but I didn't mind it at all, I realized. In fact, it was a relief to have less decisions to make.

"No, wait. I don't want to know. I'm going to assume it was wild sex, and that you should get more of it." With that, she brisked away, leaving me to take notice of my tender inner thighs as I remembered Beau between them. I bit my lip to curb the satisfied grin that was creeping across my face.

Okay, back to reality.

I walked in my office to find Mara standing at the filing cabinet; folders were strewn on top and around the desk.

"Good morning," I said as I put my bag down.

"Good morning, Dr. Wells," she replied efficiently, still pulling files out, peeking inside, then putting them back in a different order.

"How are you this morning?" I asked, gauging as I took a seat.

"Fine, thank you," she replied without looking up. She wore black slacks and a gray cashmere sweater, and her hair was down, but it lacked the buoyancy it normally had.

"Mara, do you want to sit down for a minute and talk?"

She didn't answer; she just kept fiddling with the folders.

"Mara," I said firmly.

She stopped and sighed. Her profile looked tired. "I couldn't sleep wondering what happened last night. There were times when I wanted to get in my car and drive over to watch through the window, then there were times I wish he had never booked that appointment. I keep going back and forth on whether or not I want to know anything."

"Come on, sit down," I urged.

She hesitated, then she shut the filing cabinet with a heavy click. "Did you watch?" she asked. I noticed she didn't wear mascara, but her eyelashes were still so long and black, like a giraffe's, and I thought she looked more beautiful without makeup.

I shook my head. "No."

She looked surprised. "I figured you would have. Were you here at least?"

"No," I said calmly.

"Why not?"

"I suppose the same reason you weren't," I answered. "Because sometimes the only choice left to do is to let things go."

She stared at my desk as I spoke, but I knew she was listening intently.

"I've held on to my past for so long, Mara, that I didn't even know I was holding it. I convinced myself that as long as I detested it, it couldn't affect me, but subconsciously every move that I made had my mother, or my insecurities, or what I didn't have growing up, relaying in the background. I finally turned off the noise. And do you know what I heard?"

She looked at me expectantly.

"Everything else."

She smiled.

"By letting go, I've made room for other things to come in, as cliché as that sounds," I said. "And I think maybe you're letting some things in, as well?"

She looked at me quizzically.

"Jed?" I smirked.

She sighed contentedly. "It was never the plan. For either of us. Our arrangement was perfectly professional at first and it was exactly what we both needed. Then, I don't know. We enjoyed our time together, and before we knew it, we didn't want to do anything without each other."

"That's how it happens, right?"

"I suppose it does."

"He told me he would never love again. His wife died of cancer," I said.

"I know. She sounds like she was an extraordinary woman."

"And you are too, Mara," I confirmed. "I'd say Jed is lucky to have found two extraordinary women to love in his lifetime."

She smiled. "I told him about my past last night. I thought he might think I was crazy, but he took me in his arms and said, 'I've heard worse.'"

That was so Jed.

"He wanted to know who it was, naturally, but I didn't tell him, and I don't know why," she said.

"I don't know. I'm not a psychiatrist; I can barely make sense my own problems. But maybe it's part of the whole letting-go-thing."

We pondered in silence for a minute.

"So, now what?" she finally asked.

"Well," I sighed. "We still have one more thing to do for us to move on. Because we both know that he's not letting go unless we make him."

She nodded in agreement, then we turned our heads to a tap at the door.

"Come in," I said.

Shiloh entered excitedly. "Oh, Dr. Wells. Good, you're here. I have fifteen minutes before I need to be back at the desk." She sat next to Mara. "Did you guys watch?"

We both shook our heads apologetically.

"What?" Shiloh exasperated. "You didn't watch? It was some of my best work!"

"I'm sorry, Shiloh. Tell us what happened," I said. I didn't know if I would ever watch the footage. But I still itched to know what took place, especially since I knew everything had gone to plan.

"First," Shiloh said, her red hair swooped back on the sides with vintage gold clips and her cat black glasses resting low on her nose. "Bobby smells like onions."

Mara and I both laughed a welcomed comic relief.

"And I don't know if he was fit when you both knew him, but he's not anymore. Like, not at all," she emphasized.

Mara snorted.

Shiloh went on to tell us about how Tobias met Bobby at the pizza shop. After some negotiating, Bobby agreed to get in Tobias's car and wear the blackout glasses. Tobias drove around in many loops before bringing Bobby down to the dungeon where Shiloh and Kat waited for him.

"What did you end up wearing?" I couldn't curb my curiosity.

"I wore what you asked me to: the angel costume," she smirked. "Not a look I thought I'd consider, but turns out, it quite suited me."

Mara glanced at me knowingly.

"A little homage to my mother," I shrugged. "Sorry, but the costume store was fresh out of gorgeous Azerbaijani women costumes."

She flickered a never-mind smile at me.

"Anyway, I have to hurry, so I'll skip to the good stuff," Shiloh continued. "He was a little resistant and kept looking around as if someone might walk in, but I finally relaxed him enough to get his full attention. And once I did, I asked myself, *Hmmm, what do pigs like?*"

Mara and I chortled.

"Well, they like food," she said with her finger counting. "And they like mud."

I could almost not contain my anticipation.

"So, I stripped off his too-tight, expensive suit until he was fully nude while Kat poured mud on a ten-foot area of the floor. By this time, I think he had forgotten he had come for anything else, and he happily laid down in that mud and rolled from left to right like a fucking pig in a pen!" Shiloh laughed.

I guffawed so loud that I covered my own mouth, disbelieving. Mara had her hand halfway over her mouth to muzzle her amusement.

"Then," Shiloh said through her laughter, "I started throwing him little pieces of food, and I commanded him to eat them right out of the mud with his mouth. That son of a bitch did it, too. His fat ass got on all fours and he started eating chunks of our fridge leftovers: Chinese food, grapes, and you're gonna love this, Mara — a piece of of your baklava."

Mara smiled satisfactorily. She was paid homage, after all.

"Wanna hear something really funny?" Shiloh snickered. "At one point, his knees slipped while picking up a piece of moo shu pork, and he didn't bother to get back up. He just laid there, squirming around, snorting his food," she laughed. "Then, he started humping the floor. Swear to God," she said with her hand up.

Our faces fixed in shock.

Bobby Clay, this man who had haunted our pasts and night-mared our dreams, was pathetically dry humping the floor of *my* clinic. We had slayed the dragon in *our* dungeon.

"The best was toward the end," Shiloh calmed down. "I made him sit up, his back was covered in mud, and with my finger I wrote: I'M A FILTHY PIG.

"And I angled his back so that the camera would get a clear shot of it."

Our laughter stifled as that message sunk in.

"And he left with no trouble?" Mara asked.

"Well, kind of. As he buttoned up his shirt to leave, he kept looking around again, but this time, he was a little wary. Like he realized what had just happened and he expected to get caught. He asked, 'Who else is here?' And I just smiled at him and said, 'Just us.'"

We both grinned.

"But I assured him that I had a very satisfying session and that he would see me again very soon," she insinuated.

"You did good work, Shiloh," I said. "Truly. Thank you."

Mara blinked her gratitude, and Shiloh winked.

"Okay, then," Shiloh stood up. "Back to work. You ladies coming? We have a busy day."

We both stood to follow. We gave each other a knowing nod. A nod of closure. Then, we went about the rest of our day fully in synch and with lighter steps and brighter eyes. Even Tobias lingered more than usual. The energy in the clinic was alive.

I weighed that maybe love was the cure, but today, work was the best medicine.

ONE YEAR LATER

"**D**oes this mean you won't be babysitting for us anymore?" I asked jokingly as Irena handed one of two Great Pyrenees puppies back to Juliet, who had chased them under the table.

"Because we got puppies?" Irena laughed. "No, it means I'm coming for payback," Irena gloated. "Especially for that two-week vacation! You like dog-sitting, right?"

I laughed. We were sitting at a long, provincial table made of an old barn door that rested under two giant picturesque sycamore trees. We were celebrating Irena and Josh's small, quiet wedding on their fifty-acre chicken farm just north of Doylestown.

"I'm happy for you, Irena," I said to her. "Everything is perfect."

"Who would have thought that I'd be getting married on a chicken farm, holding puppies in my wedding dress?" She threw her hands out amusedly, the sleeves of her simple, breezy dress swaying. "I've never even had a dog."

"You're going to be a great dog-mom," I chuckled. "And a great wife. And I know this because you're great at everything you do. Including friendship."

She smiled. "Thanks, Faith."

The occasion implored us to squeeze each other's hands, which was not an Irena-and-me- thing to do, but it felt good. It reminded me of how far we had both come.

"Look at them," Beau interrupted from my other side. He pointed at Matthew, Juliet, and Ena, who were rolling in the long grass with the puppies. "Maybe we should get a puppy."

I glared at him with disapproval, but then, I thought, *Why not*? I had cut down on my hours at the clinic—dedicating one day a week as initially intended—and I stopped picking up for my partner's slack at the practice. I didn't need to prove myself by overachieving anymore. I outshined them without extra effort.

"I think we have enough room in our house for a puppy," I said.

He looked at me wide-eyed. "Really? I didn't think you'd go for that," he laughed.

"Whatever you want," I smiled.

He leaned over and kissed behind my ear. "You know what I want," he said in a low whisper. My middle surged with heat as a slow smile spread across my face. The past year had brought us closer in more ways than I thought possible. We enjoyed glasses of wine on our patio and "kissed hard" often. And I now raced home for the bedroom as much as I raced home for dinner. I had never felt so full.

Clink-clink-clink. A fork hitting a wine glass interrupted our amorous moment.

"To the bride and groom!" Tobias whooped a toast to his sister. His arm rested around Kat, who smiled and raised her glass. Among the secret love affairs that happened over the past couple of years, the one that I didn't see coming was Tobias and Kat's (Shiloh predicted it, of course). But once I learned of their relationship, it made sense, like chocolate-and-salt sense.

"To the bride and groom," Mara echoed gracefully. Jed held her hand and they raised their glass to the happy couple. Mara had moved into Jed's sprawling Bucks County estate and they had become the newest partners of the Angel Clinic, securing its financial future. Mara's two boys also had joined Jed and Mara for a portion of their sailing trip to the Mediterranean. It was her first time seeing them in more than four years, and though her relationship with her kids had a way to go, it had set sail and was making headway.

Shiloh took an olive pit out of her mouth quickly and raised her glass. Her boyfriend of the month accompanied her, a striking vampire-meets-supermodel-looker with an impeccably cut blazer, tattoos peeking through his sleeves and chest. I hoped this one lasted. Beside the fact that he and Shiloh made a stunning couple, he also was a large reason Shiloh had hung up her handcuffs (for now) and had enrolled in school to pursue her doctoral degree in psychology.

I looked over at Beau, who lifted his glass with his still-tanned arm from our recent vacation, the third this year. My first time leaving the East Coast was for two glorious weeks with Beau to the gilded beaches of the French Riviera. Who would have known that I'd love the beach so much? And that I'd look so good in a beret?

And we weren't the only ones who left town. After a tasteless and untraceable video clip of an overweight attorney rolling around in mud circulated his law firm—and worse, found its way to the top of his wife's inbox—that little piggy went wee-wee-wee all the way out of Philadelphia. To where, and for how long, we didn't know and we didn't care. We knew we would never hear from Bobby again for fear that the rest of the footage would be released; and even a piggy didn't want that mud slung.

Our glasses met each other's with venerating clinks as we sipped around the table, which was adorned with eucalyptus leaves, dahlias, and candles careening to the wind in hurricane vases. Gold-rimmed plates, crystal glasses, and linen napkins laying quietly beneath gold cutlery accented the hues of the rich, sunset landscape.

"While your glasses are in hand, I suppose now is a good time for my Matron of Honor speech," I announced as I stood. The table hushed in anticipation.

"I've often wondered why a heart was chosen as the symbol of love," I started. "Maybe because it beats fast when we're falling in love, or because our hearts hurt when love is lost. But none of this makes sense to a heart doctor because those things happen because of signals from the brain," I bantered. They humored me with a mellow laugh.

I looked at Irena and Josh lovingly.

"But I have come to realize that there is a similarity between the heart and the concept of love, and it's simple: If you take good care of it, it will thrive. Caring for your relationship is much like caring for your heart. It's strong in the beginning, but it needs extra attention as time goes on. There are times when it will need something and you won't know what it is without listening carefully. There will be trial and error in keeping it healthy, but so long as you're trying, it will be resilient. And if you continually feed it with kindness, empathy, patience, and of course, love, the stronger it will beat."

I lifted my glass. "To a lifetime of full tables and full hearts."

We clinked and sipped once more, then I sat back down. I hooked my arm in Beau's and rested my forehead against his.

I still had a lot to learn about the heart. Things not taught in medical schools or books, but things you learned from the people you love: how to love them, how you need to be loved, and how to love yourself. It wasn't always a matter of facts.

But it was always a matter of the heart.

ACKNOWLEDGEMENTS

It is no small feat to thank each person who made my second book possible. Always and forever, I begin with my husband, Rocco. Your constant encouragement and belief in me matters more than you may ever know. I think back on the day I declared that I was going to write a book. "You can absolutely do it," you said, unequivocally. Thank you for doing life with me. I love you.

To my kids—Mason, Rose, and Luca—thank you for keeping me company nearly every day during the writing of this novel. One day I'll remember this as *the pandemic book*; a writing time in which I had to channel dominatrix and dungeons while in the background, one of you was screaming, "Mom! It's lunchtime!". It wasn't easy, but every day with you kids is worth it. I love your little souls.

To my mom—thank you for always being my first reader. It's surprisingly hard to get people to read my drafts, but you never hesitate. You read, then re-read, as many times as I ask you to, and your response is always the same: "That was the best book I've ever read." I love you for that. I love you for a lot of things.

To my editor—you are gem, L. By definition, a gem is "something prized because of its beauty or worth." Your beauty is obvious, and your worth is more than words could convey. Thank you for your balance of challenge and praise, and for dealing with mine, in turn.

I've become a better writer because of you. I know that one day you'll approve of my made-up words. Maybe one day, you'll even grow fond of them. That's my goal.

To a most incredible woman and cardiologist who I am honored to call my friend, MA, M.D. Thank you for the breakfasts, lunches, emails, phone calls, walks, and everything in between that helped make Faith believable as a doctor. I don't know how you juggle all those pins without dropping them, but you do. Thanks for being a badass woman, a real-life hero, and an invaluable medical consultant.

To E, my dominatrix inspiration. Thank you for teaching me to never assume anything about anyone. Like Faith, I had much to learn about the art of dominatrix; your insight opened my eyes to its psychological aspects. It was enlightening, as are you. Mad respect.

Any medical or dominatrix inaccuracies in this novel are entirely mine for the sake of better storytelling and bear no reflection of the expert advice nor critique I was given.

Thank you to my early readers—Mom, Lisa, Jen, Rocco, Michelle C.—who gave invaluable feedback and validation that shaped this book. I'm always biting my nails waiting for your responses, and nothing feels better than when you say, "I loved it."

To all my family and friends—I wouldn't be able to write books without your love, encouragement, and support. Thank you to everyone in my life. If you're in it, it's because I chose you, and I'd choose you over and over again.

ABOUT THE AUTHOR

Michelle Lee lives in Bucks County, PA with her husband, three kids, two dogs, and fifteen chickens.

She finds that most people have a story to tell if you're interesting enough for them to share it with, patient enough to listen, and humble enough not to judge it.

The Clinic is Michelle Lee's second novel in the *Secret Lives of Moms* series. It follows her award-winning debut novel *The Playground*.

Be on the lookout for the third novel in the *Secret Lives of Moms* series, *The Binary*.

ABOUT THE BINARY

Kate Salters, an IT genius, finds herself on the lonely side of divorce and the target of a partial boss. To make ends meet for her four children, Kate dabbles into the dark world of computer hacking for ransomware. When Kate realizes an opportunity to serve miscreants a dose of what they deserve, she focuses her hacking skills to serve justice, where justice has failed. Will Kate find her true self in this dual undertaking? Or will duplicity be her downfall?